B. E. Jones is a former journalist and police press officer, now a novelist and book obsessive. She was born in a small village in the valleys of South Wales, north of Cardiff, and started her journalism career with Trinity Mirror news-papers before becoming a broadcast journalist with *BBC Wales Today*.

She has worked on all aspects of crime reporting (as well as community news and features), producing stories and content for newspapers and live TV. Most recently she worked as a press officer for South Wales Police, dealing with the media and participating in criminal investigations, security operations and emergency planning. Perhaps unsurprisingly she channels these experiences of true crime, and her insight into the murkier side of human nature, into her dark, psychological thrillers set in and around South Wales.

Also by B. E. Jones
Where She Went
Halfway

(ebook only)
The Lies You Tell
Make Him Pay
Fear the Dark

Wilderness

B. E. Jones

CONSTABLE

CONSTABLE

First published in Great Britain in 2019 by Constable

1 3 5 7 9 10 8 6 4 2

A Literature Wales Writer's Bursary, supported by the National Lottery through the Arts Council of Wales, was received to develop this novel.

A CIP catalogue record for this book
is available from the British Library.

ISBN: 978-1-47212-794-5

Typeset in Sabon by SX Composing DTP, Rayleigh, Essex
Printed and bound in Great Britain by Clays Ltd, Elcograf S.p.A.

Papers used by Constable are from well-managed forests
and other responsible sources.

Constable
An imprint of
Little, Brown Book Group
Carmelite House
50 Victoria Embankment
London EC4Y 0DZ

An Hachette UK Company
www.hachette.co.uk

www.littlebrown.co.uk

For Paul – for the journey.

Prologue

No one died until six months after I saw the home video. The timing was complicated and there were important decisions to be made first, such as should I stay or should I go? Fall or fight? Mend or destroy? Curl up in a ball and die or . . .

Either way, there was no choosing on a whim, with a snap of my fingers, the toss of a coin, because what I saw in my future, if I made the wrong decision, was me all alone, scrabbling through the rubble among heaps of charred bones and the stench of death – in other words, *divorced*.

All right, perhaps it wouldn't have been like that, like the actual end of the world, if I'd just left him, but that's how it felt. So what if I wasn't the first woman cheated on by her husband? So what if I wouldn't be the last? It doesn't matter that it's a cliché, that it's commonplace, that it's glaringly mediocre. It still means the whole world and its end when it's happening to you.

That's why I'm trying to explain the last twelve months, the destruction that followed the discovery that my husband was sleeping with a skinny, skank-whore years younger than me. Because it's not always the noisiest things that do the most harm, not the havoc reported on the nightly news with footage of smoking craters and swooping aid choppers. There's the carnage that takes place in silence, in the confines of a two-bedroom condo among the steel and stone canyons of New York City.

Wars are waged inside these ordinary spaces every day, unfolding quietly within four walls, within our own heads, and there's no escape from them, no matter how many miles we travel. But we try, don't we? We try to flee. We attempt to run. That's how it all came down to one single second on our postcard-perfect 'holiday of a lifetime', our shining 'dream road trip', our enviable summer vacation – even though I knew about the affair, about Will's A-cup accomplice in infidelity. Because I'd forgiven him, except . . .

Except for that heavy-breathing doubt in the back of my head that refused to shut up and slink away, the one pawing the ground and baring its teeth all winter on the streets of New York, snarling – the little voice whispering, *Does he deserve to be forgiven? Can he ever be trusted now? Can you?*

I thought the road trip would give me some perspective, to test Will's commitment to fixing things, without more words, endless, deceitful words, so slick and slippery. I needed to know he was really sorry. And if I didn't have clear evidence of that by the end of the trip, well, I had options under consideration.

I don't mean I'd actually plotted to kill him then. Plot, plan, premeditate are such precise words, pickily implying logic and structure when all I really had were a few 'contingencies' at hand. Because it's dangerous out there in the wilderness, inside the resting jaws of the great unknown, always waiting to snap. Civilisation is flimsy at best and, believe me, you don't have to go far beyond our well-groomed towns and smartly dressed cities to watch the veneer crack, see the mask slip, the old, dark shape of the beast emerge. You don't even have to leave your own home, or what's left of it, to open a rarely used zip pocket, click on an unexpected text, then feel the hairs on your neck rise, your claws slide out, feel yourself changing . . .

Still, when Will and I set out on the first leg of our holiday it was only my usual research that had highlighted how easily people die all the time in North America's national parks, those vast areas where there are great heights to fall from, things that want to bite and eat you, and places to lose yourself in for ever. All it takes is one misstep; a slip, a trip, a flash of fangs and each can mean disaster when you're miles from help, out of sight of CCTV with no signal bars on your phone.

That's what makes it easy to die out there. Makes it easy to kill, too. Believe me, I should know.

Because by then, by the time I lost myself under the vast skies, in the empty spaces, it wasn't just about Will's survival, it was about mine and, if you're honest, that's usually the most important thing. We'll fight for that until we're bloody and breathless, or someone else is, lying open-eyed and broken in the undergrowth or splayed on a hot slab of city paving stone, until the bodies pile up alongside the excuses and you have to admit what you are – no more hiding.

Nothing makes you more honest with yourself than admitting you're thinking about ways to kill your husband, except perhaps doing it. But as I said, on a flawless June morning, with 1500 miles and four states ahead of us, it wasn't a plan, it was a possibility.

One

Phoenix, Arizona – Monument Valley, Utah

When we set out from Phoenix, just a sunscreen lick after breakfast, the day was already as hot as a stoked furnace and blinding with poured sunlight. Will was driving, me next to him with a lapful of maps, criss-crossed with the coloured lines and orange blocks of the great state of Arizona. It was his job to remember to stay in the right-hand lane and mine to navigate (alongside the intermittent satnav) through the mountains and deserts materialising through the windscreen after decades in the dreaming, years in the imagining, months in the planning.

If, at that moment, I'd taken a lifestyle photo for one of my magazine features on the 'Great American Road Trip', it would have looked perfect, both of us smiling, sunglasses on, the white glare of Will's Abercrombie shirt flaring in the lens, the gloss of my hair as it streamed behind me, chasing an unspooling ribbon of road.

Imagine the ease and eagerness of our lives, it would have said. Look at Mr and Mrs Taylor, married and loving it. Loving each other, an advert for adventure and lasting partnership. Here we go, laughing, smiling.

And it was almost like that, with the tank full of petrol, steak sandwiches and sparkling water in the icebox, well equipped like all first-world refugees fleeing our inner crisis in comfort. In our backpacks were Nalgene water bottles and vacuum-packed trail mix, wick-away micro fleeces and high-factor sun lotion, mega-strength DEET and antihistamines – charms, talismans for every eventually; as if those things could protect us from what was out there on the backwoods paths or inside the car with us, sharing every mile, licking its lips.

As we snaked northwards through the slow, sandy canyons, it seemed so much more than twenty-four hours since we'd caught a cab from Manhattan to JFK airport then jumped into the bottom left-hand corner of the country to Phoenix. The internal flight had handily chewed up 2144 miles, eight states and thirty-seven hours of drive time so we'd be in no hurry as we gazed down from the rim of the Grand Canyon into the Earth's biggest hole in the ground, dawdled through the amber dust of the Wild West captured in the red rock spires of every Hollywood cowboy movie and the grit of John Wayne's clenched jaw.

Later we'd make the long climb into the pine-clad passes of the high Sierras, tipping our hats at El Capitan in Yosemite Valley, before sliding down to Death Valley and home again. It was quite an adventure for two pasty Brits in a hired Japanese car under a Yankee sun, two people from a grey and dreary isle who until a year ago were living under the gloom-banishing electric lights of London and the constant threat of unwrapping an umbrella.

It's hard to appreciate the size of that land until you've driven across it, especially if you're from a small island that once had an empire and still puffs out its chest like it's one of the big kids. But when you realise you could fit all of the UK into, say, Arizona's jacket pocket, and South Wales, where I was born, is just a scrap of handkerchief in that pocket, it makes you appreciate the possibilities that exist, good and bad, the things that can happen if you don't keep a close grip on yourself. On the road that morning, I suppose Will and I both had our own ideas of what that meant.

As far as he was concerned it was a chance to digitally detox from the stress of New York City and his job, and for us to reconnect, recapture the romance, heal, grow, move on after the affair; you know, all that psychobabble and self-help bullshit people tell each other to give themselves the illusion of control.

I had something else in mind, something more structured – a little road-trip challenge I'd set for him, taking shape as the scenery changed and the safety and structures of everyday reality started to fall away. You could say I was offering him three chances to save his own life, *our* life together, once and for all. What could be simpler for a man who insisted, so earnestly, that he wanted to make amends than to complete three straightforward tasks:

1. Surprise me with a thoughtful romantic gesture.

2. Be spontaneous and seize a sense of occasion.

3. Stay calm if things go wrong and look after me.

Sounds easy, doesn't it? Barely a challenge at all, in fact? Hardly a fatal matter, though I can assure you everything depends on the context. Then everything seems reasonable, like the fact I hadn't actually told Will he was going to be tested and I hadn't explained the rules or penalties.

Because it's not as if we hadn't had *the conversation* before, or ones like it, back in our edge-of-Kensington, shoebox flat, rented for half market rate from a minted friend of Will's mum, the same refrain cropping up every few months across the years of our marriage, usually ending with me in tears of frustration, thinking, Why do you always take me for granted?

We'd had 'the talk' again, on those knife-edged winter nights after I'd taken him back, me explaining what he would need to do to make me trust him again. But eventually it's the unspoken things that matter in a marriage, surely? The instinct. The understanding. The offering.

That can, of course, leave you open to disappointment, and, as we sailed past the fields of tequila-bottle cartoonish cactus, upturned arms saluting our passing, the pressure of a test fail weighed almost as heavily on me as the importance of making the holiday count probably did on him. Because what would it really mean, when the final whistle blew, in Las Vegas, ten days down the road, if the judge's decision was final, no do-overs or extra time allowed? If it was game over for us? For him?

Honestly, I just didn't allow myself to think that far ahead, reminding myself I could still call an end to it all, the journey, the challenge, our eight-year marriage at any minute if I wanted to. It didn't have to mean anything that, statistically, the most common cause of death in US national parks is drowning, closely followed by fatal motor vehicle crashes, then falls and slips.

So what if my online preparations (for the tourist travel tips box in the feature I'd planned) revealed that around 160 people end up with these banal explanations on their death certificates every year, these almost no-one-at-fault, no-one-to-blame explanations in the box for *accidental* deaths, alongside a few extra for dehydration, exposure and wildlife attacks? It didn't have to mean anything. It wasn't a sign, a nod from the universe, a suggestion of any sort.

My own *contingency plan* was vague at that stage, merely something that had bubbled into being during the hazy, heart-sick hours I'd spent that winter, watching black and white films, slumped on the sofa, chugging bourbon from the bottle, crying myself to sleep. Until the very last second, in the rain, in the storm, it was only a fantasy to occupy my thoughts on those long, furtive night-walks I'd started taking through a frost-twinkled New York City, my face concealed, watching from street corners, peering in through lit windows, imagining, wondering, longing . . .

. . . imagining the sound a fist makes against bone . . .

. . . wishing I knew how to obtain a gun in the nation that loves its right to bear arms . . .

. . . longing for certainty so clean and decisive there'd be no more hoping for the best while fearing the worst – in other words no going back.

I suppose the idea, which later shaped itself into the ultimate ultimatum, was simply a way to gain some control again, because I'd had none while Will had chosen to wreck our lives, strafe through memories, explode promises, sniper-shoot my trust straight in the forehead. Will and his dick – his early midlife-crisis dick, nothing more original than that.

For a while, the rage that triggered had staggered me like nothing I'd ever felt before, that red-black, bloody taste of something primal bubbling up in my mouth, ears ringing with blood – except for maybe that one time, long ago, when I'd had the first taste of it, when James Scott had laughed at me and Natalie Lewis had been alone for once, crying . . . and I . . .

Either way, that feeling hadn't been at home in a school uniform on a warm June afternoon, nor, much later, in a silk blouse and spike heels in a smart New York hotel. But, honestly, it was under control as Will and I whizzed past the freeway signs for Camp Verde and Sedona, towards the desert rail hub of Flagstaff, turning north-west towards our new start.

Racing along the blacktop, the cares and sorrows of the months finally starting to recede before the elemental size of the land's memory, Will seemed to catch some of my thoughts. Reaching over, placing his hand on the back of my neck, he smiled tightly, swallowing before saying, 'I'm really glad we're doing this, Liv. I'm so glad you're giving me the chance to make everything right. This is a new start for us. I can never make up for what I've done but I'm going to try. I promise you that. I love you.'

'Me too,' I smiled back, taking his hand and squeezing it, refusing to give in to the familiar shock of friction, the treacherous spark that did not mean I knew him. That I never had. He didn't know me either, what I'd done in the city that winter. What I would do very soon – standing over that ravine, wind whipping my hair, clenching my jaw and my fists, feeling my feet moving forward of their own accord, one, two, one, two . . . one two three . . .

But no one could've known that, as I pointed out the turnoff sliding us north-east towards Utah, Will indicating right and grinning, 'Next stop Monument Valley. Cowboy country here we come. The Taylor wagon train is coming into town.'

Though, when we found ourselves still wheeling through the emptiness two hours later, with only the occasional green bubble of grass and stream in the expanse of dry, baked world, I gained a new respect for those first Americans who wet their toes at Plymouth Rock, pulled on their boots and pointed their wagons west.

Because we're all pioneers, aren't we? When we start out, when we say *I do* on our wedding day, when we break new ground. We set up a homestead, build fences, try to keep close to the fire where it's safe. Except, watching the buzzards circling idly over the tombstone-like landscape, the bleached skull of a horse at the edge of the blacktop, I knew it wasn't safe. Nothing ever is.

When we finally pulled up in Monument Valley just before 6 p.m., tired and hungry, there was indeed danger to life and limb but for a far more prosaic reason than I'd expected. After five and a half hours on the road, I was looking forward to some quiet time with Will, admiring those famous buttes and 'Mittens' that greeted us from the hotel terrace, immortalised by John Ford in widescreen.

With their red-rock fingers pressed into the sky, thumbs tucked at their sides, the scene was achingly Instagrammable, and, to me, instantly recognisable from an issue in my collection of much-thumbed *National Geographics* (page 39,

Navajo man in profile, facing Mittens, sunset filter). But why hadn't it occurred to me that, at a hotel with *the* ring-side seat to one of the most photographed vistas in the world, everyone else would have the same idea?

Overdressed, overloud, over-enthusiastic members of every race on earth swarmed the terrace and spacious gift gallery, wielding backpack battering rams, extremities weighted like pack horses with cameras, video recorders and newly purchased Navajo string ties, turquoise silver earrings and windcatcher trinkets.

Every corner seemed crammed with canoodling honey-mooners, grinning anniversary markers and boisterous big-birthday celebrators, jostling each other for the perfect Facebook update or bucket list fist-bump, elbows flying everywhere.

When Will and I headed outside for the nightly sunset, after sampling some Navajo fry-bread and other specialities in the crammed restaurant, in the name of research, there was even less privacy, the atmosphere resembling a rock concert with everyone popping their earbuds in and out, tapping their glimmering phone screens, sighing at the poor signal, then clicking and snapping with camera apps.

'Come on. Let's find somewhere quieter,' said Will patiently, no doubt seeing a homicidal look in my eye as I was almost blinded by yet another poking selfie stick. Leading me away from the throng he settled us into an armchair nook of red rock a few minutes' scramble away.

'This is much better,' he sighed, once I was safely ringed in his arms, head resting back against his chest. 'It reminds me of that night up on Pen y Fan? The night we stayed up to watch the Perseid meteor shower? Remember? How we watched all night.' As if I could forget that magical evening on the Brecon Beacons, snug as a bug inside one of his expensive coats, staring at the lightshow of the Milky Way as the sky dripped stars just for us.

I'd always been able to breathe up there, really breathe, never so happy as on the days the mist came down like a bedsheet, visibility vanishing save for my boots on the path until the whiteness parted to reveal a valley of tarn and field, of dazzling blue and white light. To my disgust, when we'd first met, Will, a border child from Monmouth, where much of the accent and affluence is English, had never visited our breath-taking national park, but he'd happily embraced the knee-breaking, lung-busting climbs I'd shown him after we began dating.

He was always happy for me to lead the way, map in hand, until it was time for his favourite part, making tea for us with his little backpack boiler and breaking out the chocolate biscuits.

I knew why he'd mentioned the meteor shower that night, halfway across the world under those unfamiliar Utah stars. That was the night he'd proposed, on a spur of the moment urge – no ring, that came later – and I knew he was trying to use the memory as a bandage, to close the hole he'd slashed open inside me with his infidelity. I suppose it could have counted as his first 'pass' of the road-trip test, as he kissed my neck, qualifying as a sort of romantic gesture, but it was too soon, too slight to count, the words ringing hollow like exposed bones, even as we were wound in each other's arms, the very image of a happy couple.

Because we weren't a couple by then, or at least, not the same couple we had been, not even as Will said, 'I love you even more now than I did then, and I never thought that would be possible, Liv,' because I was a stranger in his arms and a stranger was placing his lips on my cheek, warm against the chill that pulsed under my skin. Because, for a long time, I hadn't felt like his wife, the older version of that Geography student who'd twisted her ankle hauling a hired kayak out of the lazy River Wye more than a decade before, grateful for the help of a tousle-haired instructor with a mellow, posh voice and strong hands.

As the fluttering bands of pink and coral competed over the monumental buttes I tried not to think about how grateful I'd been that day, mesmerised as Will's capable fingers worked the joint under my sock, applying an efficient crepe wrap, as he said, 'Hope to see you again,' helping me hobble back to the university minibus, eager to explain, 'This isn't my day job. I'm actually a Business student in Bristol but I'm here every Saturday. Ask for William.'

Then, seven days later, I'd limped back, knowing that, though we were clearly a world apart, from very different backgrounds, it was irrelevant because Will didn't know what that meant or why it mattered. How could it? When Will had never known the girl who'd existed in Cardiff before that day, the one who'd never shown him her childhood home before they'd pulled it down, just as he didn't know the woman in his arms, shivering at the inky chill of the darkening desert.

On that first proper night of our road trip, he couldn't know I'd already sat inches away from the redheaded whore he'd betrayed me with. That for months, unseen, unspeaking, I'd assessed every stitch of her designer suits and expensive shoes, listened to her greeting clients, arranging dinners, always conscious of how I looked and sounded by comparison, how short I fell in ways that shouldn't have mattered. Had never mattered until then.

That's one of the reasons I hated her so much, I think, when I first found out who she was, with her sharp bob and young, fat-free figure. A size 4 nightmare made even worse by the fact she was the not-quite-me I'd wanted to be, could have been . . . almost . . . if only . . .

There's a green-eyed monster in us all, isn't there? Other monsters too, patient and lean, and inside me was one that had already visualised scratching out the eyes of the bitch-slut who'd stolen my husband, living in the city of my dreams with the lifestyle of my fantasies, every day rubbing my face in the fact that, because I didn't have a wealthy daddy like Will to introduce me to 'some business friends with a new venture', I couldn't get interviews for staff-writer posts ahead of the rest, couldn't move on up with a nod and a wink. That, while freelancing for travel magazines, I'd still had to work three days a week in a travel agents for a decade to bump up my salary, still chasing those glossy, high-end commissions.

Since arriving in the USA I hadn't been able to work at all, as Will's spouse, under the terms of his visa, so officially I was taking a 'career break', writing the travel book I'd wanted to for years, a guide for Millennials who want to get off the package circuit but think Airbnb is a terrifying prospect. But it was slow going, making new contacts, sending out introductions, earning no money of my own for the first time since I was sixteen.

Then there she was, that bimbo whore, 'Senior PR Executive' at twenty-six years old, for fuck's sake, in her kitten heels, with her Louis Vuitton bag and Chanel slip dress, dashing from elegant hotel lobby to uptown meeting while I laboured at my laptop in $15 leggings. That's why I'd watched her night after night since Christmas, inhaling her bubbly, flirty ease and unmistakable smell of privilege, of being 'the right sort' who has doors opened for them with a nod of the head, before visualising that head exploding from a shotgun blast, imagining how the click would feel when I pulled the trigger.

Despite the romantic, star-strewn setting of our Utah sunset, it was her I was thinking about when the sun dipped in the west, wondering if she was following her usual Monday-night routine at Ashtanga Yoga; wondering if she knew what she'd done to us, to the people me and Will had once been, to the life she'd slaughtered simply by removing her lacy pink panties.

Did she realise she was always there with us? Perched inside my chest, claws in soft tissue, even as I sat curled under Will's arm in the rocky niche, the Mittens blending red then black into the inky dark? Did she know Will and I would never really be alone again no matter where we lived, how far we drove, how many vacations we took?

As the sun finally disappeared the thought made me long for a quick, hot slug of Jack Daniel's to at least blur her from the front of my mind. Because by then I'd come to want my bourbon tranquilliser far too often, certainly more than was good for me. I needed it to help smooth the edges of the afternoons, grinding like broken glass across the approach of each evening, to help me bear the fact I was torn and bloody inside, a monster stitched back together with fraying promises, regretting the fact that the

Navajo reservation is legally as dry as the monumental valley inside it.

As the three of us climbed into bed that night, in our 'stargazer' room on the top floor, it felt crowded in the silence, under the sudden weight of the desert chill. She took up a lot of space for someone so skinny. She filled the bed and the inches between my body and Will's; I felt her warm breath on my neck. At least, at that moment, I was pretty sure it was her breath – I knew something was there in the room with us. But it was something older, something darker, something waiting. We were officially at the end of day one and it didn't have long to wait.

Two

New York City

How different it had been for me a year before, so hopeful, so guileless that I don't remember swallowing a single qualm on the day we checked into Heathrow's Terminal 5 for international departures. Will had been promoted to 'events and client manager' at last, our bags were packed and the London flat emptied. The next stop was the Big Apple and I'd never been so ready and eager to take a greedy bite.

Approaching the shimmering city that first day, in the chauffeur-driven car, the Statue of Liberty, Empire State and Chrysler buildings reared up like the opening credits of our own movie, filled with the cinematic promise of the New World. We'd been offered the use of a company apartment by Will's new employer, Piper-Dewey, for twelve months, so we could actually live in Manhattan while bypassing its sky-high real estate rates, and, unpacking on the ninth floor of a neat industrial block in SoHo, I remember laughing, swigging bubbly straight from the bottle, dizzy with the flush of opportunity.

Though our two-bed apartment wasn't one of those glorious, millionaire-only loft conversions you see in films, all soaring ceilings and light streaming through glass like water, it was roomy and charming with lots of original features and, best of all, its own narrow slice of view of the distant, shining skyscrapers of Midtown. Staring up at the iconic water towers and hoardings topping the loft spaces and designer shops, I loved it with every humming fibre of my being before I even opened the door. Will put his arms around my neck, and said, 'Well, we're here. Welcome home, honey,' in a terrible mock Brooklyn accent.

The neighbourhood itself was wince-inducingly trendy. Back in Kensington we would've sneered at the hipsters tapping on their laptops in the Portuguese delis, stroking their beards sipping $8 soy lattes or cycling in neon regalia through the shopping-bag weighted tourists. But it wasn't London, it was New York, and the new and the strange is the same as exotic and charming, at least for a while.

In those first weeks, with the city caught in the sticky, blue-skied hug of a June heatwave, we were overwhelmed, overexcited tourists. Pattering ant-like and eager through the clatter and chatter of the sidewalks, the honk and swish of yellow cabs, Will making me chuckle by being unable to stop looking up at the buildings soaring in stone and glass around us, mouth agape, betraying he was just off the bus from Hicksville USA, or in our case London, England, via Monmouth, Wales.

In fact, he was so very 'Englishman in New York' back then it was endearing, even though he wasn't really English, just sounded as if he was when answering everyone who asked, 'Hey, where are you guys from?' I guess having the right public school 'British' voice is as good as the real thing out there and Will did look a bit Hugh-Grantish in his long shorts and short-sleeved shirt, fumbling when ordering complicated coffees and debating over the exact number of dollars to leave for the tip.

I used to like that about him, the fact he made no attempt to blend in or hide who he was. Unlike me, he was comfortable in his skin. But that was before he became a cheating wanker, when everything about him became self-conscious in a new way, the unironic button-down shirts he'd favoured at university, the refusal to stop wearing a parka after thirty, throwing on his public school scarf with jeans and a sweater for a trip to the pub.

That stupid red parka was one of those affectations, bought that summer because we were already planning our road trip and 'broken in' during the drizzly autumn, Will sticking out like a hot, Gore-Tex thumb among the hipsters and urbanites.

'Well, at least the wildlife will see you coming, and the mountain rescue team,' smirked the brawny man in the outdoor pursuits shop, all of us oblivious to how prescient this remark would eventually become.

Still, we had fun. We were happy.

Or I thought we were, as we road-tested the delicacies at the Dominique Ansel bakery, home of the 'cronut', and took snorty-horse cabs through Central Park. Will even rowed us around the boating lake in a little two-seater skiff, glad to have a set of oars in his hands again, taking a thousand photos, caught up in the novelty. Then it was

handshakes, 'Hi there's and icy Manhattans as we toured
the Lowbeck Hotel, Will's new place of work, the restored
art deco gem that lived up to its sleek new silver and gold
branding like a starlet on Oscar night.

Before the soft opening, Will whisked me up the staff
stairs for a peek at the suites, perhaps in response to my
complaints that, 'you never do anything spontaneous. You
never surprise me,' and other remarks I'd come to hate
myself for during our last few months in London. Sharing
a bottle of chilled champagne on that wrought iron and
blue velvet bed, we felt like filmstars; treated to welcome
drinks in the leather nooks of the speakeasy-inspired lobby,
eating burger sliders and tuna sashimi, we felt cosmopolitan
and successful; sipping negronis under the twinkly lights
of the roof terrace bar, we felt younger than our years, a
couple going places.

And there was Will in the centre of it all, blond and
preppy, meeting and greeting, making the most of his typical
British charm and suggestion of Ivy League comportment,
chosen I'm sure, to win over the fashionistas soon to be
buzzing into that beautiful lobby. Watching him, I still
didn't know how it had happened. How we'd found each
other and hung on for dear life, through the wind and
waves. I used to think it was fate, that something brought
us together to save us from ourselves, from the uncertainty
and unfathomability of other people, a self-sufficiency of
two. Then I grew the fuck up.

How stupid was I? How naive had I been?

Why hadn't I minded being on my own so much after
Will's job started? Suspicious when he worked late nights
with clients? When on his cluster of days off he was so

exhausted he'd crash into bed, a grumping, snoring lump of bedcovers and stale breath until well after 1 p.m.? Because I told myself it was the price to pay for the stellar opportunity we'd been handed. The least I could do was give Will time to decompress when he was so busy, making sure I changed into a decent top and put on some lipstick before he came home from work, so he could see I wasn't becoming a slob 'working from home'.

So I threw myself into the role of good wife, taking care of everything, cooking healthy meals that could be reheated when his appointments ran over and he'd rock home, ravenous and wired, to an immaculately neat apartment. I was supportive because he was supporting us, because he was the one within striking distance of finally making some decent money. And because he loved me and I wanted to show I loved him.

Then, in a New York minute, the holiday was over, with the arrival of just three text messages – not many, perhaps, but enough, the magic number, the evil charm – on that light September evening, as summer starting packing up and moving out for the season.

We were eating dinner at the kitchen table as usual, Will annoying me by constantly checking his phone when I was trying to tell him about the great little gothic church I'd found that afternoon, on one of my solo adventures in the city. Because that's how I'd been filling my Will-free days until then, exploring the sidewalks and alleyways, blocks and crosswalks of our new home, making a point of absorbing the different voices with their lilts and inflections, getting to know the lie of the land, blending in.

In fact, I'd got so good at acting like a local that, just that afternoon I'd been paid the ultimate compliment by a delivery guy who stopped to ask, 'Hey, miss, do you know where the Sushi Shack is?' Without thinking I'd shot back, 'Sure,' in his own New York brogue, as if it was my own. 'Go two blocks over and cross the street, over by the mailboxes,' buzzing with a moment of belonging when he winked back, 'Thanks, honey. Even us New Yorkers can't keep track of these new places, huh?'

As Will's phone buzzed for the dozenth time my good mood faded and I snapped, 'Who *is* that? Is it the hotel again, at this hour?'

'Just work,' he replied, not looking up from the screen, 'Welcome to twenty-four/seven American work culture . . .'

'Really, Will, I know you want to make a good impression but it's eight-thirty and it's your day off. Who is it this time?'

'Sol,' he said, without hesitation. 'What's wrong? Don't you appreciate my newfound dedication to climbing the corporate ladder? Back in Kensington, you always said you wanted me to push myself forward more, climb the greasy pole. This is the price we pay.'

He went to the bathroom then, leaving his phone on the table, and, irritated, I snatched it up to see what could be so important. He must not have realised I knew his PIN number, my birthday, otherwise he wouldn't have left it lying there, out in the open, undefended, primed for disaster unleashed at the input of four digits. Even so, when the message flashed up on the screen, ending the world, it took me a few moments to work out what, if anything, was wrong. All it said was, 'I need you xxx', the name Sol Adler flashing in the sender box.

I knew Sol, the dapper night manager who offered me coffee when I occasionally popped by, who I'd once given some 'English tea' and a jar of Marmite prompting the return gift of one of Brooklyn's finest giant pretzels. The message didn't sound like him. Not *we* need you, or *I need you down here, buddy*, as you might expect, and I couldn't imagine fifty-plus Sol adding three kisses at the end.

So I clicked into the message app I hadn't even known Will used and scrolled backwards through the feed. The rest of the chain was empty, deleted for obvious reasons, but it was clear what the last three texts meant.

I need you. ☺ What are you doing right now?
Guess what I'm doing? Xxx ☺
Don't ignore me for too long. I'm already wet for you.

Will froze in the doorway when he saw the phone in my hand, when I said, 'You and Sol are cosy all of a sudden,' even though a fist had been driven into my gut, leaving me winded and punch-drunk dizzy. My hands began to shake, fight or flight adrenaline, meant for something older and more visceral, flooding every nerve and muscle, that survival instinct, once used to save our lives, left with nowhere to go as I stared at the remains of the haddock fillet I'd cooked not an hour before, praying I was wrong, that there was an explanation. There was one, of course, just not one I wanted.

'What are you doing?' demanded Will, snatching the phone back. 'You went through my messages?' and I let him have his moment of denial because, when it ended, I had to somehow believe that, in the spasm of the clock between his going to the bathroom and returning, he was no longer the man I'd married, no longer my good Will, my loyal, honest Will, shaking his head at the antics of friends and colleagues screwing around on their wives *because they didn't know when they had it good, led around by their dicks, the fools,* each new tale of someone caught out, leaving us smug and superior, convinced, *That'll never be us. Thank God. We know what matters.*

All that was shattered as he scanned his phone, pretending he was affronted I'd invaded his privacy, his usual attempt to make me think I was in the wrong, in any confrontation, when he'd snap, *What are you talking about? I don't understand. You always think the worst of me. What's the point of even trying to explain if that's what you think?*

It was always that way when he was scared or felt threatened, chin thrust out, demanding, *What are you playing at?*, fight first, flight later, usually with the slamming of a door. I, on the other hand, always stood back, took a deep breath, needing ever so long to wind up into an explosion – facing off, we were two instinctive animals, protecting ourselves. But we weren't supposed to be animals, standing in our American dream apartment in our supposedly dream life. We were supposed to be civilised, a devoted husband and wife.

'What's her name then?' I asked quietly.

'I don't know what you're talking about,' he insisted, but didn't ask 'Who?' and that was when I was sure, when I said, 'Show me the other messages,' steely and calm.

'What?' he bluffed. 'What are you on about? Why are you snooping on me? Checking up on me?'

'I saw it, Will. I saw the last message. Who's *wet for you*? I really hope it isn't Sol or there's something important you need to tell me.'

I could see his fingers flying across the screen then, deleting, deleting. If I could have, I'd have lunged forward and grabbed it from him, but how could I? I knew how it would end, him pushing me back easily with the hand of one angry arm, the shameful knowledge that we'd descended into something sordid, something out of control, something hands-on and physical.

'Who is she? How long has this been going on?' I yelled, impotent at arm's length. 'Don't think I don't know what you're doing.'

'Look. You've got it all wrong, Liv, as usual. It's a stupid girl from work, that's all. She messes about with all the guys, sends them texts. I've told her not to, but you know young girls today. It's a laugh to them – they don't think anything of it.'

'It's a laugh? She sends sexts to married men and that's a joke?'

'Lighten up. It's a generational thing. Tinder and hook-ups and all that. It doesn't mean anything. Look, if you're going to be like this I'll get rid of them. There, I've deleted them all, deleted her number too. OK, does that satisfy you?'

I was so far from being satisfied I could easily have ripped his face off, clawed his fucking skin from the bone and smashed his skull with my foot. Instead I asked, 'Why would you do that if there's nothing to it? So what's her fucking name?'

He looked up from the phone then, looked me in the eye for the first time.

'It's Kath. She's just one of those girls who thinks it's cool to be all upfront and flirty.'

'So why is she hidden under the name Sol in your phone?'

'What are you accusing me of?' he yelled, running out of corners to defend. 'Whatever it is, you've got it wrong. It's always like this with you, Liv. It's always the third degree, a hundred questions, when I've done nothing wrong.'

He was still protesting his innocence an hour later when I called him a piece of shit for the third time, shoved his stubbornly braced chest with my hands and asked him to leave. Asked, not ordered, mind you, my manners still more infallible than my judgement because, even though I knew what was happening, I couldn't believe it.

And because he had to leave, right then, that second, because of what I might do if he didn't, because the shove I'd given him felt like the first of many gathering behind my ribs, deep in my core.

I managed to hold it together that day, to rein in what was struggling inside, trying to escape. As Will grabbed his keys and stomped out, I shackled it deep down so it took months to get free, to run wild. After that, there was no way to coax it back inside and make it sit quietly in chains. By then there was already one dead body and I was in trouble.

Three

Monument Valley, Utah

When our Navajo Wind Spirit guide arrived in a dramatic, jeep-generated dust cloud at 8 a.m. the next day, I was glad I'd taken the initiative and booked a guided tour for the second day of our holiday. After a quick clipboard namecheck and safety briefing, 'call-me-Brogan' bumped us, and eight other older, and thankfully quieter, tourists away from the oasis of the hotel complex and right into the deep, red bowl of their sacred valley.

Clinging to the guardrail, hanging on to our hats, we wound downwards towards the monoliths that had only seemed pocket-sized because they were deceptively far away. Nothing short of an avenue of stone tower blocks emerged from the sweep of dust devils and tyre smoke ahead as we made our first stop at a traditional Navajo Hogan, the round stone and clay dwellings the original natives lived in.

Listening to Brogan's laconic history lesson, about how, despite Hollywood's insistence, there were never any swingporched cabins picturesquely situated there, I marvelled at how anyone could set up home in such a barren place where plumbing was a luxury and the very existence of water seemed a shimmering mirage. Wales is one of the greenest places on earth, where you can practically inhale water and absorb chlorophyll through your skin, so there was something chastening about standing in the quiet, beating heat, nodding with the over-sixties leisure seekers at the harshness and ingenuity of Native American life.

I remember thinking that, while one room with no idiot noisy neighbours and an unbeatable view was a fair trade-off for TV and electric lighting, I'd miss a shower and a fridge. To be honest I was already missing the hotel air con as, at barely 9.30 a.m., the sun was already scouring us remorselessly from its eyrie and the valley's fine, floury dust was sieving its way into the creases of my eyelids, catching in my throat, prickling my salt-encrusted skin.

As Brogan had warned us in his safety briefing, at that level of low humidity you simply don't sweat, the liquid evaporates instantly from your pores. That's why it's so easy to dehydrate and suffer heat exhaustion before you even realise you're thirsty – something I'd definitely have to mention in my 'Travel Safely' tips.

Though, as I sipped my coolie bottle, seeking shade whenever possible, Will seemed in fine fettle, playing with the cheap, white Stetsons at the unexpected gift stand, doing cowboy finger-shooting impressions with a bandanna tied jauntily around his neck.

Blue eyes laughing, he looked handsome, cool almost smiling, 'Back of the neck, don't forget,' adjusting the neckerchief he'd insisted I wear to keep the heatstroke at bay. *My* Will, who, minutes before, had helped an elderly Texan woman down from the back of the jeep into the soft sand on the valley floor with his usual chivalry; my Will, who then tried to tempt a nervous pony, tethered at the corral, to eat an apple out of his hand with cooing noises.

'You've got a good one there,' said the skinny woman from Iowa who'd sat opposite us in the jeep, now in line for the last Portakabin loo in the West. 'A sweetheart.'

'Yeah. He's a star,' I muttered, thinking of the nine minutes of film I'd watched on my laptop the previous December in which Will had a starring role, nine minutes of footage I'd never un-see where he was anything but a chivalrous hero in a white hat.

'Smile, Liv,' Will insisted, raising the camera he'd borrowed from work, the kind that takes short videos as well as photos – the 'crime scene' camera as I'd come to think of it by then. Seeing it, knowing what *it* had seen that winter, made me suddenly want to smash it, and Will's head, against the Hogan wall. Instead, not wanting to make a scene, I watched as Will used it to take some landscape shots and capture the petroglyphs etched into the rocks by hands older than language. I still have the sequence he filmed with it half an hour later, of Brogan cross-legged, playing a Navajo flute inside the sacred 'eye of the sun', a water-formed fissure that opened like a squinted eye to the blue sky.

I remember the red-rock ceiling above us prickling with water run-off eyelashes, how it was all I could do not to cry along with it as we lay on our backs as instructed, closing our eyes to *commune with the ancient ancestors*. Will reached over and held my hand as the flute notes floated up on the breeze, circling the smooth stone walls, though I wished he hadn't, since I knew where that hand had been and had the video evidence. That was one of his biggest mistakes, I remember thinking, head on the warm red rock, memory in New York, not covering his tracks properly.

Everyone knows that, in the wild, you should never leave evidence of your passing, a trail that something with bigger teeth can use to track you down. You should always shovel over your shit, bury your food waste, douse your fires at dawn – any good camping guidebook will tell you that. I remember thinking later, much later, that if Will had only learned that first lesson, perhaps it would have burned itself out between him and her without my ever knowing. That way something more of us might have survived that trip, instead of letting us run headlong into trouble so much harder to spot than the signposted warnings of 'unstable road ahead' or 'falling rocks' – there was nothing to warn us about the hidden dangers, lying in wait, patient, cunning, creeping.

Like the ratty coyote I spotted on stop number three, languishing on the rutted track close to the soaring 'three sisters' rock formation, prompting Brogan to remark, 'Ah yes. We are being watched. Of all the figures in Navajo mythology, Coyote is the most contradictory, a god, a trickster. He cannot be killed because he is too powerful.'

Making his voice low and ominous, a kid telling a campfire ghost story, he whispered, 'They say that if Coyote crosses your path, turn back and do not continue your journey or something terrible will happen to you. Perhaps we should return to the hotel while there's still time.'

Everyone grinned then, except me, wondering if Brogan was trying to tell me something as he tipped me a wink. Everyone laughed as we watched the balding fleabag decide our fates, oohing and aahing in a *we're all doomed* sort of way when it got up and trotted off into the dunes, and while I felt a weary longing for our cool New York apartment and bottle of Jack Daniel's.

It was 11 a.m. by then and even Will, who'd been having a great time quoting lines from John Wayne and Jimmy Stewart westerns to anyone in earshot, had started to get tired and crotchety.

'I know I should probably check my white privilege,' he muttered, as we trekked towards Teardrop Arch, 'but what's up with this Brogan guy? This guilt-trip about classic Hollywood westerns misrepresenting Native American life is a bit of a downer. I mean, I'm not defending colonialism but I didn't disenfranchise anyone, and does Brogan really have it so bad, waking up to this every morning, teaching, sharing all this history? It sure as hell beats a suited nine-to-five in an office, right? This jeep ride cost us fifty bucks each and if it wasn't for bloody white-centric 'classic westerns' no one would know about this place anyway.'

'Yeah, well. Some things are so unforgivable you never get to stop paying for them,' I snapped, surprising myself with the verbal slap that turned Will's cheeks pink in an instant.

'I just meant, we get the point, that's all,' he muttered, staying on safe ground. 'This is meant to be a holiday. He doesn't have to keep going on about it. I feel enough of a prick most days without paying for the privilege.'

And then I wondered for the millionth time why I hadn't just left him, at moments like that when every word out of his mouth made him seem like a stranger – even worse was that he was making me a stranger to myself, making me think things I'd never have thought before, making me see something unfamiliar in the mirror each day that had nothing to do with the blue undereye rings beneath my carefully layered concealer, the tightness in my jaw.

It felt like something shifting, something watchful, surfacing. Like the coyote, perhaps, which I realised was still observing us from a tump of boulders nearby, nose in the sand, body motionless. His camouflage was almost perfect, yet I could see him, maybe contemplating all the tricks he could play on the unsuspecting white folk. Guess it takes one to know one, since I'd been playing a few little tricks of my own by then, back in the city, in the months leading up to our vacation, tricks such as delivering presents to a doorstep under the cover of darkness; such as popping a tiny white tablet into a drink on a bar then standing back to watch the aftermath. Such as leaving messages on a phone with a 'smiley face' emoticon added for good measure – all good fun until someone gets hurt, that is.

'Laughing leads to crying,' my mother used to say, and she was right for once. Pretty much everything turns to crying in the end, laughing included.

As the coyote and I stood locked in a staring standoff, Will was too busy admiring a sculptural cluster of wind-smoothed rocks to notice. When I smiled as the coyote saved its fight for another day, slinking soundlessly away between the boulders, he was too distracted to care, or to have the first idea that I was idly trying to estimate how long he might survive if I slunk away too, leaving him out there in the baking desert all alone.

First, I'd have to convince Brogan to let us hike back to the hotel, just the two of us. My holiday preparation had revealed that pre-booked permits were available for a fee, and a few extra bucks would probably grease the wheels for us at the last minute. After that it would be easy because, as usual, Will had no idea where we were. He was relying on Brogan to get us back to the hotel and without Brogan he'd be relying on me.

Will knew I had a map of the valley in my pocket, had, as always, looked over the route, scouted the ground in advance because I like to be prepared. Once the jeep trundled off surely it would be easy enough to slink away, hide, coyote-slick behind a rocky outcrop, in a box canyon, until, panicky and bone dry from searching for me, Will would be forced to find his own way back.

Would the sun and dehydration get him first? I wondered, playing a little theoretical game of how and what if, as I pretended to admire the span of burnt orange stone stretching against the sea of sky above me. Or would it be the snakes and scorpions we'd been warned littered the valley, as he blundered about looking for landmarks, trying to gain a sense of direction from the sun he might be vaguely aware would eventually slip to the west behind that tall red spire?

Something about it made me smile, the idea of testing his John Wayne grit against the landscape and his insect-repelling shorts against the lurking creatures of the red rocks. What use would his cheap Stetson and jaunty bandanna be then? But, before I could think it through properly my daydream was broken by Brogan, honking the horn and calling the group back to the jeep.

A very special tour upgrade was available, he said, the chance to spend the night in a Hogan with a Navajo family, to eat at their hearth and experience their hospitality. It was a great honour on sacred land.

'No thanks, mate,' grinned Will, shaking his head immediately. 'Time to take my pampered white skin home for a shower and some aloe vera gel, I think. I'm waving the white flag and hanging up my spurs while I'm ahead,' generating a polite ripple of laughter from the now weary crowd.

And that was it, the moment I put the first definite cross on the left-hand side of his test column. Because the test was up and running, the clock was ticking, and what was Will's self-satisfied response in that moment if not a clear fail – an immediate rejection of spontaneity, to respond to a unique possibility, to seize a sense of occasion?

Yes, it was probably a twee marketing exercise designed for naive city dwellers (as Will would remark after dinner) but wouldn't it have been romantic? Hunkered down together around a crackling fire, the night unfolding above? What visions of the future might we have seen there? What silent starscapes exploding above us, away from all light pollution and noise of the hotel terrace?

Out there maybe *she* would have had to stay outside at least, uninvited, excluded. Just for one night. The ultimate gesture.

But it had passed us by with one flippant comment, still sticking in my throat as we bumped back along the rutted sand towards the hotel and Will leaned over, tying a clean neckerchief around my mouth and nose, as he'd done with his own, to keep the swirling dust at bay.

'Stick 'em up,' he muffled through the cotton, making the older ladies laugh, smiling beneath the mask, but all I could think of was the smile on his face the night I'd found those texts. The night he'd insisted, 'You're crazy.'

I was glad my face was hidden as I was swamped by the memory of how, in the days afterwards, he'd insisted on the phone, then in the apartment, that *Kath* was just someone he'd met on a conference, that he'd only slept with her once, after the delegates' leaving dinner. *We were drunk*, he said, and *she started it. She made the first move*, like he'd been involved in some schoolyard spat that got out of control. Like it meant nothing.

It had been so pathetic, hearing him pour out cliché after cliché at the kitchen table, I'd wanted to kill him, then and there, for his sheer lack of imagination, the laziness of showing himself to be *one of those men* after all, *led around by their dicks, the fools*.

How had I possibly missed it, all those years? I asked myself, as we began the long climb back towards the park barriers, back to The View's car park.

But the unthinkable is unthinkable until suddenly it isn't and it's smacking you in the face, leaving your head ringing as you sob, 'Do you want to be with her? Are you leaving me? Do you love her?' Even when he insists it was a mistake. He was a fool, flattered, that the texts just kept popping up long after she went back to San Francisco, titillation, nothing more.

'I know it was wrong but she was in another city, it seemed . . . harmless . . .' he'd sighed across the table, not able to meet my eye, 'because it was never going to happen again. She meant nothing to me,' tears wrinkling down his face in the sunlight filtering through the apartment windows, the tower blocks blackening against the evening sunset.

I swallowed mine down under my cowboy neckerchief, turning away from him, from the Iowan lady and her sharp knees opposite, from the memory of the snot string stretching from Will's nose in sticky slow motion, through the orange October twilight because I couldn't tell him it was OK. It wasn't OK at all. And it wasn't harmless. What did he know about the definition of harm? What could I still teach him?

While we were bumping back to the hotel dusty and sulky, I was one day closer to finding out.

Four

New York City

After two weeks staying in a cheap hotel, bombarding me with begging messages, Will had returned home, laden with dirty shirts and golden promises. We had several 'big talks' over those long nights, when the crisp, dry sounds of autumn drifted up through the open windows, reminding my brittle heart of the hopes he'd crushed underfoot.

Those were the nights when I laid down the 'ground rules' of 'trying again', warning Will he could expect to be made to feel like the absolute shit he was for some time to come. After that we made a 'to do' list as the self-help, 'fix your marriage in five easy steps' websites I was obsessively Googling suggested, hoping someone better equipped to deal with this than I was, someone who'd seen it all before, could tell me what to do.

Over the weeks the benumbed and frost-glittered city iced over and Will and I reassembled the broken pieces of our lives into fragile versions of their old selves a careless word might still destroy. During that time I reminded him, every day, that he needed to stop taking me for granted, that I needed to be convinced he was really sorry with a gesture or two, to be made to feel special, so I could believe he really saw and heard me again.

Over time 'the talk' became part of the verbal 'give-and-take' contract we drew up, to 'emphasise the positive' while coming to terms with the negative, like the self-help gurus advocated. So, as I'd asked, we cooked together again as the nights drew closer and tighter against the windows, started planning a proper holiday, *the road trip* I'd always talked about, and Will promised to do something spontaneous, once a month, to take me out, surprise me.

In return I put the laptop away on his days off, tried to stop 'envying other people's lifestyles' and stop bitching about not being able to work in America.

It was working for a while and Will seemed to relax, talking to me more than he ever had in the months before, sharing funny stories and embarrassing mishaps that all hotels hold secret. We were rediscovering each other, relearning who we were and that was reassuring. When he was there, that is, when I was looking into his *trust me I'm a good guy* eyes and couldn't imagine they would ever lie again.

But, when he wasn't there, in the hours I'd once relished for my solitary city adventures, the thoughts kept coming, buzzing, stinging, swarming, swooping, attacking. Thoughts such as, Where are you now, Will? Was it really a one-time thing, a digital flirtation? Is she really in another city? This girl you call Kath but I don't think is called Kath? Is she still hiding in your phone under a different name? Is it really over between you?

I suppose that's always been my problem. Maybe it's a writer's curse, but I remember pretty much everything ever said and pick it all apart endlessly, things such as, *Stop crying Olivia, what good will that do you? Stuck up little tart. Who do you think you are? What the fuck are you looking at? Can I play join the dots on those spots on your face? Are those tits or fried eggs?*

I love you. It didn't mean anything . . .

They're all there, all the time, the words and promises, lies and excuses, swooping, spiralling. Soon it was all I could do not to scratch the doubts out of my own skull with bloody fingers. So I put the thoughts to work, carrying out little reconnaissance missions inside the apartment, trying to gather evidence and come to a conclusion. It was one way to fill the hours suddenly pregnant with threat, the anticipation of fear, the suspicion of the unknown as yet unrevealed. Of *the other woman*. When and where she might appear next.

So I went through Will's trouser and jacket pockets, sometimes two or three times a day, despite telling myself it served no purpose; if it was over, as he promised, I wouldn't find anything. If it wasn't, he would be careful now.

Logical yet doomed, I hunted and sought, a slave to the failure of magical thinking, of looking on the bright side, of hoping for the best. I looked through his messenger bag, his wallet, hunted down evidence in every flap and fold, envelope and notepad, clothes drawer and wardrobe, searching for something out of place, something unfamiliar, something deadly.

I looked at his emails when unattended, checked the sent and deleted boxes, sneaked a look at his phone messages so I could be reassured there was nothing to hide, relieved when I found nothing, frustrated when I didn't, because that might mean he was cleverer than me now, better at hiding in plain sight.

It was no way to live, on a knife edge, on a cliff ledge, on a rope bridge swaying and fraying underfoot. 'Hyper vigilance', the support blogs call it, the instinct skewed by the knowledge of lies, leading to suspicion everywhere. Each one assured me it was 'perfectly normal' but it didn't feel normal, the war being waged inside my skull, armies clashing, trying to gain ground, gouge out answers to the questions, How do I get over my husband's affair? Should I give him a second chance? Once a cheater, always a cheater?

And of course, worst of all, What if this isn't the first time? Will he do it again?

Trust your instincts, the agony aunts say, but that's easier said than done when your instincts are screaming that there's a knickerless tart opening her legs for your weak-willed husband around every corner, so you ask a hundred times a day – Should I stay or should I go? Fall or fight? Mend or destroy? Curl up into a ball and die or . . .? Can I live like this?

Exhausted by the questions, by the uncertainty, I tried to make a list like the gurus suggested – two columns; good things in your relationship on the left-hand side; things you'd like to change on the right. Consider if one outweighs the other. Which aspects are non-negotiable? And in those darkest of New York twilights, there was something appealing about that, a tally sheet that could be logically assessed, ticked, totted up – a decision reached.

So, I made a list.

The good things in our relationship

>Will was kind.
>Will was a good listener.
>Will was not a football fan.
>Will was generous with money.
>Will was really good in bed.
>Will always supported my work.

The bad things

>Will was a lying shit.
>Will chose a skank over me.
>Will pretended to be a good person.
>Will took me for granted.
>Will often made me feel bad for wanting more.
>Will made me feel like I was a bad person for not always being happy.

Then I stopped writing, hurled the pad across the room, not just because I was writing in the past tense, as if my marriage was already over, but because I realised just how fucking pathetic I'd become. How could a list quantify the daily dynamic between two people, all the small things that make a relationship? I'd already made my decision. I'd taken him back instead of giving up, moving on, which I easily could have, after shredding his shirts first, of course, or posting his face on a roadside billboard under the words 'lying cheating adulterer' and sticking the photo on Facebook, as is the twenty-first-century way.

But I didn't want to give up. I wanted to believe him when he said he'd made a terrible mistake. After all, I wasn't perfect. I'd done things I'd regretted, things I wasn't proud of. Like what happened with James Scott, on the evening of my sixteenth birthday . . . James and his pretty eyes . . . Natalie, in tears for a change . . .

I hadn't allowed myself to think about James Scott in twenty years, but suddenly he was there, skulking behind my back, just out of sight, reminding me how I might fare in a tally list of my good and bad points if someone was to draw one up, when right at the top would sit the words, *Liv once killed someone.* That'd pretty much be non-negotiable for anyone, I think. Who would bother to read on past that?

So I told myself one bad decision didn't have to define me for ever, or define Will, as we kept trying, and I kept fighting the attacks of dislocation and detachment that began to ambush me without warning, that feeling that I was somehow existing in an alternate universe, living a life no longer mine, getting stronger every day.

It's a strange sensation, watching a hand that's your own and not your own, reaching for a pack of supermarket chicken breasts, the sweat on the top of the cellophane in sharp focus alongside your wedding ring, still on your finger, thinking, Will likes the way I cook them, with tomatoes and black olives, a hint of rosemary, then realising that Will, while he'll still come home for dinner that night, is also gone, missing in action, and another Will-like man has body-snatched him, one you know nothing about any more – who he is, what he might do.

Then the panic attack would sweep in like a tornado, head whirling, lungs wheezing. Caught out in the dizzy open, keeling slightly, I'd find myself wishing a door would open beneath me, swallow me up, thinking, Please don't let me pass out here in the frozen food aisle. Someone will probably steal my purse and that gritty floor isn't that clean looking.

It happened so many times that winter, buying a coffee and choosing the caramel syrup Will liked, seeing an advert on TV we'd laughed at, hearing a song that meant something to us both, a TV in-joke, a phrase triggering nothing less than grief, real throat-clenching grief. It was hard to keep moving, from bed to shower, grocery store to desk, in that state, but I did. Because it was impossible to ask for help aloud, when Will had always been the one I'd always turned to.

My friends in New York were few. Pilar was my only acquaintance in the apartment building, eight years younger than me, a fiery and free-smiling artist who'd invited me in for coffee after a chat by the mailbox revealed a mutual love of Frank Lloyd Wright and Edward Hopper. She hung out with a rather handsome man with an artfully groomed beard who rolled from 'great guy' to 'no good loser' with regular ease. If she'd found what I had in the 'no good loser's' phone I've no doubt she would've *kicked his lousy ass out*, and, viciously dabbing her brush at one of her colour splodge paintings, would tell me to do the same.

But I couldn't bring myself to say the words aloud, to tell anyone my marriage was failing. So, despite the give-and-take pact, the peace talks, the temporary lull in hostilities, I was somehow gagged and tethered, trapped in a silent place where words such as I love you, words that had once carried the weight of worlds, shored up our lives, were unable to hold up their heads and look me in the eye.

Voiceless for the first time in my life, vibrating at a level too high or low for the human ear, I imagined the street dogs of the city snuffling in the newspaper-blown alleyways, the silk-cushioned pets of the New York high rises, howling in sympathy with me as I slid past in the darkness, moving through the night, mute.

That was before I found the support group, of course, before I could talk about it, though I knew I shouldn't talk about it. But I really needed to talk about it.

It was before I changed my name, my voice and my story. Before I became a widow.

Five

Grand Canyon National Park, Arizona

When we pulled up outside the El Tovar Lodge in the mellow rust-tinged twilight there was no chance I would simply wait in the car until Will had checked us in. Because I knew it was there, just across the tarmac path, hidden from sight by a quirk of geography and the handful of T-shirted tourists strolling past the gift shops along the promenade. Unable to bear it any longer, I jumped out of the car and ran right to the edge of the Grand Canyon South Rim.

Tears caught in my throat as my eyes adjusted to the landscape hacked out of the rock before me, so much more heart stopping than the crowded arrival at Monument Valley that I didn't know where to cast my gaze first. The vista was, in the true sense of the word, awesome, more than living up to the promise of page 38, *National Geographic* (storm clouds over North Rim, American Condor and thunderhead), that once graced the mildewy walls of my childhood bedroom. In fact, it was almost too beautiful to bear, too overwhelming, as a great ball of gunmetal clouds built in the north, churning the canyon into a sea of rolling colours.

As the pressure in my chest rose, I felt myself going thin all of a sudden, struggling to draw in air before the stark brutality of a world with barely a tree, barely a patch of green grass or shade, dust-dry, sharp toothed. I'll say this for the Americans though, they have a practical approach to health and safety, relying on people's common sense to tell them that a massive hole in the ground equals danger. Apart from the low wall I gratefully steadied myself against, the edge of the abyss was completely unfenced, not a single sign planted to keep people back from the jagged drop where the skin of the earth, the layers and striations of once tremendous seas and fossilised forests, peeled back a million years before my eyes.

Will came to find me then, bags speedily dropped in our room, beaming, pulling me towards him so we could admire the view, silently folding into each other, no words needed, at least none we could say. I wanted to stay there for ever, captured insect-like in the amber of the moment, preserved with no past, no future, no regrets. But dusk fell like a flicked switch, as it does that far west, and dinner beckoned with a rumble of Will's ever-empty stomach.

We were staying at the El Tovar for three nights, a welcome throwback to the rustic elegance of pioneer days with a few mod cons thrown in. The great, dark wood and stone shell of its interior, housing brittle-haired animal heads and huge sooty fireplaces, had welcomed travellers as far back as the 1900s, when tourism first hit the area and the railroad reached out to ferry the rich and curious up from San Francisco. Will was in his element again, threatening to wear his Monument Valley souvenir Stetson to dinner or buy a furry Davy Crockett hat from the gift shop, while I was more interested in finding the bar and ordering some cowboy bourbon.

Dinner in the darkened restaurant that night felt atmospheric and intimate for once, as we dissected our rare steaks under the rafters. Whispering, smiling, we recalled a not so different lodge in the Austrian Alps, near Berchtesgaden, where we'd once ended a day's hike with schnapps and schnitzel under a grinning stuffed boar's head Will had christened Trevor, after his dad, the ultimate 'stuffed bore'.

'Tell me, Trevor, where do you see yourself in ten years? What's your five-year plan?' he echoed with a grin, and, armed by the memories and several glasses of smoky California Pinot Noir, I was finally starting to relax.

So it would've been the perfect time for Will to summon a little surprise to reinforce the moment, to rise to the ongoing challenge. Surely it would be a moment's work to speak surreptitiously to the waiter and ask him to bring over a glass of surprise champagne, and I was optimistic that, at any minute, Will might even clear his throat and produce a little pre-wrapped love token from his pocket, that would've taken care of the 'romantic gesture' and 'sense of occasion' elements of the test in one go.

Instead, I was left hiding my disappointment as he enthused about our hiking plans, telling myself there was still time for him to raise his game, that perhaps he had something special planned for me when we arrived in the Sierras.

We'd learned from our stay in Monument Valley that most people simply head to bed after dinner when there's little to do but stare at the stars, banking early nights for payback sunrises. So the only sign of life as we strolled on the canyon rim, swimming in milky mist between threatening storm clouds, was a huge elk grazing by the Hopi House Gallery, its soft, dark eyes seeming to question what right we had to be there, interrupting his meal.

As Will and I froze, the animal's eyes locked with mine and suddenly I felt like an intruder, under scrutiny. There are no large predators left in that part of Arizona; wolves were hunted to extinction centuries ago, but all animals sense the scent of a predator, and after a moment he lifted his head and bounded away to a little stand of trees.

'We scared him,' said Will with disappointment, as we padded across the low boundary wall onto the rock formations beyond. I clutched his hand tightly as we clambered right to the precipice, unsettled by the look in the elk's eye, by the smell of cooling stone, reminding me of forgotten summers out among the trees and shrubs of the little wilderness behind the housing estate in Cardiff. Of a night on a rooftop, staring downwards, memories merging, questions hovering like vultures above me, waiting to swoop down.

All at once that fist was back in my chest again, squeezing, and I couldn't quite bring myself to look down into the canyon's open maw, nor even to smile when Will said, 'It's magnificent, isn't it?' as the moon skittered across the yawn of the canyon's stone teeth. 'I'm so glad I could share this with you, Liv, that you've let me. This is as it should be. As I always want it to be. Just the two of us,'

'Hmm,' I said, face pressed into his fleece jacket, not trusting myself to speak, not to lean out, fall from the edge, to see the ground swirl up towards me, because it wasn't just the two of us there, far from it, not just because I could still sense the elk, watching silently from the blackness of the trees at our back.

We headed back after a few minutes, ready for our early start, and I slept that night spooned into the crook of Will's body, dreaming of dark birds and feathered beasts, images of the gift shop gods of the Hopi House awash with Native American art and legend, smoke-fuelled memories of prayers past.

We spent the next morning taking a sleepy sunrise walk along the rim, before heading to the airfield for our pre-booked helicopter ride in the afternoon. Despite the queuing at the reception centre, the awkward safety weigh-in for balanced seating and being squashed into a rotor-driven tin can alongside three plumply grinning Germans, it was a breath-taking twenty minutes of bird's eye swooping over the rifts and cracks stretching as far as the eye could see.

But you can't really appreciate the scale from above. You have to trek down from the rim, like all the good guidebooks insist. So that's what we did, on our second day, after sampling buffalo burgers and Monterey Jack fries for that night's dinner under the guise of getting our carb levels up.

We set off down the donkey track of Bright Angel Trail at 6 a.m. sharp, through the candy-striped layers of rock, time and history. Sinking down through millions of years was a bit like time travel, a moving archaeological excavation, not unlike excavating a marriage, I suppose, or its corpse. At least, that's what I found myself thinking as we dipped down through the Coconino sandstone and hermit shale, the Redwall limestone and Bright Angel shale, the sun throwing a blanket of rosy dawn above us.

With each step we left behind our phone reception, internet data connection and the helicopter whirrs from darting black tourist drones forbidden to dip below the rim. Will kept turning around to grin at me, eager to lead the way for a change on a path that went straightforwardly down forever, his neck growing pink as the world filled with sun and birdsong.

At first, I was glad to see him enjoying himself, so keen to share every detail with me, pointing out a rock formation here, a flower there with childish happiness. But, as the silence let the space inside my head expand away from me, I found myself thinking how unfair it was that he was getting to enjoy our adventure with a clear mind when mine was still so addled with noise.

Hearing his breath quicken as he picked up the pace, I found myself re-hearing it as the sound of his breath on the memory card I'd found in his pocket, on the day before Christmas Eve. It had been a surprise, certainly, to see the cause that day, to watch them screwing on the screen in front of me, Will and the skank, his breath ragged and hitching. At least the mechanics were dull, nothing kinky or disturbingly *Fifty Shades* of pervy, that was my first thought, a few moments after pressing the play button on my laptop, though that didn't help much in the moments that became months afterwards.

I'd found it by accident, while wrapping Will's Christmas presents, a smart blazer from Saks, some nice aftershave. That's how these things happen, they creep up on you when you're off guard, when you're not looking, pounce, claws out, then shred you to pieces. In this case, it was a moving image of *her*, her pink mouth open, panting, her face sheened with sweat.

I'd been looking for quarters for the basement laundry machines, and there was the memory card, in the zip pocket of the fleece Will occasionally wore to the gym, with a crumpled buck and a clutch of cents. Without thinking I took three dimes and got as far as the apartment door with the dirty clothes under my arm before I stopped, the hairs on my neck prickling.

I put down the basket, retraced my steps, and fished the memory card out again, wondering what it could be when we didn't have a camera. Wondering why Will might have taken the card out of the camera he used for work and brought it home. Fingering the plastic square, I thought of the great meal Will had surprised me with the night before, actually making a reservation for once, unasked, in the trendy little Italian place two blocks over.

Sipping salty Margaritas I'd finally started to feel as if we'd lived through something terrible and world-altering but ridden it out, survived. Yet I still carried the card to the kitchen table and opened my laptop. An unnamed file came up as soon as I stuck it in the flash-drive slot, the date stamp showing three weeks before, after Will had supposedly broken off all contact with you-know-who for over a month. It was when he'd said he was meeting those Dutch clients uptown, while I'd been planning our first New York Christmas; champagne and lobster in the apartment on Christmas Eve and lunch at the Lowbeck on Christmas Day.

I recognised the room as soon as I clicked *play* – number 717 at the Lowbeck, where we'd made love, right after we arrived in the city. We'd 'christened' the hotel on that same wrought iron and blue velvet bed, under that exact arty, black-and-white skyline shot of the Manhattan water towers and SoHo midrise.

The composition of the little masterpiece on screen was terrible in comparison to that impeccable studio shot, off-centre, with something blurring the outer corner of the lens. Her bikini-line shaving rash was clearly visible though as she fingered herself, hand between her legs, the butterfly tattoo on her left buttock coming into view as she straddled him, a ripple of sinewy thighs flexing.

The camera must have been set to record on the table under the window, to catch the action from that low, long angle, the grinding, the sighing. He was open-mouthed in anticipation, his hands reaching to grip her waist. Will, *my* Will. My husband.

'I love you, Will,' she said, her face in profile, red hair swishing, pausing, pulling upright to look into his face, cupping his face with her hands. 'Do you love me?'

The moment hung there and I hung with it, swinging to and fro from the chain of my discovery, my destruction, 'Oh yeah,' he said, after a moment, 'but don't talk, just keep doing that.'

'Sure, sure,' she answered, 'but since we're on camera,

why don't we liven this up a bit? Let me give you something to fantasise about later.'

Sliding off him, ignoring what sounded like his huff of frustration, his protest that 'you know, I'm not really . . . can't we just . . .' she moved to the edge of the bed. Repositioning the camera, shifting it into a close up, kneeling in the sheets, she said, 'I'll show you something sexy.'

After another minute or so the images cut out, low battery perhaps. But in my head everything was already laid waste. I smelled burning and blood, though I clicked restart and watched the segment twice more before I could move. I remember thinking, staring at the Christmas tree I'd just hung with silver baubles, the evergreen garland over the apartment fireplace, This is not happening. That is not my husband. This is not my life. He promised, he promised, he swore it was over.

That day in the canyon, trekking down into the red-rock heart of eras long past, I had too much time to relive the smooth contours of her pale thighs in a flashback that refused to end, to see and hear the sound of shared saliva in digital high definition. Too much time to look at Will's hairy legs marching ahead, his familiar hands, filling my bottle for me at the water stops, the same hands I'd seen on her schoolboy tits; the hands brushing a stray hair from my forehead when we stopped to admire the acid-yellow butterflies, the arc of an eagle riding the morning air currents, the hand that had slid between her legs.

By the time we reached the cool, watery green of Indian Gardens, I could hardly look at him for fear of what would show in my eyes when he grinned and said, 'Alone at last,' pulling an apple from his rucksack and handing it to me.

And I was glad of the sudden privacy, the absence of other early-bird hikers and the clop of plodding, sure-footed donkeys and their guides we'd passed in the upper canyon, ready for the unfit or lazy tourists, resigned to their early start.

Once or twice we'd passed upward climbers who'd spent the night at the Colorado River still far below, returning before the heat rose. Though I reminded Will of the signs dotting the rim above, warning hikers not to attempt to reach the river and return in a single day, Will still wanted to press on to the plateau edge, to get a peek at the great Colorado.

As we trekked out of the leafy shade, the vast flank of rock rim behind us, we were suddenly invisible to all but the birds, and perhaps the pinprick people with binoculars moving on the rim above. The sound of the crickets, or whatever those things were that screamed their high-pitched electric hum at us, was relentless, the flowers and fragrance giving way to barren rock and air so dry my eyes were stripped back in minutes.

That's when I really started to panic, to doubt I could go on any further or make it back, not just out of the canyon and up the four-hour climb behind us, but ever; back to New York, back to a life that suddenly felt as empty as the track beneath the lonely tramp of our boots. While Will ploughed on oblivious, towards the edge of the false lip, where the plateau plunges to the green snake of water at its base, my chest began to seize, my pulse quicken.

It wouldn't have been so bad, the sun hammering on my baseball cap, the wings and trilling that sounded like laughter, if Will had just shut up for five minutes, but he simply wouldn't stop talking, offering platitudes and advice, as I puffed and fell behind.

'It's a mental battle, you can do it, Liv,' he repeated, evidently pleased I was puffing and finding it tough for a change; 'One foot at a time, like you used to tell me on those hikes up Corn Ddu, remember? One foot in front of the other, you used to say when I was blowing like a whale. It's a mental test, right?'

He was right, of course, and those had been my own words, yet that was then, in the time before, when I knew him, and in my head everything had suddenly split in two. I wanted him to stop speaking, to give me two minutes to un-rattle my brain, restore some sequence to my breathing. To banish the sight of her butterfly tattoo, the spreading flesh, from behind my eyes. Why did he have to be so damn practical about everything? Why couldn't he see I was in as much emotional and mental pain as lacking lungfuls of oxygen?

If my body was shutting down it wasn't only because I'd eaten nothing since coffee and cinnamon buns at 5 a.m., apart from a bite of apple, it was because of all those nights I'd believed he was safely at work when he surely wasn't, when he'd sat on the sofa and played on his phone for hours and I'd assumed he was reading the news. When he'd lied to my face about everything that mattered.

When we finally found a spot to rest by the edge of the cliff, he sat next to me, rubbed my back. But still he kept talking, opening a Clif Bar he'd packed just for me, handing it over, ordering me to eat, prattling about our walks in the Beacons, comparing them to our fantastic adventure, even though he'd poisoned all the air and every touch between us.

I felt my head pound, suddenly owning and observing a pair of hands that weren't mine, detached hands that wanted to roll him backwards and shove him off the edge of the rock escarpment so I could just sit there, letting everything end in peace. How was this prattling thoughtlessness showing me he loved me? Showing me he understood what this had cost me? Showing me he was really sorry?

How was it *taking care of me*, looking after me, point number three of the test, suddenly more important than either of the others? If there was ever a chance to put a tick in the pass column that was it. But how was it anything but yet another fail on his part – failing to have the first clue what I needed without my having to yell it at him?

I tried to focus on my Clif Bar, on the peanut-butter stickiness clinging to my tongue, Will asking if I was OK, me saying, *I'm fine, I'm fine*, two of the most treacherous words in any marriage.

Then I wasn't really thinking about the trip any more; I was wondering if Will was really possibly still allergic to peanuts, like he occasionally claimed to be when he remembered, if he'd only been exaggerating when he'd said he'd had breathing problems once, on a canoe trip when his teacher had offered him trail mix, had really got a hot, tight feeling in his throat and chest at that seventh birthday party with the peanut-butter cupcakes.

Will still carried an old epi pen around with him, though he'd never once used it, and I wondered if it was in his rucksack, and if he could get to it in time if I smeared some of my peanut-butter bar onto his water bottle. If he touched his mouth would there be any reaction? Enough to cause a swelling and tightening, perhaps, like the one in my chest that very minute, like that day I'd seen the memory card show and every day since?

It would be easy for something like that to happen in an isolated spot, an accidental exposure to an allergic substance down to carelessness, or bad luck – a blameless explanation in the 'accidental fatalities' box on a death certificate. Because we were an hour's walk from Indian Gardens by then and, if Will were to unexpectedly fall into the dust clutching his chest, there was no way to summon speedy help. If his throat clenched out of the blue and his lungs closed off, once again *I* was the help, *I* was the rescue.

If I just left, tossed the epi pen into the rocky clefts way below us, took the water with me . . .

It was a logic problem really, I thought as I ran through the story; I could tell the park rangers when I arrived at the first water station, tearful, breathless, screaming the words *hurry* and *please help, we forgot his epi pen, he hasn't needed it for years.* I smeared some of the sticky Clif Bar between my thumb and forefinger as I chewed it over, torn for a minute or two, remembering the ant people on the rim above us, invisible but possibly still watching through binoculars. And the drones, the ones we'd seen taking aerial footage at dawn. What if one shot overhead? Zoomed in on my 'panicked' progress back to Indian Gardens, alerted a chopper?

'Ready then?' said Will, holding out a plastic bag for my oily wrapper, though he was never that careful at home.

I dropped it inside, before cleaning my fingers and the flawed idea away with a wetwipe.

'Do you love me, Will?' I asked, as he got to his feet,

thinking of the whore's panted question to him in the video, his hesitation.

'Of course I do,' pulling me up, cupping my face without a second's pause, planting a kiss on my brow. 'You're my whole world.'

But after that, every foot of the trek back to the top of the rim was like lagging through lead, trying to still the panic, trying to breathe, Will finally becoming anxious that I'd actually passed the extent of my strength.

'Come on, Liv. You can do it,' he coaxed. 'You did six hours on the Fan Dance, remember? It's just the altitude. We'll take our time.'

Yeah, but I wasn't dragging the naked body of your mangy slut behind me every step of the way then, was I? I thought, dry tears evaporating invisibly.

'You know this is your fault, don't you?' I snapped. 'That this is happening because of you?'

'I know. I just wanted to see the river. I thought you were up to it. We should have turned back at Indian Gardens.'

And I couldn't look at him then, as he made me drink a glucose packet from his pack and, after a while, a little bit of energy returned to my legs. I think it was only the thought of the sheer humiliation of possibly having to be rescued by donkey train or air ambulance that made me get to my feet and finish the hike in an unspeaking, unthinking trance.

By the time I collapsed outside the coffee shop at the top, while Will was getting sandwiches and soda, I'd emerged from the climb as something other than myself, something worn and hard, beaten glassy black by the sun and the disappointment of reality.

'Tuna or cheese?' grinned Will, showing the sandwiches and offering me a bottle of my favourite iced tea like the very proudest of hunter-gatherers. 'You've earned it, today.'

And I knew that, in his mind, it was all a great success, while in mine it was nothing more than yet another epic fail.

Six

New York City

The night I discovered the home movie I know I didn't behave rationally. As the low December sun had fallen across the kitchen, signalling the false sunset of the tower blocks, I got up, got dressed and went to dinner. Bonnie and Oliver, the Lowbeck's PR team, were tasked with making sure the other halves of new, out-of-town employees had company while they were settling in and, once a month, treated me to dinner and a 'catch-up'. We'd made a longstanding arrangement for sliders and Christmas cocktails that night and I couldn't think of a last-minute excuse to cancel.

I actually liked Bonnie. We shared a love of reading and she'd shown me several great bookshops, not to mention the Victorian marvel that is the Morgan Library near Grand Central Station, housing JPMorgan Chase's collection. Olly was charming too, great at celebrity impressions and sarcastic asides.

Their names were always spoken as a compound unit by

anyone who mentioned them – Bonnie-and-Olly – the well-dressed, well-connected young couple, smiley and 'super-stoked' to be working for such a great firm in the greatest city in earth. And they both loved Will. Like most Americans they adored his accent, mistaking upper-class diction, and slightly old-fashioned manners, for integrity and honesty. So of course I couldn't tell them what I'd seen on the laptop, what a lying, cheating shit their lovely, amiable, British Will was. Instead, in a numb trance, I changed into a silk shirt and heels, applied my most festive red lipstick and spent the next three hours watching myself chatting cheerily under the art deco Christmas lights of the Lowbeck bar.

'Where's Will tonight?' they chanted in unison, immaculate and white-toothed across the booth.

'Working,' smiling, the image of a happy wife.

'Good man,' said Olly, pushing a pre-ordered 'dark and stormy' across the table towards me, chinking with ice. 'Glad you two are settling in now.'

'We just *adore* Will,' said Bonnie, '*so* nice, so helpful and funny. You've got a good one there,' clink, clink on our glasses, *Merry Christmas everyone*.

I think I got away with it, though, honestly, I could hardly bear to look at them, one year into their own marriage, their own pioneer odyssey, and still so in love. I wanted to take their hands and say, we were like you once. We *were* you. We held hands under the table when we thought no one could see. We arrived at double-date dinners with time to spare, to have that first drink together. Like them, we'd go home at the end of the night and kiss on the doorstep like first-date lovers, sit on the sofa watching black-and-white films, eating cheese on toast, or whatever Bonnie-and-Olly's private rituals were, the ones that told them they weren't like the other couples, they 'got' each other, they'd last the distance.

There were no words at the table to warn them.

Later, after we'd finished our fourth round of drinks and small-plate medley, we air-kissed goodbye and wandered back to our own neighbourhoods, frosted with picturesque snow flurries and festive-lit windows. Then I waited on the sofa for Will to come home, my holiday mask sliding off to reveal something solid and stubborn with cool, sharp teeth.

When he finally appeared I didn't rave or rant. He didn't arrive to find I'd finally thrown his suitcase onto the stoop with a theatrical clatter, making Pilar's eyes widen with shock. I didn't ask him to explain. I asked to look at his phone.

'This again? Seriously, Liv, it's been a long night,' he sighed.

He handed me the phone though, after a brief resistance and, after scrolling, I found a receipt in his emails, in the deleted items box, for a necklace from a place called Silver Soul. I saw the message thanking him for his customised purchase. Then I discovered *her* message, a few lines below it. 'I love it. When can we have a replay?' dated three weeks ago.

Careless, careless, so careless, to delete the email but not take out the trash. So complacent, so sure of my belief in him that he'd only made time to half cover his tracks. He never did have great attention to detail. I suppose I should be grateful for that, considering what I got away with later.

'A silver pendant? A classy early Christmas gift?' I said, as he snatched the phone away, and, as if in rage at its gross betrayal, smashed it against the tiled kitchen floor. He lied then, while I waited for an explanation, a truth that might give him an out, something to show that it was over between them despite the video. He lied while I walked into the bathroom and splashed water on my face.

When I returned to the kitchen, I told him to get his stuff and get out. He begged. I stood firm. There was nothing else to say.

I waited while he sat, head in his hands, muttering to himself, 'I'm so sorry. I ruined everything. I don't know why I did this.'

I stood marble-still, drinking a glass of wine, staring at the water tower one block over and the moon behind it, until he went into the bedroom and put some items into his bag. When the door had closed and the sound of his feet had died away in the stairwell, I upended the stupid Christmas tree in a flurry of needles and baubles, grabbed our wedding photograph from the mantelpiece and put my fist through it.

I learned in the weeks afterwards that Will had stayed at the Lowbeck over the Christmas break, in one of the staff rooms reserved for back-to-back shifts. Sol had sneaked him in because everybody loves Will. During that time he left me constant messages and apologies. I didn't reply.

At 11 a.m. on Christmas Eve I opened the bottle of Jack Daniel's we'd been keeping for the holidays and invited it to stay with me, learning for the first time that bourbon is one hell of a counsellor. Firey-woodsmoke-ish and cara-melly with latent sympathy, it possessed a raw kind of patience that was something like understanding. From then on the next-day hangovers were medieval in their sadism but the nights were . . . an experience.

You know the Ancient Greeks believed that imbibing wine could bring you closer to the gods and the elemental soul of divinity? They took part in drunken Dionysian raptures to release man from his civilised self, unleash the base beast within (page 35 of the *National Geographic*'s 'Ancient Civilizations' issue, photo spread of the Acropolis). You can't argue with the culture that produced democracy and theatre, so Jacky D and I had quite a lively time, ignoring Will's lengthy repentant messages on his work phone.

Jack comforted me as I spent twelve straight hours crying and dozing through the old movies Will and I used to watch together, wishing I could be Bette Davis in *All About Eve* warning her guests to buckle up because it was going to be a bumpy night, or cool Grace Kelly in *Rear Window*, icy stare, glistening eye, dignified in rejection, instead of sobbing, throwing up and falling asleep on the sofa.

Later that night, as Christmas Eve gave up the ghost and Christmas Day ticked in with carols soaring from the TV, I found myself struggling to breathe in the screaming silence of the apartment, desperate for cold air and the sight of some sky. That's how I ended up on the rooftop of our apartment building, a Christmas miracle I didn't kill myself in the attempt.

At the time it seemed quite sensible to climb out of the kitchen window onto the scrolled iron fire escape that scaled our block, with half a bottle of bourbon inside me. The window was often pushed wide open because the apartment was so hot, and, occasionally leaning out to water the rangy yucca plant someone had left in a terracotta pot, I'd often thought about sitting outside on the iron bones zigzagging upwards.

I'd got as far as the windowsill once, during that first sticky June, putting my feet on the grille outside but afraid to test my weight against something that looked a little rusty and rickety. In the moonlight slanting down between the tower blocks and flat roofs opposite, it looked much more robust, a ladder to the stars. So out I went, knowing no one would care, even if they saw me, tucked up, waiting for Santa Claus. The only apartment above ours, right under the roof, contained a dapper pensioner called Mr Luigi and his poodle Poppet, who I said hi to when collecting mail in the hall and had once collected a prescription from the drugstore for when he was full of a cold.

I was pretty sure he'd said he was spending Christmas with his son in New Jersey; if not, he was almost certainly in bed in the back of his apartment. So, oh so very *Breakfast at Tiffany's*, I pulled on my giant cardigan, pulled a bobble hat onto my head and climbed out. In my tatty trackies, gloved hands sticking to the frosted iron, I no doubt lacked Audrey Hepburn's elegance, but there was no one to care as I climbed past Mr Luigi's closed and darkened windows.

I never knew the rest of the tenants in the block below. Pilar, who lived on the ground floor, once told me the whole building, owned by the Piper-Dewey company, was earmarked for renovation, so most of the apartments were unoccupied. Some, on the lower floors, were occasionally rented to professionals like me and Will staying a few months at a time, but Pilar and Mr Luigi were the last 'original' tenants, among the empty units, untouched since the eighties.

So there was no one to disturb or alarm as I climbed above the streets of SoHo, laying themselves out along the grid lines of the streetlights and upscale heritage facades, dressed for Christmas. Most of the windows along the block were dark, no strings of fairy lights in the rooms above the retail spaces, the windowless warehouses.

Sitting on the top-floor grille, already dizzy from the climb and the rush of icy air, I noticed a few people about at 6 a.m. on Christmas morning, the tops of their warmly hatted heads moving hurriedly on their way, not looking up. To my right, a narrow set of iron rungs was bolted into the stonework, rising the last seven feet from the top window to the edge of the flat roof above, and I had the sudden urge to see what was up there, to stand on the roof and survey 360 degrees of the new world I'd found myself in.

Testing the iron, it felt solid, more solid than anything else in my life, so, hand over hand, I heaved myself up and over the low wall onto the flat roof.

Panting, on my haunches, I realised I was in a frozen garden, well, what had once been the beginnings of one, tucked inside the tarred roof area about as big as a tennis court. No one had been up there for a long time but they had once planted pots of rosemary shivering along the opposite wall and a stunted olive tree in a tub in the middle. Then there were the cannabis plants, wilted and overgrown, trailing winter-shrivelled skeletons from three shallow wooden pallets, hardly suited to growth in the cold New York winters, though I'd never done any drugs.

There was also a small brick structure releasing a heating-system-inspired hum from a fan turning in a recess, and a door, presumably to the inner stairwell, which I tried but was bolted. It felt like a hidden hideout high above the city, the skyscrapers splitting to show a great, all-knowing moon, the aerials and telephone lines almost trees and creepers, a wilderness within a wilderness where I could disappear, lose myself.

Stepping up on the low brick parapet above the street, my toes peeping timidly over the edge at the pavement ten storeys down, a thought slid quietly into my head. I thought about taking a leap, ending it then and there, soaring out on the night air, arms wide, silencing every voice and shutting off every image I was unable to blackout in the never-ending show reel in my brain.

I'd died anyway. Will had killed me, or at least set me up to endure a slow, lingering death. He'd committed a murder of his own over the months by choking me with his lies, taking me apart piece by piece, his deceit flaying me raw, down to the bone of my belief, my confidence, my self-esteem. Why keep splitting hairs, keep breathing and putting one foot in front of the other?

Do you know that you're pretty much guaranteed a quick and fatal result if you fall from 76 metres or higher? And I was about that, above the street, so it seemed like a restful idea, a more permanent peace than Jacky D could afford, than the course of another unconscious pass-out and addled wakening to the head-splitting truth of a lonely future.

On a whim I looked up at the setting moon, raised my arms in supplication, then opened my mouth and howled from my belly, from deep in my DNA, a roaring wind of pain across the shuttered windows and star-spackled sky. Though I didn't actually make a sound the first time; I didn't want anyone to look out of those windows or up from the street below and wonder what drugged-up madwoman was going werewolf on the apartment roof on Christmas Day, above the artisan bakery and the outrageously expensive sneaker store.

Then I thought *fuck it*, opened my throat and keened, waiting to see if a light would flick on, if anyone would come out on their fire escape. Nothing stirred. Not even when my scream raised itself towards the constellation of Orion, firing his arrows into the heart of the Milky Way and beyond, warning the gods of my wrath.

I was a little disappointed actually, as the faintest finger of dawn poked the eastern skyline, half hoping someone might come up and talk me down, call with a loudhailer crackle from the street, like in a movie, where an American cop, ready for the holidays and carrying parcels home for the kids, might be diverted to the call. Then he'd appear from the doorway behind me, stretch out his hand and say – *Tell me what's wrong, ma'am. You don't need to do this.*

But survival is a funny thing, a base instinct; I didn't really want to plunge onto the pavement, a posthumous plea for pity, I just wanted to not feel that way any more, broken and beaten, lost and discarded. So, after a cold and frozen minute, I got down. I knew it didn't have to be me whose life was snuffed out and I wasn't the only one who thought so.

Maybe it should be her, honey, not you? whispered Jack Daniel's, waiting in his bottle on the roof ledge where I'd left him. *Maybe it should be that filthy whore who pays.*

That was the first time he offered me actual advice, his voice, low and slow like molasses, with a touch of Tennessee road gravel beneath as he said, *Maybe it should be her, the skank who stole your life away with a flash of her crotch, or maybe it should be Will? Till death do you part and all that. After all, he should be the one to pay, shouldn't he?*

From then on he became more than my silent partner in misery, because that's where it was born, I think, *the third option*, after *forgive Will* and *leave him*, in the sloshing of the half-empty bottle that vibrated through the days and out onto the open road in the form of three simple tasks. It showed me the opposite of uncertainty, the idea of a clean break, no aftermath of the end of the world, no rubble and stench; no divorce.

The possibility arrived as a shuddering relief that let me step down from the edge and slump onto the rooftop; the perfect get-out clause I'd longed for since seeing the words *I'm already wet for you*, even before the image of the wet, dark hole of her mouth opening to take Will's cock inside it.

That's the moment it became a matter of survival, my own – life or death, jump or push, sanity or insanity – an end or a beginning?

Sometimes they're the same thing.

So I climbed down from the roof, back into the kitchen, plugged in the laptop and started hunting down the whore.

Seven

New York City

I found out where she lived easily enough. It helped that I knew her name. It wasn't Kath. I recognised her from the home video so I looked her up online through the Piper-Dewey website's useful staff thumbnails. After that, it was easy to trawl her social media profiles, tumbler of Tennessee courage in hand, tracing her steps.

Her Instagram account was the most helpful, making it clear from the start that she was what I would call an 'indoorsy' girl, a joke Will and I had about *that* sort of woman, the sort who have manicures and wouldn't be found, makeup free, sweating their way up a hill in hiking boots.

Sure enough, in every photograph on her feed she was perfectly groomed, self-snapped wearing recognisable brands and labels in filtered, high-end shots, *aspirational*, with price tags to match. Her most recent yoga shots showed her tight, ten-year-old-boy arse sheathed in skin-tight Lycra, to stunning effect, the after-workout epitome of 'clean' living, glass of matcha powder in hand.

Way down on her Twitter feed, under the busy, busy, New York trendsetter-in-the-office sheath dresses and heels shots, were more interesting, seemingly older snaps of her apparently on vacation, among immense trees that looked like San Francisco's Marin Headlands or Muir Woods, her thumbs aloft conquering a rocky escarpment in expensive trainers.

It was all vanity stuff really, with the exception of one or two family birthdays on a mostly defunct Facebook account and one, more recent image, with her arms around an uncomfortable-looking older man being forced to smile for a selfie.

What hurt most was that she personified everything Will had always claimed to hate about the girls he'd gone to college with, and the women he'd worked with since, the image of the ones he'd dismissed with the words, 'They're just so shallow, it's all about appearance; where you shop, what clothes you buy, the gym you belong to. There's nothing appealing in that at all.'

He'd always said he loved the fact I didn't care about 'stuff', was more interested in experiencing the world, seeing, touching, tasting it than wearing it. So much for that! Unable to stop scrolling, to stop torturing myself, I thought, If that's what Will wants now, how am I supposed to measure up?

Because I know I'm not 'hot', the most reductive term of the twenty-first-century culture cycle so far, and I'm not whip-thin. I'll never stop traffic in a Julia Roberts, *Pretty Woman*, head-turning-at-the-Rodeo-Drive-crosswalk kind of way. I'm attractive, I scrub up well and own far more lipsticks and plumping mascaras than I'd ever admit, but I was thirty-two when Will upgraded to a fitter, younger model, just old enough to realise I didn't look quite like that fresh young thing any more, a few pounds heavier, a few frown lines forming. Unlike that tramp, no doubt, not a fledgling crow's foot in sight, jaw as taut as a drawn bowstring, posture screaming success.

I hated her for that too, for reviving something old and painful in me, making me feel invisible, inadequate, like the girls at school, back in Cardiff, girls like Natalie Lewis. Of course, she was a cut above them, above their cheap trainers, over-linered eyes and over-processed hair, but there was something in the pose, the smile, the 'queen bee' look shared by the pack of girls I'd learned to avoid, if I wanted to limit the number of times my already dog-eared class books were dumped on the waterlogged playing field, sticky, pre-chewed gum thrown into my hair, and guttural jibes like, 'Hey Olivia Cum-suck, show us your fried egg tits. No wait, don't. I just ate lunch. We know what Cum-suck eats for lunch, don't we, girls? Mmm, mmm, mmm. Spit or swallow, baby?'

Because there's always a pack, isn't there? In every school, inner city or otherwise, in each office and work-place? We're all animals, ranging like prairie wolves across territories shrunken with small victories, like the smug recognition that 'her arse is bigger than mine', or savouring tiny, alpha-dog triumphs over who gets to hold the remote control.

At Grange Road High School the pack was led by Natalie Lewis. The alpha male was, of course, James Scott Thomas.

Ah yes, James . . . tall, broad, rugby-thickened by the approach of sixth form but lean and lithe enough to have a certain elegance. Good on the ball, good with the girls and the worst of them all, in a way, though he never took part in the actual ribbing, just watched. Leaning into Natalie's bulimia-frail shoulders, he'd keep his eyes fixed elsewhere until they'd accidentally catch mine with a look that offered something like *Sorry*, like *What can I do about it? Natalie does what she pleases.*

Is that what Miss No-Tits Whore thought about Will, I asked myself, looking at her concave six-pack, that she could do as she liked and no one would challenge her? The slut, the whore, because there was no way I could say her name. To name her was to conjure her – to speak of the devil was to make her real.

At first, to Will, those are the names I called her. Will didn't know I knew her real name because I never told him I'd found that memory card with the video they'd made. Instead, the night after the dinner with Bonnie and Olly, I'd returned to the apartment, copied the file onto a memory stick and put it back in Will's pocket before he got home.

At first I'd wanted to throw it in his face right away, let him know I'd seen the filth he'd brought into our home, but it was all the proof I had, the only edge and advantage, and I wanted to see if Will would confess without it, how many lies he'd cling to, how convincing they'd seem, were it not for the flesh and fluids I'd witnessed with my own eyes.

Then I'd found the deleted jewellery receipt in his emails, the message from *her*, and there was no need. No need to say the words, to have to acknowledge the truth, because I feared what it could lead to, if I fired that loaded gun in his face, let go of my restraint, smelled blood.

Of course, in a way it was already too late the day I
started following *the slut*, because online reconnaissance
was never going to be enough. Because you need to see
someone in the flesh to catch their scent, assess them. You
can't size them up through a screen, examine the threat
level, decide if you can take them in a fight, and, eventually,
there has to be a fight.

So, after New Year limped in and slept itself off, I followed
the whore home from the Lowbeck for the first time. I think
I intended to confront her, ask her who the hell she thought
she was, but I didn't want to rush it in anger without proper
preparation and research. Instead, I trailed her around the
city, every day for weeks, doorway dodging and sidewalk
crossing, following her to appointments, sliding onto a bar
stool in a crowded lobby, lipstick armour on for urban
combat, 'Berry Nice' plum, and 'Smooth Operator' pink,
drinking a Manhattan two booths across from her or
reading a magazine on a Subway car one carriage down.

Stalking is a harsh word, one we've all seen on the
nightly news. But before it was a crime it was a necessary
animal instinct, a slow following of prey through the
undergrowth, tracking its movements, up until the moment
came to pounce. That was me then, following the skank
through New York's narrow passes and steaming streets,
Subway juddering and screaming beneath us, January and
February gripping the city, freezing its breath, the streetlight
shadows affording me cover.

Few people stand out more than those trying to look
inconspicuous; the trick is to simply look like you belong
and I was an expert at that, at blending in. Camouflaged in
a black coat, scarf and hat, like all the other New Yorkers

scurrying from door to door, office to bar, station to station, I became a player in a film noir of my own making, a sequence of trench coats and shadows and cigarette smoke in huddled doorways, the clip of shoes on a frozen street.

I was glad I was anonymous, glad that, if she ever tried to Google *me*, to see what she was up against, she wouldn't find much 'online presence'. I had my own website page and Twitter feed for a travel blog I updated now and then, but no images of me on them. In that way I was protected and, later, that helped a great deal in keeping me invisible, barely related to the police investigation that would begin in the wilds of California then follow me back to New York.

As I said, leave no trail, cover your tracks, douse your fires at dawn, delete the evidence.

So, in those brittle weeks, when I was a ghost in the city, inside my marriage, I didn't change my movements, update my defunct Facebook status to 'separated', or add teary emoticons to a 'wine o'clock' selfie. I guarded my own privacy even as I thought about the best kind of revenge to inflict on @AshtangaYogaLover3.

At first I thought about showing the sex video to her colleagues, a nice little Monday morning, espresso-beating wake-up call in all its graphic, legs-akimbo glory. It would've been easy enough to copy the segment then post a disk out the old-fashioned way, in an envelope, leaving no digital footprint. Or I could go to an internet café and upload it as an email attachment, and send it to everyone on the hotel's universal address list, easily copied from Will's phone, allowing her colleagues at the Lowbeck to click open the link onto the sequence of her working her fingers in and out of her smooth shaved slit.

76

Because Will's colleagues were her colleagues, of course, that's how I'd recognised her in the first place, because she'd worked with him before we came to the US. She'd helped him get his visa. I'd seen her in the Lowbeck lobby the day after we'd arrived from London and remembered that henna-red hair I'd seen the year before, in San Francisco, when I'd accompanied Will on a work trip.

The firm had paid for the flights and I'd gone along on the understanding that I'd spend most of the days alone while Will attended workshops and meetings. So, while I'd bobbed on a boat to Alcatraz, Will was discussing marketing strategy. While I was flying over the burnt red expanse of the Golden Gate Bridge on the open-top tourist bus, in the freezing sun, Will was exploring social media penetration figures. While I'd roamed Golden Gate Park and the waterfront with its 'tsunami escape route' signs, suggesting something brewing out there, turbulence coming, gathering speed and deadly momentum, Will had been working.

Or had he?

During my night walks through Manhattan I realised Will had probably been in a room, or at least a conference centre every day, with *that woman* eighteen months before we'd even left London. On the last afternoon, I'd seen her smiling and flicking her hair at him in the lobby, as the minibus was loaded with our luggage.

Had it started then, between him and her? asked the Jack Daniel's voice in my head, even when I was almost sober, *Something semi-innocent at first? Maybe a swap of details, a keeping-in-touch connection? A flirtation that became something else?*

The idea contaminated my thoughts like a virus, multi-plying while I sat in the lobby of the hotels she visited during the working day, sipping a bitter coffee in my good slacks and jacket, watching discreetly from wing-backed chairs. I wondered if they'd screwed during the stolen hours after the late drinks receptions, in a room alone at lunch break, clothes heaped on the floor, while I'd sipped Pinot Grigio with the hotel rep in a wine bar in Washington Square.

I wondered about it as I roamed the streets as the skank's shadow, watching the swing of her hair, thinking how easy it would be to grab the back of her head and ram her face into one of the lampposts. If I timed it just right, with the squeal of the Subway at the crosswalk, no one would hear if she cried out. No one would see as she dropped to the floor and I landed kick after kick in her taut, yoga belly.

I wondered about it after I took Will back for the second time in March, because he pleaded and promised and seemed so distraught. Because in the twelve weeks I'd become her shadow I'd never once seen them meet or speak or even share the time of day. And because the alternative was frankly unthinkable, the prospect of heading home to Wales alone, at thirty-two years old, too horrific to contemplate.

My mother would insist I move back in with her, of course, while the divorce came through, perhaps a hint of pity in her voice rarely heard during our twice-yearly phone conversations that supplemented the large cheques I sent inside birthday and Christmas cards.

The alternative wasn't much better, renting a shithole flat in London, sending out CVs, stalking features editors from office to 'accidental' meeting in cocktail bars over-looking the Thames again, as I had in my twenties, skirted and shirted on uncomfortable architectural chairs, portfolio in hand, in the hope of a commission. Trying to stay positive, trying to cover the bills . . .

So I hoped for the best, that it was really over this time, that he was telling the truth when he said he'd never lie to me again. Though he never changed his story, still insisting it had happened when 'Kath' was in town from San Francisco, never admitting she worked at the Lowbeck, I suppose, by then, he was practising damage limitation.

He insisted the 'second lapse', the one he thought I knew about only from the receipt and the emails, had happened when she'd come back into town, caught him unawares, rekindled something that was only about sex, nothing more. A terrible mistake, after she'd asked to talk.

Certainly, he should have said no, had hated himself afterwards, had cut off all contact completely the next day, the pendant just a little gesture to ease the brush off, though I knew deep inside, even if that was true, he'd probably continued the cyber affair in some fashion until then, right under my nose. That there must have been nights in our apartment while we were 'mending things', when his face had been intent on his phone screen, that he'd been messaging her. Shamelessly, without conscience. Who does that? Maybe everyone, now? If it makes you feel good it's probably all right, even if you bring your affair into your living room, in the same breath as your wife asks if you want coffee or tea; while you watch your skank finger-fuck herself twenty blocks away, across the city.

But, deep inside, I still wanted to believe him when he said it was really over. That it had never really started. I already knew better than anyone that it's hard to pinpoint when a temporary lapse of reason becomes a decision. I've asked myself in the months since, if that moment came for me on that first trip to the apartment rooftop or when I actually began looking at pistols and automatics in the windows of tatty pawnshops in the shadier back streets of downtown.

I was always too afraid to go inside, to ask how much, to ask about the ammunition I'd need – what did I know about guns? Though I walked up to the glass-paned door of the whore's apartment building one night, thinking I might pretend to have a gun in my pocket, to make a two-finger shape and poke it into the material – force her to see me, hear me at least – the woman she'd failed to give a second thought to.

One night I actually walked up the three shallow steps, put my finger on the doorbell and kept it there, imagining the pithy *stay away from my husband – it's over, sweetheart* speech I'd give, like Lauren Bacall emerging from under a New York streetlight, trench-coated, lipstick immaculate, femme fatale red. Then I'd light a cigarette, blow smoke in the face of the dishevelled slut in her dressing gown, barefaced as befitted someone with no shame, caught unawares by the visit and the right hook that followed it.

In the end, I hesitated when I saw a light come on in the hallway, a voice in my ear saying, *Bide your time, honey*, over the dying trill of the brownstone's bell. *Stay in the shadows. Wait a while.*

So I walked away, quietly clipping down the street, just quickly enough to hear a male voice say, 'There's no one there, hon,' already thinking of better ways to fight back, of some hit-and-run tactics all my own.

Eight

Yosemite Valley, California

I remember the police officer's words clearly now, almost the same questions that would be asked the second time, as it happens, though there was no way the officer could've known, when he asked 'Where were you at the time? Did you see anything or hear anything?' that I was lying when I said, 'No, I wasn't there.'

For some reason I was thinking of those questions as I peered down from Glacier Point, in Yosemite, the grande dame of the national parks, the crowning highlight of our, until then, raw and unromantic holiday. When we'd checked into our lodge the night before – exhausted from the nine-hour drive, from how much I'd underestimated the distance involved in visiting Yosemite before Death Valley because the accommodation was booked solid on the dates we'd wanted – we'd only wanted to shower, grab a snack and crash into sleep under darkness of a kind unknown in cities.

It was only when we journeyed into the valley in the

morning that its true majesty revealed itself, Bridal Veil Falls, Half Dome, El Capitan emerging from the towering pines as if from a myth of the wilderness, and my favourite *National Geographic* spread of all time (Half Dome on a winter's day, wide angle lens).

Windows down, my breath stolen by the sheer immensity of the wild, green world around us, I felt I'd come home at last, returning to somewhere remembered from a dream, or the idea of one, a wooded landscape buried in my DNA memory, where my ancestors might once have roamed, without language or learning, in the forests of an ancient dark Europe.

The green tunnels of trees, flanked by soaring spires of granite and ozone-scented rivers, were breath-taking, spectacular, stunning, though none of those words did the sight justice or acknowledged the feeling in my bones, the low vibration that could only have been a resonance of joy.

'We're here, we're actually here,' I said to Will, reaching across and putting my hand on his neck, though he was too busy trying to left turn into the caterpillar of crawling camper vans and cars on the valley floor to notice.

'Jesus, there'll be nowhere to park if we don't get down there soon,' he huffed instead, edging forward. 'I told you we should have been up earlier but you just had to have another latte.'

I really hated him then, his impatience, treating the expedition like a chore instead of the adventure I'd dreamed of for decades. With a single stroke his lack of understanding pricked me like a pin, bursting me open, and I hated him, even as I hated myself for letting him do it so easily, even as we parked up to make the pilgrimage across the greenest meadow in the world to the base of Yosemite Falls on what should have been one of the greatest days of my life.

'Don't get too close, folks. It's slippery and the snowmelt is freezing,' warned a ruddy-faced ranger, tipping his wide-brimmed hat to us, then nodding at the spot where the water plummets 700 metres, through five falls. 'Remember three people died at Vernal Falls across the valley in 2011, trying to take a photograph when the rivers were in spate like this.'

We heeded his words as we edged carefully around the freezing, frothing base and gingerly walked the slick plank bridge through the icy spray, bickering drowned by the thunder and roar. Afterwards, we ate lunch in the amphitheatre-like forecourt of the market square, perhaps the most spectacular place in the world to munch a sandwich. But Will was still annoyed, fussing about mosquitoes, popping antihistamines and complaining his baguette was giving him indigestion.

He wasn't much happier as we drove out to the base of El Capitan to watch the ant creatures, high above us, slow-crawl their way up the giant's granite face. Perched on a fallen trunk, light sifting through clouds, it could have been a bucket-list moment in itself. Instead it was spoiled by the bears, well the possibility of bears, the invisible, gnashing threat we'd been warned about.

There were cautionary photos at every information hut of eager claws tearing the doors off cars to get at snacks they can scent miles away, which was what threw Will into a panic when I remembered I'd left the last few bites of my beef salsa wrap in the glove compartment. Though our SUV was parked on the busy valley floor, hardly bear-creeping country, Will didn't want to take the chance of even a scratch rendering our insurance 'fucked', shooting to his feet and huffing, 'For God's sake, Liv!'

By the time we'd trekked the fifteen minutes back to dispose of it, Will complaining like every step equalled a mile, we were both openly cross and sulky, him because I was a 'dopey woman', the ultimate unfair insult, me because I felt that, if I could overlook three months of infidelity, he could overlook five minutes of forgetfulness. I wanted to yell at him but he hated arguing in public, even in a car where people might see and smirk, and knew if I did the day would no doubt be officially destroyed.

So I swallowed my anger with my tears, the vibration of joy that had thrummed in my bones changing pitch to that low, slow sadness of the winter city streets. A sleepy-eyed spaniel came up and licked my hand, in what might have been sympathy, or it could just have been the lingering scent of the beef sandwich.

Will was apologising by the time we drove up the hairpin switchbacks, past Tunnel View towards Glacier Point, explaining he was just tired and burnt out from yesterday's marathon drive, so, with the sheared white egg of Half Dome standing to attention opposite us, bald and smooth, I tried to focus on the 3D Imax show around us instead.

Staring down to the campground at the base of the sheer drop, it was impossible not to marvel at the toy houses, the matchbox hotel tossed against the valley floor, the improbable blue rectangle of a swimming pool among the trees. Perched on a crop of rock like a bird in a nest, the scale of the place slid into perspective, making everything else seem tiny, diminished, and I envied the eagles their ability to launch off and soar above the insignificant photo seekers clustered at the viewpoint.

Without intending to, my mind fell into its old groove of idly working out the equation of distance times speed of a falling body down the vertical face, holding tightly to the guardrail. You'd have plenty of time to ponder the meaning of life on the way down, I realised, if you took a wild leap. Too much time maybe, to count your blessings, to ask for forgiveness perhaps, and also to scream, all while the end is racing up to meet you at 10 metres per second, at aptly named terminal velocity.

That's when I thought of the officer asking, 'Where were you at the time? Did you see or hear anything?' Too many words, swooping, attacking, making me struggle to keep my balance. So it was probably a good thing that Glacier Point was one of the few places health and safety had taken a reluctant stand in the wilderness, the edge fenced off, though you can still find the photos online of the time when daredevils dangled over the tiptoe edge of the granite overhang, free-climbing kids from the school of free kicks held gasp-inducing handstands on the lip and sepia-clothed aliens in Victorian finery posed stiffly above the chasm.

Even without the threat of immediate death it was still vertigo-inducing, its postcard-perfect composition designed specifically for the ultimate selfie and one I'd longed to see first hand since I was a child, mesmerised by how such a place could exist outside the concrete and cooking-smell world I inhabited, the grey day, stale bread, avoid-the-used-syringes-in-the-stairwell world of my youth.

After I'd met Will I'd always imagined standing over the valley with him beside me, snuggled into his warm flank, him kissing my brow, the perfect couple's moment, and he must have known that. I'd hinted at it often enough, usually when we were halfway up one of the Brecon Beacons, buoyed by the feeling of rising higher and higher above the world, and at last having someone to share it with.

But it was all going wrong. It was not supposed to feel like that after all the years. Because of Will, because being somewhere with someone, occupying the same two-foot space at the same moment, is not the same as sharing it; not like the grey-haired couple in their sixties holding hands and bird-kissing each other's tanned faces, not like the Chinese girl and her boyfriend, angling themselves into the exact perfection their grins suggested – that was seizing the moment, a sense of occasion.

Instead, Will was ten feet away and spent the whole time with his binoculars and camera alternately planted on his face. Even when I tried to take his hand, sidled up behind him, sliding myself into the curve of his hip, he just kissed the top of my head and fiddled with the buttons and knobs.

Eventually I retreated, wrestling back tears to the sound of my mother's voice suddenly sneering, *Stop crying, Olivia, it won't change anything. Grow up, don't be so sensitive, or you won't get very far in this world*, hating her too, just as I'd always hated the memory of beer on her breath after the sound of those late-night keys in the lock. She of all people was not supposed to be there, even though she was right – it shouldn't have mattered so much, any of it, what had happened that day or the ones before, not in Monument Valley or the Grand Canyon, things so small they barely qualified as a rejection, let alone a pass/fail tick on a life or death challenge I'd created.

But it did, and Will had failed again – because everything matters all of the time and how could Will still not know that, test or no test? How could he not realise, after all he'd put me through, that this was the shining moment to take me in his arms, burn the togetherness of the moment into our flesh and say something, *anything*, as long as it was, 'I'm so lucky to have you for my wife. No one can compare to you. I was such a fool I'll never stop being grateful for this second chance.'

Watching him, as he leaned across the guardrail to get a better angle on the string of hikers cresting Half Dome, I wished the wooden slats would give way before him, or that someone would grab his feet in their designer hiking boots and tip him over the barrier for me. No one could react in time to stop it, as he sailed down like a drop of blood in that stupid red anorak of his, glinting for seconds only before splashing onto the valley floor.

And for a second that was the answer – as I saw hands going out, shoving, using his weight against him, a lift, a heave, his body bending in the middle before up, over, down, almost like . . . the rubber soles of those Adidas three-stripe trainers rising, the mud in their treads . . .

But I looked away, because it was still *my* moment no matter how hard he tried to spoil it. I'd made it, finally, and that was a triumph of sorts. I'd come a long way, so much further than an ocean, eight states and 600 miles, further even than suggested by the map at the ranger station showing the park and, in the north, that vast green chunk of trees and ordnance lines ominously labelled 'wilderness'.

I heard my mother's voice again then, sniping as I'd packed my bag for the last time, *Well, you've certainly done well for yourself, Olivia. You've landed on your feet all right with Mr Posh Prince Charming. Hope you're finally happy.*

So I sat and waited, until Will came back from the edge and sat next to me, hugged me and said, 'You're right, it is spectacular here, Liv. These photos I've done should come out really well. You can have a real one for the wall of the apartment now, instead of those crappy, magazine cutouts you had stuck everywhere in Kensington. I'll get one framed for you.'

But it was no longer a moment I wanted frozen in paper and glass. I didn't even want it in my head and that was the worst thing of all.

Nine

Yosemite Valley, California

By the time we returned to Pine Lodge that evening I was more than ready for a shower and at least half a dozen shots of bourbon. Luckily, with its rustic cabins among the fragrant pines, our campground would've made a great chapter in my travel book's 'glamping' demographic, and I made a mental note of the diner's appetising bistro menu and the rustic bar's huge demijohns of herb-infused cocktails for the 'Where to Stay' and 'Where to Eat' sections.

Further up the hill from the main square was a shabby-chic rec room, a lounge with a roaring log fire and firepits, and picnic benches outside. The whole site was rimmed by a three-mile ridge trail with soaring views across the sharp cliffs and ravines, but the best thing was our cabin, set just off the path, surrounded by whispering pines and chattering blue jays. If you didn't squint your eyes through the screen of trees opposite, and ignored the very tip of the roof of the cabin a few hundred yards away, you could imagine it was safe from the world and its haste and hurry.

In that way it was almost the perfect hideout, like the ones I'd fantasised about escaping to as a kid, flying up and out of the door of our council flat. I'd prepared for it too because, before I'd even heard the term 'go-bag' on the news and packing one became common advice for people living in areas at risk of natural disasters, I liked to itemise what I'd need in an emergency, just in case.

How far could I get from Cardiff? I always asked myself, and where would I go, given the chance? The answer, always a picturesque log cabin with a view of a rippling lake; a wooden dock over cold, clear water. A place to go to ground. Like my first childhood den tucked under the hill of what was called the 'wilderness' behind the Pen Dinas estate, a patch of land at the edge of the old mine workings, seeded with trees and the gash and gouge of an old quarry.

Set back from the dog-walking path snaking over to Penarth, the Second World War pillbox was my first secret hideout, only visible as a low rectangle of concrete slabs, flush with the ground. One wonderful winter, when the bushes hiding even that tell-tale sign were bare, I'd spotted the little cutting on the left-hand side and realised it led to a recessed doorway, a single room and two open 'windows' facing the sea, where guns would've been mounted if the Nazis had actually invaded Britain.

Concealed, it had an uninterrupted view down to the glinting water of Cardiff Bay, and it was the perfect place to hide when it all got too much; the taunts from Natalie Lewis and co, lying in wait in school stairwells, science labs and sports fields, from the yelling then the silence after Dad skipped out with the woman from the Co-op checkout.

Though my homelife back then was hardly one of abuse, my mother wouldn't have won any awards for parent of the year, not when the only food in the cupboards was bought and cooked, by me, with the Giro cheque she left on the table. As for my clothes, I mended and washed them myself, when the washing machine was working, scraping up my savings for new shoes once a year, for second-hand books once a month.

Being trapped between those paper-thin walls, drowning in the soup of muttering TVs, screeching laughter and raucous domestics, was almost too much to bear, at its worst when my mother's friends came over, slumped on the settee, and 'Downstairs' Mae, our raddled, cigarette-skinny neighbour, would scowl at me for breathing while they watched reality TV and drank cans of Stella.

By then I'd become a lodger, invisible, a hindrance, a reminder of what my mother had lost with my fleeing father. That was worse somehow, to be unseen, unheard, invisible – sometimes I wished she'd yell at me or hit me so at least I existed.

So, every day I fled to my den with my 'go-bag', aka my school rucksack filled with a bottle of water, a bar of chocolate, a warm sweater and a hat in winter. I always carried at least one *National Geographic* magazine with me, in rotation from the pile I'd rescued from a skip, plus £43 I'd saved from working in the corner shop hidden in a couple of sanitary towels.

When I felt my head would burst I'd go for the pillbox in the overgrown hummocks, safe as long as I stayed away from the paedos and weirdoes, druggies and crackheads rumoured to skulk its paths, hungry for lonely little girls.

And if you were soft-footed and knew the lie of the land, it was easy to avoid the clutches of squawking teenagers that congregated on the quarry side, smoking pot, armoured with confidence and cruelty, blowing out clouds of smoke like mythical beasts.

If they spotted me, Natalie Lewis, usually at the head of the pack, would resume her tirade of taunts in my direction. Same words, burned into my brain.

'Hey Olivia Cum-suck, show us your fried egg tits. No wait, don't. I just ate lunch. We know what Cum-suck eats for lunch, don't we, girls? Mmm, mmm, mmm. Spit or swallow, baby? Hey Olivia, bend over will you, I need somewhere to park my bike and that fat arse will be perfect. What you looking at, Cum-suck? If you wanna lick my fanny you could just ask, though you'd have to pay me for it. You're too fucking ugly to get it for free. You're too fucking ugly to even rape.'

Apart from the big tits, I never understood what James Scott saw in her, when I followed them out there sometimes, hidden in the scrub, watching them shoving their fingers in each other's underwear as they sat on the low, crumbling wall ringing the quarry. Once, I actually saw him screwing her against an oak tree, the back of his neck tensed, shoulders rigid as he thrust in and out.

It wasn't erotic though; it was educational, like observing animals in their natural habitat, hoping I might learn their weaknesses, something to armour me against them, to strike back with. Like the time I saw James getting a blow-job from Gail Swan, so comical standing there, making faces, such silly sounds, I'd laughed to myself, waiting for the moment I'd tell Natalie exactly what her boyfriend had been up to with 'Gail the gobbler' when no one was watching.

But most of the time I was alone on my solitary adventures, watching the blustering clouds from the roof of the pillbox, sun-hot in summer against my back, racing south towards the Bay. If I could, I'd have stayed there for ever, cross-legged on the old sofa cushions I'd dragged in, with my drinks and snacks, magazines and books, plotting journeys out into the world after college, itself a mythical place in a fantasy realm of books and dreams.

I always knew I'd have to live at home until I graduated, since there was no money not to, but it was only three years and all day, every day off the estate, even with the chance of meeting a nice boy. But that was later. James Scott was my first love who said we'd be friends for ever, and I'd believed him because James was a good person.

Throughout junior school we'd idled in the wilderness together in the long, empty summers; I'd even shown him my pillbox den, the only honoured visitor, where we'd played 'Conquest of the Seas' and other old board games he'd stolen from the school library, marooned together in our little patch of green among a concrete sea, where he was in love with me.

But it all changed in secondary school. There was no big break between us, just a slow drifting away, towards Natalie and the rugby boys, though I knew he missed me underneath his bravado, his play for popularity. I never gave up on the fact he might return to me, because he was the only one who seemed a little bit different.

He wasn't though. I got that wrong, though it wasn't my fault he was so disappointing. I was reminding myself of that on the night I left our Yosemite cabin to explore the rim trail while Will was showering before dinner. Staring down into the ravine, tumbler of red wine in my hand, the colours of sunset creeping up from the quiet world below me, I tried to push the memory of James away once more, forcing myself to think of the present instead, of New York, lighting itself up 400 miles behind me.

It was a Sunday night so I wondered if the tart was halfway through her impeccable downward dog at yoga class, or if Gus would be in grief counselling again, starting on his second coffee and third donut.

In a way, I already knew that Gus was the biggest regret of the months behind me, next to my cheating husband of course, that Gus was my unfinished business, the loose end, all too easy to trip on. I knew he wouldn't be expecting me at support group that night, not after what had happened between us two weeks before, and I told myself it was for the best. Standing there, I made the mistake of assuming he was the sort of man who'd do the least dramatic and most sensible thing when faced with rejection. That he'd be easy to keep quiet.

But I was wrong, because by then Gus was in love with me, and there's nothing more dangerous and unpredictable than that.

Ten

New York City

I should say, right now, that I never intended to visit the support group, it just happened in January, while Will was still in disgrace at the cheap hotel for the second time. I certainly never meant to lie to those poor women, to pretend. I just got carried away, listening to them talk, listening to the stories of the widows.

They weren't like any widows I'd ever imagined, not a clutch of old women in flat shoes and black dresses, but smartly coiffed hairdressers and CEOs, trendy accountants and shop assistants, old-fashioned dog walkers and teachers. In other words, people like me, of all ages, with great skin or sagging jowls, tinted hair or gym-honed abs, some with children without fathers, others with grown families and grandchildren, but all with empty halves of beds gaping at home.

To be one of them was a privilege of sorts, after I first heard Angel ask, 'What about you, hiding at the back? Come and join in. Would you like to introduce yourself?'

There was something inside me that night, with Will still six weeks away from slinking home for the second time, after a clutch of nights spent on the roof of the apartment building like that first one, that wanted, needed, to speak up. Sometimes I'd danced up there, swigging bourbon like soda, earbuds in, volume up, soundtracking my silent misery with music, occasionally howling at the sky, often weeping, but always with no one to see or hear me, and I wanted to feel my pain acknowledged, that the gaping hole in my chest getting more ragged by the day was real and I was entitled to it.

What better place was there to do just that than a grief group full of women going through the same thing? Well, almost the same, except they had the benefit of never having to suffer the humiliation of explaining, of having to justify why their husband, the man they gave their life to, failed them. By contrast, though people mean well when you tell them your husband's a lying, cheating shit, insistent that *you deserve better*, they just can't stop themselves telling you that there're plenty more fish in the sea, you'll find someone else, someone who deserves you, and what use is that?

That's what my mother had said when I'd finally crumpled and called her at 2 a.m. in the Welsh morning, heavy with whiskey and self-pity. It'd been a couple of months since I'd heard her voice by then and her accent was harsh against my ear, still seething with disappointment and Regal cigarettes until she realised why I'd called.

Of course, I couldn't tell her the whole truth about Will – that would've been admitting that her stuck-up daughter had been brought down a peg or two, put back in her

place. Instead, I'd pulled in the deepest breath I ever took
and said:

'I think he might be seeing someone, Mam. I don't know
what to do. I found some messages on his phone. I could
be wrong but I don't know what to do.'

'When are you wrong, Olive?' she'd asked simply, after
a long silence, her voice cracking a little at the sound of
mine breaking. 'You should trust your instincts, love.
Dump the lying bastard. I always knew he was one of those
guys. You deserve better. Rich buggers think everything
can be bought and everyone's disposable. They're just used
to having their own way,' though how she could've known
that, when she'd only met Will twice, once at our engage-
ment drink in Cardiff, once more at the register office the
day we married, I don't know.

Even then, the old embedded instinct wanted to defend
him but I stayed silent until she said, as I'd known she
would, 'You could come home, love. I have a spare room
here now, you know, in the new flat. It's a nice flat. I've got
the little job still. Take him for everything he's got and
come back home.'

'I can't. I don't know, I don't know what to do. I feel ...'
beginning to cry, but how could I tell her, I feel as if the
world has ended?

'You feel too much, Olive, cariad,' she replied, when it
was obvious I wasn't answering, 'you always did. That's
why I tried to toughen you up. I tried to warn you. Make
you independent. The world chews up people like you.
Stop crying now. It won't help. Move on, there'll be
someone else out there for you. Smart girl like you.'

Because that's what you get, platitudes and clichés when

what you really need is for people to understand that you're a fucking wreck and things will not be all right.

The widows understood though, how *nice* people are when they hear that Todd had a heart attack on the Stairmaster, Aaron was hit by a crosstown bus, or Julio was eaten from the inside by bowel cancer. And I wanted a share of that priceless compassion, just a sliver of it, in that airless, gothic church on 12th Avenue at 8 p.m. on a Tuesday evening.

I'd only ducked inside so the whore wouldn't see me following her as she suddenly crossed the street and headed into the 7-Eleven instead of straight home as usual. That's when I heard the voice explaining how dear Joshua had died six months before but it wasn't getting any easier, each morning still rising as raw as sandpaper and as empty as his side of the king-size bed.

Listening to that voice from the porch was like listening to the dark thoughts that had driven me up into the roof garden, night after night. The loss, the fear, the anger, the feeling of being bent backwards over the knee of fate and broken in half, until, hanging on every choked word, I slid through the door and into the back pew.

I stayed for three confessions after that, three rounds of hugging and support, realising how much easier it would've been if Will had just died too. How much simpler if he'd been hit by a car like Mitch, choked on a chicken ball at the Tai Pan buffet like Chad. A tragedy yes, a grievous loss, but a clean one, instead of this dirty, stained alterative, letting Will go, knowing all the time he was out there somewhere, walking the streets of the city, eating dinner, going to work, carrying on without me.

The thought of even passing his hotel and seeing him in the lobby was enough to make me hyperventilate, the idea of bumping into him in a bar somewhere unbearable. Or worst of all, seeing *them* together, Will and her, in a coffee shop or on the Subway, possible because, in a city of eight and a half million people, on one spit of land with five brim-filled boroughs, my daily world was still a grid of around six and a half square blocks. Beyond that it would always be where he was and where he wasn't.

Death seemed an easier option, as the streetlight glow sifted down through the patient, patchwork Virgin Mary in her stained glass window, bringing comfort with the thought of a modest black dress, flowers arranged in vases, commiseration casseroles and handkerchiefs in the hands.

I imagined Bonnie or Pilar, tears in their eyes saying, *I'm so sorry, honey.* Never another question asked, never the truth known. And later, a place to visit, words on a stone that could not be erased, *devoted husband of Olivia, loving wife . . .*

So when the group leader stood up and asked me to *share my pain, set it free,* I found myself raising my head, smiling bravely and, in a perfect New York accent, like the ones they'd all spoken in that evening, telling them my name was Bonnie and my husband Oliver was two months in the ground.

'It was cancer,' I said, 'testicular, aggressive,' a blameless death, brave and smiling to the end, down to the skin and bone sack he became in the hospital bed, then I was bathed in the scented water of their sympathy, rinsing off the shame, letting myself cry and be held.

By the time I left I was feeling decades lighter, shorn of the urge to visit the skank's apartment building yet again, for once not wanting to watch her eat dinner through the window where the curtains were never drawn, wondering if the message she was tapping on her phone screen was winging its way to Will.

I didn't see Gus there that first night, the only man in the group of women, apart from Angel. I smiled at him two weeks later though, when I somehow found myself on the back pews once more. On the third visit he smiled back and came up to me at the coffee and donut table, saying, 'They're a great group, aren't they? Pleased to meet you,' sticking out his hand.

I recognised Gus right away, though he had no reason to recognise me. He couldn't know I'd seen him in his apartment on the ground floor of the brownstone, at the kitchen table where the curtains were never closed.

Eleven

New York City

Gus really was a widower, genuinely grieving, as much for his unwise life choices as his dead wife I suspect, but that's neither here nor there. I suppose that's all we had in common really, our lost loved ones, but sometimes that's enough.

His wife Hallie had died three years before in a car accident, I learned the first night he was at the group. It wasn't until much later that he told me he'd been out in a bar with the woman who later became his girlfriend the night they'd peeled Hallie's Chevy from around a telephone pole.

He and his 'girlfriend' had 'fallen into a relationship of mutual comfort' he said, in San Francisco, she getting away from her previous abusive boyfriend, he dealing with the distance and resentment that had crept into his six-year marriage without children.

Hallie had been undergoing chemotherapy for several months, given the all-clear at last. But it had been so difficult. He'd only started meeting the other woman to feel something again, hadn't meant to take it any further, let it become physical. She'd just made the first move, come on strong. Things had got out of hand.

If I'd felt anything for Gus at that point, which I doubted, it had drained away by the end of that self-serving sentence, delivered after we'd rolled apart on the bumpy mattress in that in-need-of-an-update hotel off Times Square. Lying on his back, me next to him, he gave his confession staring at the ceiling, though I'm not sure how he expected me to react to the revelation he'd been stepping out on his cancer-surviving wife.

Still, I realise now that people don't often think of themselves as the villain of their own story. No matter how selfish or deluded they are. Will hadn't when he'd cheated on me. Gus clearly thought he was justified in his infidelity, and me, well, I hadn't got as far as considering that.

'You understand, right, how you can grow apart in a marriage?' Gus asked.

'No, not really,' I answered, in my New York accent, 'Oliver,' my fictional dead partner, 'was a good husband and he was taken from me too soon.' It wasn't the answer he wanted, naturally, so I snuggled up closer so he'd keep telling me all about his girlfriend, *the whore, the skank, you-know-who*, all the things I wanted to know.

'I felt sorry for her,' he said. 'She seemed so vulnerable at first, really seemed to need me when all Hallie did was push me away. Nothing I could do for her while she was ill was ever right. I was too smothering or too worried. I was too positive, looking on the bright side all the time when she wanted to acknowledge it could be the end and I didn't. And then, well, I met Jenna through a work thing, when

102

we were still in San Francisco, and I thought I could help her. We could help each other.'

Jenna, that was the first time I'd heard her name spoken aloud, heard the devil summoned, and I didn't like it.

'She's quite a bit younger than me,' he sighed, as if that explained it. 'She'd been in an abusive relationship. Her last boyfriend beat her up pretty bad. She'd suffered depression and made a suicide attempt just before we met. We'd meet and talk and then it just started to become something else, you know, it wasn't deliberate, I didn't mean to cheat on my wife.

'We were both doing too much weed then,' he added, the excuses continuing, 'me and Jenna, and drinking, to help us cope. Eventually we went to counselling, detox together, got straight.'

So I learned how, six months after Hallie's funeral, Jenna had moved into Gus's one-bed apartment in Sausalito, leaving her parents' place in San Francisco Bay, but had 'changed' over the next year. He'd tried everything but she seemed so clingy one minute, indifferent the next. He had no idea what each day would bring. He'd even moved to New York for her, just over a year ago, though he hadn't really wanted to. He was in start-up IT and everyone knows San Francisco is the place to be, but she'd had a great opportunity with her hotel firm and he'd given in, to a change of scene, a new start.

But he'd been suspicious, not long after they'd arrived in New York, that something might be going on, she might have been seeing someone else, glued to her phone all the time, out at all hours. He'd followed her once or twice, to the hotel where she worked, found nothing. They'd fought about it constantly and he'd tried to give her an ultimatum, said something had to change, explaining, as he stroked my hair, that he was starting to think about going back to Sausalito but wasn't sure how she'd take the news if he left her.

'She seems paranoid, fragile lately,' he sighed, 'making a huge fuss about little things, going on about how she thinks someone has been targeting her, carrying out a vendetta against her, saying weird shit like that, just because she found a dead bird on the apartment doorstep and totally freaked out, because someone stole her clothes from the locker at yoga and she went crazy, accusing people there, and was banned.'

He wondered if she was sneaking out to smoke weed again, as that had always made her crazy and weepy. He just wanted to make her happy, but he was failing at that so he might as well stop hurting her altogether.

Poor bastard, I thought, listening to him talk, wishing he'd stop fiddling with my hair. He was clearly in the grip of Sir Galahad syndrome; sweep in and rescue the damsel in distress then become disappointed when she's not the fragile little princess you thought she was. He clearly couldn't see his damaged girl was something else entirely, what I was beginning to see, a quiet, manipulative sort of predator in her own way.

Whatever had or hadn't happened between her and Will in San Francisco, she'd known he was coming to New York and it looked like she'd gone there with her boyfriend in tow, fleeing to the safety of the next married man whose bitch wife just didn't understand him, six months before we'd arrived.

I wondered what she'd done to the previous abusive 'boyfriend' Gus mentioned, if he'd existed at all, since she'd told the same pity line to elicit Will's sympathy. Some people draw violence towards them though, so maybe I wasn't the only person who wanted to beat the living shit out of her, seeing her mouth-breathing face every Monday at my boxercise class in the precise spot on the punch bag where I landed each jab. Her ribcage had become the object of my dummy punches – Hook! Jab! Uppercut! – Die! Skank! Whore! – as Kim Lae the instructor prompted, 'Let's hear it, ladies. Bring the noise!'

Poor Gus. He was so limp, so limpid by comparison. It might have done him the world of good to punch the shit out of a gym bag once in a while. It might have even prevented what came later, if he'd channelled all that angst and insecurity in another direction. Gus who'd kissed me in the coffee shop an hour before, shyly suggesting we 'go somewhere more private', expecting to be rejected. Gus who didn't know my real name, or who I was, who didn't know his girlfriend had screwed my husband.

Listening to his breathing slow into a doze, I tried to gauge how long I had to lie there before I could leave. I'm still not sure how I'd allowed myself to let it go so far between us. I wasn't even that attracted to him, but the idea had felt good an hour before, daring, even, after our fifth 'date' in a line that included one chaste walk in Central Park, one handholding stroll around the Museum of Natural History, one heads-together meatball feast in Little Italy.

Will had been back in the apartment for a month by then and I'd relished the feeling of having a secret of my own. Getting close to Gus seemed like a step up in the guerrilla action I'd promised myself I'd carry out on that January night on the skank's doorstep, but as the clammy sheets cooled in the city's April fug it already felt like a mistake.

Hoping I could soon slide out from under his arm and dress silently, I wondered if Gus would feel the same when he woke to find me gone, if his conscience would prick him when he went home to *her*. More than hers had when she'd gone home to him, fresh from Will's bed?

Would he tell her about us then? Confess after he'd dumped his hipster messenger bag in the hall, pulled that faintly sad smile onto his face, speaking words to salve his conscience? How might she take that – being on the other end of the equation for once? In her supposed fragile state? I was half curious to find out, remembering what Gus had said about her being upset and paranoid.

My other guerrilla tactics were clearly starting to pay off, the ones that had started with a visit to that cheap shop in Little Italy where I'd bought a pay-as-you-go phone. I'd started sending her the one liner texts in February, every day at first, then sometimes twice or more. Nothing too specific, nothing to reveal my hand, just things like, 'Nice butt tattoo, bitch,' 'Nice performance, slut,' 'Eager to see more of you and I bet your boss would be too,' carefully calculated to shock and alarm, to invade her privacy, and sense of safety, as she had mine.

Like the dead blackbird I'd shoved on her doorstep in March, after I'd found it, feet up, wings stiff on the apartment rooftop, merely a piece of luck that, the day before, she'd posted an Instagram photo of her new yoga gear with blackbirds on.

Then, two weeks before I'd slept with Gus, I'd stolen her yoga bag and clothes from the gym I'd identified on her Facebook post as 'Birdies' on 8th, with its little blackbird logo. Sometimes there are nice symmetries in life and it was easy to pay for a quick 'taster' spin session at 9 a.m., then hang around until she was in the hot yoga room. No one there locked their lockers or checked entry ID it seemed, too Zen for that. I didn't even have to break in.

Best of all, some weeks before, and again seven days later, I'd sent a printout of a cropped section of one of the sex video stills to her office, addressed to her in a plain brown envelope. I'm sure she must've known what they were when she opened them. You'd recognise your own tits in front of you, probably, even if your face was struck out with black marker. I was very careful with fingerprints and didn't lick the envelope.

All in all I was pleased with myself, until Gus tucked his head into my neck and murmured, 'I really like you, Bonnie,' nuzzling up to spoon me. 'You're such a good person. You deserve so much. I don't really know what I'm doing but I'm glad I met you.'

That was the moment I knew I'd taken things way too far, glad he couldn't see my face or its ragged expression as I clenched my eyes shut and squeezed his hand in reply.

I waited until he was sleeping soundly then crept out and left him.

Twelve

New York City

After leaving Gus that night, I wanted nothing more than to get home, take a shower and wash his smell off me. I knew Will wouldn't be back for hours, hosting a reception for a Japanese delegation, probably rolling home after midnight reeking of whatever they'd been drinking. But I was eager to get to the apartment roof, to share some quality time with Jacky D, give myself time to think.

Hurrying into the foyer of my apartment building I headed for the stairwell only to jump in alarm as a dark figure separated itself from the semi-darkness. But it was only Pilar's guy, the one called Beau, with the impressive ginger beard, grinning 'Sorry babe,' hovering on the bottom step, seemingly unclear whether he was going up or down.

'Waiting for Pilar?' I smiled, glad I hadn't overreacted and landed a Kim Lae kick straight to his groin. I liked Beau, who always opened the door for me when we met in the foyer and, because Pilar had obviously told him I was a writer, always asked how the Great American Novel was coming along.

'Yeah, well . . .' he sighed, shifting the brown bag tucked in the crook of his arm, smiling ruefully, 'actually she's not answering right now.'

'Did you knock hard enough?' I asked, spotting a packet of Twinkies on the top of his bag and a few packets that smelled like the expensive herbal tea she liked. 'She probably has her headphones in. I saw the light on outside.'

'She's in there, all right,' he smiled. 'But I'm not "in favour" right now. She's on a total detox and I'm a bad influence.'

'A detox? Pilar?' I laughed, pointing at the Twinkies, thinking of the girl who always offered me a puff of her joint at her kitchen table when we were drinking tar-black coffee, eating cookies.

'Yeah, you know,' he mimed a toke, 'a *recreational* detox, so she still needs the sugar.'

'Well, you can't hang around here like a sex pest startling lone women,' banging the door with my fist as I called out. 'Hey, Pilar! Open up. Give a guy a break, huh? He's making the place look untidy out here.'

Sure enough, after a few seconds, she opened the door a crack, clad in a paint-splattered apron, yellow daubs on her cheeks and forehead.

'Sorry if this dead-beat has been harassing you,' she smiled, pushing the door open and taking the Twinkies.

'No harassment has taken place,' I replied.

'Well, OK then,' twitching her head a fraction to indicate he was allowed in. But, as he sidled past me the bottom of the brown bag he was carrying split and a little packet of pills dropped out as he bent over.

'That'd better not be ecstasy, Beau Jackson,' said Pilar, swooping on the packet in his hand, voice molten with threat. 'You said you were over that retro crap – that we needed to be clear headed and ready for the creative process.'

'You said that, actually, sweet thing,' grinned Beau, 'but hey, they're not mine,' giving me an earnest stare. 'Right, Liv? They were just lying in the hallway.'

'Oh right,' grinned Pilar, not in the least taken in, 'so you won't mind if Olivia tosses them down the pan, then?'

'Yeah, sure, better than some kids finding them, right?' green eyes twinkling.

As she waved me goodnight and started to close the door she offered as an afterthought, 'Art show on June tenth, sweet thing? Edward Hopper's legacy? At the Guggenheim? Should be fun and there's free wine.'

'Sorry,' I said, already five steps up the stairwell, 'I'll be halfway up El Capitan by then, remember?'

'Oh yeah, the great American Road Trip. Raincheck then?'

Fifteen minutes later I was in my favourite cardigan and leggings, on the rooftop, fingering the pill packet in my hand. I was half thinking of sampling one to take the edge off the evening, ease the sensation that, when fleeing the hotel bed with Gus in it, I'd somehow fled a crime scene. Like that day in the wilderness with James Scott, the day I'd run away.

It all came flooding over me then, the memory of how, that evening, after school, after hockey, I'd watched him arguing with Natalie in the wilderness, seen him shrugging her off, her crying and begging him to *come back, come back, don't leave me*. I'll never forget the hope in my heart as I followed him when he strode into the hummocks, because he'd finally seen Natalie for what she was.

I was hiding, of course, in the bushes on top of the pillbox, when he stopped to strike up a cigarette, beautiful in the rare, hot afternoon light, until he said, 'For fuck's sake come out, Liv. I know you're up there.'

Slipping obediently out of my hiding place, refusing the fag he offered me, he grinned. 'Why are you always lurking around out here, anyway? Little sneaky spy, eh? You saw that then, the bust up with Natalie? Don't worry. She's probably run back to her mates. You're safe with me.'

He looked much older than sixteen that day, nearly six feet tall, almost a man. I hadn't been that close to him, alone, in years and I was suddenly conscious of his muscled torso shifting under his tracksuit top. The way he was looking at me.

'She's such a bitch,' I said, because it was true and I needed to say it.

'You got that right,' he frowned. 'She's wrong, you know. You're not ugly. You're not fat. You're, well, you're you, right?'

Flushed with joy, I moved up closer, because I knew he'd finally come back to me at last. Maybe not for ever, not with wedding bells and babies, but for the rest of my school years at least, my legs trembling as I imagined walking into the schoolyard next morning, me and James, lining up for registration, obviously 'going together', revelling in Natalie's fury, her impotence instead of mine for a change, with James on my arm, all her insults silenced, exploded.

So when I moved in to kiss him, lifted my face to his, I fully expected him to grasp me in his arms, press his lips to mine, not jerk away, and laugh. 'What the fuck are you doing, Liv?'

'What you've wanted to do for years,' I whispered, sliding my arms around his waist.

'What are you talking about?' He stiffened. 'Get off, Liv.'

'It's OK. Nat's not here now, like you said. It's just us. No one can see.'

'See what? Jesus, Liv.' He grinned. 'You didn't think . . .? Just because I said . . . Come on, love. You didn't think I'd actually want to go with you, do you? Fucking hell, Natalie will just love this.'

Stunned, my arms dropped away as I struggled to form the words, 'But you broke up. You said she's a bitch.'

'We're always breaking up. She'll come crawling back tomorrow, eager to show me how much she loves me, as usual.'

'But you *said,* she's a bitch.'

'Yeah, but she's my girlfriend and you're . . .'

He broke off. It took me a second to find a reply. 'I'm what? And what's the Gobbler then? If Natalie's your hot girlfriend why are you meeting up with Gail out here?'

'Yeah, well, that's different. She just gives really good head on tap, that's all. It don't mean nothing. She's a slag. I'm not *with* her.'

'But you came out here on purpose. You left your girlfriend back there. You knew I was here. This was our place, remember?'

'Jesus, Liv, that was years ago. Grow the fuck up. We're not ten years old any more playing dens and all that shit in a war bunker.'

'But Natalie isn't . . .'

'What? I know what she is. She's the fucking fittest girl in the school and you . . . well, look at you, love. No offence

112

or nothing.' Me with my fat arse and spots, too ugly even to rape. 'Jesus, I'm not desperate, like.'

When he laughed I saw the casual cruelty in it, turning away, so he wouldn't see the tears in my eyes.

'Look. Don't fucking cry, now. Don't be a stupid girl,' dragging on his Regal. 'Just grow up, OK?'

'I won't cry for you, ever again,' I said, turning around, blood beating in my head, 'you shallow, selfish piece of shit. Fuck you!'

'Aww. Liv, love. Come on now. Don't be like that,' making a half-hearted attempt at an apology, reaching out for my arm. There was nothing half-hearted about the shove I gave him though, slamming my hands into his chest with all my might, the oof of air that came out of him, winded, startled, the most gratifying thing I'd heard in months.

I'm not sure what I thought I was doing. I think I just wanted to knock him off balance, push him off his feet into the mud and quarry scree, wipe the smirk off his face once and for all. But he didn't fall down. After the initial shock, he seemed to think it was funny. How could he not, I suppose? Big old him, little old crying me?

He didn't think I could hurt him, and perhaps I couldn't have, wouldn't have, if things had been different. If the thought of him laughing about me with Natalie, my humiliation complete, hadn't made me angrier than I'd ever known, raised that thing not at home in summer school uniform, that scalding red-black taste in my mouth and howl in my head.

The low wall behind him, skirting the lip of the quarry, had been crumbling for years, barely separating us from the sheer drop to the old machinery, abandoned like rusting dinosaur bones below. On my second shove, my hands driving into his chest like the head of an enraged bull, it gave way under his weight, his arms reeling comically for a moment as his centre of gravity shifted backwards and he started to fall.

His feet propelled above the ground, his bulk pushing the stones back with him before they parted ways. With a flash of rubber soles, he and his Adidas three-stripe trainers, mud in the treads, went down with a crumble of dust and gravel, leaving a smash-toothed gap in the stones.

I stood there unmoving, my heart thumping against the walls of my chest, aware of sun on my face, a tanker trawling its way across the grey edge of the horizon, a plane arrowing onwards into the western sky. The world had split in half, into the moments before and the moment after, but no one had seen it, no one was watching. No one had noticed.

I walked forward then, looking over the drop, straight down the quarry side. I'd never seen a dead body before but I knew I was looking at one below, on its back, head lolling at an unpleasant angle, half obscured by the bushes that had rooted themselves at the base of the rock.

I knew I should do something. I should raise the alarm. But I didn't, didn't even move until I heard Natalie calling from across the waste ground behind the copse of trees, calling for the smashed figure far below, 'Jay, Jay, come on. Don't be a prick! Jay? Let's go and sort this out. I've got a spliff, yeah?'

I hid then, darted into the shrubs and onto the pillbox where I'd watched James a few minutes and a lifetime

114

before. Still, silent, my hands clenched in fists, she walked right past me, half in tears, not stopping to look over the wall, trailing miserably back towards the estate, wiping her nose on her school shirtsleeve.

I waited as the day cooled and dusk came down, carrying the sounds of cars making their way home across the bay. I didn't know what would happen next but something in me knew I shouldn't stay to see the carnage discovered, that I needed to be somewhere else when that happened, that I needed to cover my tracks.

So I started running and didn't look back.

On the roof of our apartment block, a thousand miles from the Pen Dinas estate, I tried to tell myself that I'd come a long way since then, that I was not that Olivia any more. What had happened with Gus, what I was doing to *you-know-who*, was not a crime of that sort. I had nothing to be ashamed of.

But I also knew there are things we carry with us, always, and others that follow of their own accord. And something was following me then, through those long winter days, something that found a snarl of pleasure in playing my little tricks. Its teeth were waiting to be bared some more and I wasn't sure how I felt about that because, whatever that thing was, it wasn't afraid like I was. That was either something to envy or something to fear.

Swigging down some Jack Daniel's, I forced myself not to think about it, to think instead what I should do about Gus, now that things were getting out of control. I'd been taking a risk all along by returning to the grief group, leaving myself exposed. I knew I had to step back, break it off, think of a way to let Gus down gently so he'd never find out who I really was and Will would never find out who he was.

So, a week later, with my break-up speech prepared, I seated myself at the back of the grief group and waited for Gus. I knew something was up when, at one second to eight, Gus walked in, clearly saw me, but carried on down the aisle to a seat in the front, alone.

Seemingly unwilling to even look in my direction while Angel talked again about the five stages of grief, Gus pulled a piece of paper from his pocket and started folding and unfolding it between his hands. This went on for a whole half an hour, even when Marianne, Chad's widow, gave an alarmingly distraught testimony, three feet away from him in floods of tears.

'Hi Gus,' I said, friendly but not too friendly, as he finally approached me at the coffee cart, only to frown, take my arm and steer me to the privacy of the corner by the confessional, right at the back.

'Bonnie, I . . .' he began, still using my fake name, of course. Here it comes, I thought, as he pressed the scribbled note into my hand.

'Am I supposed to open it now?'

'No. Yes. No. I don't know. I was going to give it to you at the end of the group and just walk away. I thought it would be easier than having to see your face when you read it but it isn't. I owe you this much. I'm so sorry. I've thought long and hard about it and I can't do this any more. I'm not a good man. I have to end it.'

OK, I thought. Thank God. 'But Gus . . .?'

'I know, I know. I'm sorry to be such a shit when you're going through this massive loss. You don't deserve this.

116

I care about you, Bonnie, but I just can't be *that guy* again. Jenna is going through a bad patch and I have to be there for her. I have to fully commit to this or it's Hallie all over again. I can't be a cheat in my heart. I think it's best if we stop being friends.'

Righto, I thought, impressed he appeared to be a man who actually learned from his mistakes. Though our flirtation, lasting so briefly and brokenly, was hardly an epic romance, I knew he needed something more than a quick *thanks, see you around* and a civilised handshake to make himself feel better.

'I'm sorry too, Gus,' I said, trying to look suitably teary, 'but I understand. I don't want to be *that woman* either. I think you're right. We should stop this before anyone gets hurt. Give it all you've got. Try and make it work. Jenna's a lucky girl.'

'I think I love you, Bonnie,' he said sorrowfully, 'but it's all or nothing now, isn't it? With me and her? But then, who knows? Fate brought us together once, you and me. If we're meant to have something more then perhaps we will, in time. For now, though . . .'

'It's all right, Gus,' I said, 'I'm taking a trip upstate next week to see my sister. You won't run into me here again. I understand.'

There were tears in his eyes and I tried not to cringe as he kissed my cheek, saying, 'Do what's right for you,' as he clearly intended to do just that, adding as an afterthought, 'Maybe in the future there'll be a better time.'

Then I couldn't take it any longer, couldn't stay until the end in his earnest and sorrowful presence. I squeezed his clammy hand, because Angel was looking over ready to start the second half, pocketed the note he gave me and walked away.

Striding home, fingering the paper rectangle in my cardigan pocket, with Gus's words *I'm so sorry, I have to end it* scribbled on it, I thought about throwing it in the trash but hesitated for a moment, pushing it back down among the loose change and receipts, part of me wondering if I could find a use for it, send it anonymously to the whore perhaps, and see how she felt about it. I doubted Gus had come clean yet but she'd know her own boyfriend's writing, surely? Even if he denied it?

But by the time I got home my heart wasn't in it any more. Better to let Gus slip away with no one any the wiser than to overplay my hand. There was no reason for me to bump into him again, or so I thought, letting out a great, long-held breath to make smiley small talk with emerging Mr Luigi and Poppet off for a stroll. Though, as it turned out my relief was misplaced. I'd bump into Gus again soon after, in the most unlikely of places.

Thirteen

Yosemite Valley, California

As Will and I fell into bed that night, after our visit to Glacier Point, and a barbecue dinner of gourmet hot dogs and mac and cheese under the firepit smoked pine trees, I found myself seriously questioning the point of the trip. After the day we'd had, how could I ignore the fact we were more than halfway through our journey and, so far, all Will had done was spectacularly fail every challenge I'd set him?

Perhaps impossible challenges can only result in disappointment though, even if they seem so simple to deliver – such an easy way to show someone you really hear them, see them, think they are special. That's what the test had come to symbolise, I suppose, because, even before the affair, Will had refused to see why these things mattered to me.

He'd never understood why I'd get so upset when he'd pick up a last-minute birthday card and bunch of flowers on the way home from work, or why I wasn't enthusiastic when he'd ask, 'So what do you want to do tonight, Liv, since it's our anniversary?' instead of surprising me once in a while, laughing it off like he was such a lovable dunce.

He never seemed to understand that it wasn't about receiving expensive treats but about reversing the usual role in our relationship where I organised and took care of everything. It was about *taking the initiative, making the effort*, that was the test Will had refused to participate in since the day we'd met and, when it had become too much effort to tell him yet again how that made me feel, I'd learned to tell myself he was right – 'Romantic gestures' were clichéd, not like the things that really mattered.

They were not like the Sunday mornings cuddled in bed with books and papers; the Saturday night filmathons at the old cinema in Ealing where he introduced me to Hollywood classics; not like the way he laughed at the dumbest things and loved my scrambled eggs with alarming passion, or, when I was confronted by a hairy, eight-legged intruder in the bathroom, he'd always get a glass and envelope to humanely trap it for me, though he was afraid of spiders too.

That's why I'd given up on being romanced and spoiled for so long, in exchange for something more genuine. Except it wasn't, was it? When it all came crashing down. When I found out about the affair and realised I'd got neither gestures nor loyalty, romance nor fidelity. I'd thought it was an either-or deal. Turned out it was a neither-nor.

Even worse was the knowledge of the time and effort he must have put in to keep the indoorsy slut, the high-maintenance whore, a secret. How much preplanning and preparation had been involved in arranging hotel rooms and ordering her silver customised pendants? That's why, even when the outcome seemed so obvious, the holiday a disaster and the totting of the crosses in Will's fail column so inevitable, I still couldn't let him off the hook and abandon the test.

He had to make amends – in the way I needed – give me my second chance at being wooed and won, the least I deserved. Even though the reality of who Will was, and what he would never be, was becoming clearer by the minute.

Naturally, we made love later that night, because it seemed the thing to do on a dream trip, on the vacation of a lifetime, urgently grasping for each other in the dark warmth of the sheets, bodies moving in familiar rhythms. Unusually for me, I didn't come, probably because it was *her* face I saw in my head as my eyes closed, wearing his silver pendant, his carefully selected romantic gesture.

'What are you thinking about?' I asked, as we drifted off to sleep, listening to an owl hoot in the woods above the cabin, the most dangerous question of all in a marriage.

'I'm thinking I need to try harder for you, Livia,' Will whispered. 'We have thirteen years behind us. I don't know how it will work out but I want it to, Liv. Let me try. We can move forward, I know we can.'

Except that wasn't the immediate problem. It was no longer just about us. Things were about to catch up with us, to catch up with me, because you can only run for so long before whatever's pacing you, waiting for you to tire, finds your heels and snaps its teeth.

So, the next day, parked at the side of the road approaching Mariposa Grove, home of the fabled giant sequoias, I assumed the people in the other hire car, parked ahead, were also avoiding the teeming car park, disinterested until

I saw the dark-skinned man leaning against the bonnet. That's when I realised it was Gus, actually Gus, halfway across the continent from New York, at the side of the shady road. And *she* was with him, *the skank, the whore*, right there.

There was no doubting it was her, even though she'd swapped her usual nip-waisted dresses and click-clack heels for tiny hiking shorts and boots. The expensively labelled ensemble might have been intended to suggest 'sexy lady hiker', but somehow only managed to draw attention to her hollow cheeks and the thinness of her toned legs; lucky legs, I thought randomly, as my mother would have said, 'lucky they don't snap'.

Snorting with inappropriate laughter I watched her lean against the fence, drinking green gunk from a transparent plastic sports cup, while Gus, like I'd never seen him before, out of his usual chinos and jacket into hiking shorts, a faded Death Metal T-shirt and backwards baseball cap, stretched out his hamstring, one leg on the wheel arch.

He looked glaringly self-conscious in his outdoor gear, like a geography teacher caught in the Spar by his pupils on a Friday night, in his off-duty tracksuit, buying a four-pack of lager. When he spotted me, holding the car door open, waiting for Will to stop fiddling about and grab his rucksack, I had no idea what to do, panic flaring, wondering if there was time to get back inside, slam the door, and tell Will to drive to the swimming hole down the highway instead.

But then Will got out, grinning like a child, looking forward to the visit because he said the giant trees looked 'like a scene from *Vertigo*', his favourite Jimmy Stewart movie we'd seen half a dozen times, and it was too late.

Looking back, I think Will still fancied himself as a sort of Jimmy Stewart everyman then, a do-right kinda guy, always the first to help a woman down from a dusty tourist jeep, to stand for a pregnant woman on a packed train.

I wonder if that's what Gus saw when he finally spotted him, staring from me to Will then back again, a clean cut, nice guy, while I looked at the ground and held my breath. Either way, there was no way to retreat without causing suspicion but I knew that, when Gus opened his mouth, things were going to get very complicated, very quickly. He was going to say something like, 'Hi, Bonnie, fancy seeing you here,' calling me by a made-up name, asking who I was with and then what? Should I deny all knowledge of him, claiming instead to have a doppelganger like Kim Novak in *Vertigo*, or a twin sister called Bonnie who spoke with an American accent?

For a moment neither of us moved until Will broke the standoff, spotting *you-know-who*, blanching, then recovering with enough impressively British self-control to walk towards her and say, with his best client-greeting voice, 'Well, hello. Fancy seeing you here? Long time, no see.'

Long time, no see? I thought, stifling another snort of laughter. Next thing we know he'll be going all doubly Brit abroad, saying *It's frightfully good to see you*, or something equally *Brideshead Revisited* and then I really won't be able to keep a straight face.

Because there really was a note of black comedy about it, of a 1970s *Carry On* movie, as the skank opened her mouth, closed it, raised her hand in a wave then dropped it. She regained her poise while Gus kept up his thousand-yard stare, his eyebrows raised, running her gaze up and down me from head to toe. Though, for once, I actually felt I had the upper hand. Tanned from the desert, hair tinted by the sun, a smudge of sunrise coral on my lips I looked pretty good; that and the fact she didn't know I knew who she was, or had seen her in all her nakedness, surely gave me an advantage.

She must have assumed I was the dumb wife, still in the dark, though she had the good grace to drop her gaze from me for a second before her professional manner kicked in with, 'You must be Olivia? I've heard a lot about you.'

I bet you have, I thought, saying, 'Oh, yes,' brittle smile in place, 'don't think I've ever heard of you, though. And you are?'

She looked taller when we were eye to eye at last, as tall as me in fact and, at five eight, I'm only a couple of inches shy of Will. I'd never been that close to her before, in daylight, so it was the first real chance to see her without the flattering Instagram filter, to notice, alongside those skinny legs, the shiny, open pores on her nose, stripped of makeup, what looked like a coldsore in the corner of her mouth.

I was almost tempted to reach out and touch it, the soft brown crust at the edge of her lower lip, touch *her*, the demon made flesh, blood and blister in the sunlight, hoping to break the spell with my finger, watch her crumble from existence in a puff of green smoke. Instead I clenched my hands as she said, 'I'm Jenna. I work in PR, at the Lowbeck and the other hotels. Me and Will have done a couple of little jobs together. You two enjoying a vacation, then? Good! You guys need a break and you should get out and see the country while you're here. There's so much more to the US of A than just New York City, as you can see.'

As she waved her arms like a tour operator, I almost expected her to pull out a microphone pack and regale us with facts about the national park system. 'You're heading to the valley, then?' she carried on, as we nodded and Will tried to find something to say. 'Taking in El Capitan and Half Dome? It's stunning, really, trust me.'

'We've come from the park, actually,' said Will, keeping remarkable control of his facial features. 'We're staying there a few nights. What are you doing here? Jenna and . . .?' Gus forgotten, until now, at her shoulder.

'Oh, sorry,' said Jenna, placing a hand on his arm, 'this is my boyfriend, Gus.'

'Oh, hi.' A pause from Will, a nod from Gus. 'You guys just started dating then?' Looking surprised, when Gus said, 'No. We've been together three years next week, actually. This is kind of an anniversary trip for us.'

Gus looked at me as he spoke, for just a fraction too long, before he asked, 'And you guys?' forced and bright. 'Old flames?'

'Almost fourteen years,' said Will, 'and it's Liv's birthday on Friday.'

'A birthday celebration? How lovely!' grinned Jenna, also too brightly, each of us blinding the other with our mega-watt civility. 'Hope you've got her an awesome gift, Will. No slacking now.'

God, it was a torrid moment, so sharp and strange I wanted to spit up a thousand black and blue curses, while somehow stifling the desire to snigger like a fifteen-year-old, every second waiting for Gus to say, 'So your name is Liv? Strange, because you told me your name was Bonnie, remember? At grief counselling? I must say, your dead husband is looking remarkably well, and, by the way, how come you're British all of a sudden?'

He didn't though as he walked towards me, put out his hand and said, 'Nice to meet you, *Livia*.'

'So, how do you and Jenna know each other?' asked Gus towards Will, keeping his gaze on me.

'Like I just said, Will works for Piper's too, at the Lowbeck,' said Jenna, staring at Will, California smile at full blast.

'Right, of course,' said Gus, as if a penny was dropping somewhere behind his wide, brown eyes, rattling down to ground zero. 'You two work at the Lowbeck together.'

'Uh, yeah. We work at the Lowbeck, check that,' grinned Jenna, though I could see her perfectly manicured fingertips whiten as she gripped her green gunk cup.

'You're on vacation too?' I asked, to break the smiley but stiffening silence.

'Yeah. Getting some R and R in before the big conference in August and the renovated suites finally open,' said Jenna. 'You'll still be with us then, right, Will? Piper's is renewing your contract for another year?'

'We'll find out officially next week, when the contracts come through,' said Will. 'But yes, I've been led to believe so. You?'

'Yeah, well, I think so. I mean, there was that fuss with the thing at the Temple Hotel the other week. I'm sure you've heard about it, everyone else in New York has. The night the Germans were over? I'm sure my drink was spiked but, well, I'm hoping that'll all get sorted out and it won't be a problem.'

'I'm sure it won't,' said Will, as if he had no idea what she was talking about.

'Guess you'll be looking for a new apartment, then? Out of the Piper holding pen at last? A place of your own in midtown or one of the boroughs?'

'So you drove all the way out here from New York?' I interrupted, not wanting to talk about where Will and I would be in a month's time.

'Hell, no!' laughing at the suggestion they might have driven almost 3000 miles just to see some really big trees. 'My folks still live in San Francisco. We used to live there,' gesturing to Gus. 'I used to drive up here every summer with my dad when I was a kid. It only takes about three or four hours but Gus has never come, imagine that? Even though he's from Sausalito, across the Bay. So we've been to see my folks and now I'm introducing him to the delights of camping before we head back on Monday. Well, actually, he suggested it this time, as we had a few days to spare. I've been telling him forever that everyone should see Half Dome at least once in their life. But Gus is such an urbanite. He thinks a stroll in Golden Gate Park is the Great Outdoors. He's about as indoorsy as an IT geek can get.'

She grinned wider then, but Gus didn't and neither did I, registering the word 'indoorsy'.

Not taking his eyes off Will, Gus said simply, 'Nature's not really my thing.'

'*Movement* isn't really your thing, hon,' she laughed. 'Yeah, I can't get him to even go to the gym with me. Healthy body, healthy mind, right?'

She seemed to realise she was babbling then, closing her mouth to allow Will to say, 'Well, we should probably be going. The next shuttle up to the grove is in five minutes. See you around, I'm sure.'

'Yeah, sure, yeah,' waving her hand at the approaching bus, kicking up dust in the distance. 'Oh, the grove is awesome. Make sure you get all the way to John Muir's cabin at the top, the guy who wrote all the wilderness philosophy. It's just gorgeous, with this little stream and everything. You'll love it, and don't forget to go over to Hetch Hetchy reservoir. It was a whole valley once, like Yosemite Valley, drowned in the 1920s to provide water for San Francisco. It was super-controversial at the time but it's super-beautiful and you can walk through the actual waterfall. You'll get off on that, Livia.'

I almost did it then, covered the three paces between us in one second and smashed my clenched fist into her face yelling, *Don't* – Pow! – *Presume* – Smash! – *To tell me* – Jab! – *What I will* – Cross! – *And won't* – Jab! – *Like* – Smash! – *You manky, anorexic, stupid slut! I didn't like you telling Will you were wet for him, or care for the sight of your skank arse riding him like a bucking bronco, so don't assume you know the first fucking thing about what I'd get off on.*

'We'll try,' said Will, before I could answer, smiling as if grateful for the travel tip, while Gus at her shoulder stood dumbly, diminished somehow without his city uniform suit, skinnier than he'd seemed in the sweating darkness of the hotel bed.

Poor Gus, biting his tongue even harder than I was biting mine, because he still didn't say anything as Will added, 'We're staying up near Hetch Hetchy actually. The valley hotel, the Ahwahnee, or whatever it's called now, was full. We'll take a look,' pointedly hoisting his rucksack onto his shoulder.

'Well, I'll leave you to it, then,' said Jenna, her smile folding, as if she'd actually hoped she might be invited to join us, make a friendly foursome for the day. Taking Gus's hand, she said, 'We'll be under canvas tonight, at Camp Curry. Think of us in our sleeping bags when you're in a king size,' then blushed, because I assume the last thing either of us wanted to be thinking about, ten hours from now, was who the other was in bed with.

Somehow she looked so much more human in that moment, cheeks flushing, something snagging at her smile, more real in the real world beyond the cinematic pavements and tower blocks of New York. There was something hollow behind her eyes as she said, 'See you next week then, at work. Have fun,' and Will replied politely, 'Enjoy your camping. Nice to meet you, Gus.'

As we turned away she didn't look like a cheap and clichéd sex bomb any more, like the siren who'd lured my man away. She looked like an underweight seventeen-year-old girl who wanted to be invited to the prom by the jock she was crushing on and had just been told she had to stay home instead.

She loved him, I realised, she still loved him, and in that instant the tricks I'd played on her in the city, the texts, the photos, the dead bird on the doorstep, seemed childish and spiteful. I was old enough to know better, better than that and better than what I'd done at the Temple Hotel in Tribeca ten days before.

It had seemed a thing of beauty at the time, during the reception for the Hamburg delegation, watching her wobbling, spilling her cocktail, sprawling off-balance into the arm of the sofa, the look of alarm on Dieter Petersen's face priceless, as she lumbered into him, slurring.

I'd kept the little pills, the ones I'd appropriated from Beau that night in the stairwell, after sleeping with Gus. I didn't throw them down the pan as I'd promised Pilar. Too cowardly to try them myself, I'd kept them tucked in the side pocket of my handbag. I'd only followed her that night to make sure she wasn't meeting up with, or going anywhere near, Will, relieved when I saw him sit down with his boss Toby in the bar, from the safety of the taxi rank opposite the lobby.

Too jacked up to go straight home and, by chance, smartly suited for one of Pilar's art shows on the Upper East Side later, I'd followed her when she left the Lowbeck, all the way to the Temple, three easy Subway stops down. Then I slipped into the crowded lobby and ordered a cocktail with the rest of the guests, looking the part, playing it, as she lorded it over the clients in her black silk sheath dress and Jimmy Choo's.

Watching her at the bar, fawning, flirting, I'd thought about sidling up to her to see if she would recognise me, if I could throw her off her stride with a few well-placed words about butterfly tattoos and cellulite, but she was in full PR mode and the room was jam-packed. She didn't even turn her head as I ordered two Manhattans, her obvious drink of choice, one already in her hand, at the far end of the bar, then slipped one of the pills into the cloudy glass.

So very femme fatale, so Lauren Bacall cool, I asked a waiter with a tray to send it over to her, my face half hidden by my fall of hair, an elegant flick of the hand accompanying the words *courtesy of the tall gentleman in the grey suit.*

I couldn't be sure she'd actually drink it but she didn't waste any time nodding her thanks to the waiter a few seconds later and knocking it back. I stayed just long enough to watch the effects start to manifest, sidling past her black silk jacket on the back of a chair on my way out, slipping the plastic bag, wiped clean of my prints but with three pills still inside, into her pocket.

Bonnie was the one who told me about the aftermath, while we were sipping almond mocha lattes at the coffee shop the day after, her face twisting into a swirl of pity and distaste as she related the vomiting incident by the buffet table, the way Jenna had insisted Mr Petersen, the German CEO, had put his hand on her ass, then called him a slimy, Nazi pervert.

'Not like Jenna, at all,' Bonnie had whispered. 'It was all very embarrassing. I mean, Mr Petersen's *wife* was there and we're a wholesome brand, you know, at Piper's. Not *that* sort of place at all.'

Olly had seen it happen, told Bonnie the gory details, how he'd helped Jenna into her jacket and noticed a packet in her pocket, *with pills in, you know, drugs*, searching for her phone to call her boyfriend. And, across the table from Bonnie I'd suppressed a smile, glad I'd made Jenna look like a fool, put a chip in her glossy image.

Except, she didn't look glossy any more, at the side of the road in Mariposa Grove and I didn't feel so fiendishly clever. As Will locked the car I felt petty, degraded, especially when Gus called after us, 'Nice to meet you, *Olivia*,' and she waved.

It had all been so polite, that meeting under the majestic trees, by the burbling river. So *civilised*, none of us wanting to make any sort of 'scene'; Will, scared of betraying himself with a wrong word; Gus, clearly too surprised and confused by my sudden appearance to ask, 'Who the fuck are you, lady? What kind of sick game have you been playing?'

So, all I could say to Will, as we waited for the shuttle to disgorge the returning tourists from the grove, was, 'Wow! Who was that? You really work with her?'

'Yeah. She's . . . we don't work together any more,' he muttered. 'We did in the beginning. I can't believe we bumped into them all the way out here. She's kind of hard work, to be honest. One of those high-maintenance types, very *American*,' as if that was dismissal enough.

'No kidding,' I snorted. 'Does she ever eat? Those were definitely lucky legs. Her thighs were as thick as my arms.'

'Yeah, they all look like that, the younger execs, zero carbs and so forth. Quick, jump on before that big party of Japanese gets in front of us or we'll have to wait two hours for the next shuttle.'

Hanging on to the straps above us, as we trundled up the valley to the redwood grove, Will leaned across and put his arm around my waist, kissed my forehead.

'I love you, Liv. I really do. I wish I could convince you of that. I want to try no matter how long it takes. You're everything I want.'

If only that were enough, I thought, hiding my face in his shoulder thinking of her wistful smile as we'd walked away, knowing I wasn't the only one he'd hurt.

Fourteen

Mariposa Grove, California

After that, I didn't really enjoy the stroll through the giant trees. With their impossibly broad trunks and foamy green heads they could easily have been plucked from a children's story about a land of giants and magic trolls, yet all I could do was run through the encounter back at the roadside, picking through the bones of what had been said in my head, who had said it and precisely how.

Will must have been doing the same, quiet and distracted as we left the copses of the valley floor and headed up one of the steeper routes to the upper grove, where we'd find John Galen's cabin, rather than John Muir's as *she* had claimed. I'd read up on Muir before the journey, one of the first men to head into Yosemite and pioneer for the protection of one of the last chunks of genuine wilderness. I envied him that, when it's hard to find really wild and lonely places anywhere any more, and, the more I thought about it, the more it struck me as odd that we'd just happened to bump into Gus and *her* in the mountains, 200 miles from her parents' home, 3000 miles from New York City.

What if it wasn't merely chance? asked the Jack Daniel's voice in my head, though I was twenty-four hours on the wagon then and starkly sober for once. What if she'd known where to find us because Will had mentioned something to her about us taking a trip? If so, that would mean they were still in touch, wouldn't it? Or that's what the snarling, green-eyed monster suggested, waking up, stretching out its legs again. That would mean they were still in contact, even just casually, something I'd expressly forbidden in my winter non-negotiable 'ultimatum list', even for work reasons. Even for just an awkward shooting-the-breeze and making small talk at the water cooler moment in full view of their colleagues, because it would have been too much to bear. And what if it was more than that? What if . . .?

But I mentally slapped myself, telling myself in the sternest voice I could muster not to tread that path again. There'd been no sign of a continued affair in all the weeks I'd been watching her so closely. If they'd tried to meet up I think I would have seen it. Besides, however she'd found out, surely she wouldn't have decided to just 'bump into us' way up there? What could she hope to gain? She'd seemed genuinely surprised, awkward.

Gus on the other hand . . . Some little glitch on his face had bothered me. He hadn't seemed that surprised to see us, or more obviously, to hear me speak in my own Welsh-hybrid accent. I wouldn't say he was a man I'd expect to have a well-developed poker face, so maybe he really was just too startled to respond, but, whatever the reason, I knew his reticence wouldn't last, that he'd have to have it all out with me at some point, face to face, though that would have to wait until we got back to New York.

As we hiked up the staggering, pine-clad incline through shady glades and light-littered clearings, I pushed the pace, trying to still the buzzing, darting doubts in my head with bursts of oxygen. It almost worked. Sweat sheening my chest and back, lungs opening to accommodate the altitude at last, it felt good to feel my body moving after that surge of unreleased adrenaline at the roadside.

Birds chittered in the otherwise silent grove as Will huffed up the track behind me, saying, 'This is amazing. I keep expecting an Ewok to fall out of a tree in front of us,' surprising me with an unusually lowbrow pop-culture reference. 'Like, *Return of the Jedi*,' he prompted, as if I'd forgotten. 'I'd love a speeder bike ride through these woods right now. How much further to the top, do you think? Is it left or right up here?'

Because, as usual, Will had no idea where we were going. As usual, I'd done all the planning, read the travel guide, had the map in my hand. Though, for once, I wasn't completely convinced I was steering us along the right track. We'd only been walking for an hour but I was starting to question if we were still on the path marked with a yellow zigzag on the pictogram. The fact we'd seen or heard no one since leaving the photo-opportunity crowds swarming the felled giant on the valley floor made me think we might have taken a spur track off the official route.

For that last twenty minutes the path had kept hair-pinning upwards over fallen trunks and along dizzying little ravines, falling away here and there down cuttings of sharp rocks and fern-green watercourses. A slip or a trip could easily result in a plummet and crash here, I thought, a broken leg, a fatal head injury, watching my step, leaning in to the incline, hand out at the ready. It would be hard to tell later if a head injury, sustained in the middle of leafy green nowhere, had come before or after a fall, a terrible accident. *If someone needed to be disposed of... if someone else were so inclined ...* whispered the voice in my head, though I told it to shut the fuck up as we approached an almost invisible fork in the path.

Pausing for a few seconds, Will overtook me, then stopped ahead where someone had placed a wide, fallen tree trunk over one of the ravines to act as a bridge. Perched on the edge of that cliff side, looking down into the mossy bite of stone cascading to the flash of stream below, I suddenly had a flashback of Will's flushed face as he was screwing *her* in Room 717 of the Lowbeck.

The memory hit me with the force of a fist all over again, almost doubling me over, reeling, as it was replaced by the memory of the look on Will's face when he'd met Gus on the road far below. Chest screaming for air, vision greying before the familiar panic attack's approach, I realised Will really hadn't known that *she* had a boyfriend and, when he'd found out, looked as if he hadn't liked it a bit. *Not one bit,* whispered the voice in my ear, *and you know what that means, don't you?* snickering.

Did I, though? Did I know what any of it meant any more? I suppose it might have meant that Will, like me, had been 'doing the math', as the Americans say, realising that if it was Gus and the skank's three-year anniversary as he'd claimed, she'd already been living with him when we'd made that trip to San Francisco. She'd moved to New York with Gus just before she'd told Will she was getting over an abusive boyfriend.

So was it jealousy I'd just seen behind Will's discomfited politeness, suggesting he still cared for her? Or was it simply male pride that loves to be adored, even by the thing it's rejected?

Then the old fear was back, bitter and metallic in my mouth, hackles raised; the voice that said again, *Is it really over between them, then? Will it always be? Could it ever, really, if they work together in the same city? In the same few blocks, at the same hotel at least a few days a week? If she still looks at him like that, after all this time?*

As Will swigged water from his bottle and reapplied DEET spray to his shins, all words finally seemed to fail, reason and logic crashed and burned. Maybe it was time to restart the system, to 'force an unexpected reboot' as Gus might have said in his IT capacity, time to break the endless loop of uncertainty in my tortured head, so much worse than knowing – to make that clean break, flick the off switch and wait for what might happen next.

Will was off balance at that moment, peering down into the granite narrows to the rock-strewn water, and I knew it would be the work of a moment to end it. There was a rumble of thunder somewhere above us, the approach of rain filling the air, fat drops sizzling into the leaf litter, making it even easier to claim he had simply slipped, down, down, a cry, the frantic flutter of birds, then silence.

I could walk on, up the hill afterwards, say we'd got lost, terribly, impossibly lost, that I'd left him on the trail after a disagreement about the path and then . . . and then the scurrying feet with medic bags and stretchers, the drone of a chopper overhead, the tea and sympathy, the solace of a widow.

It didn't seem like an equation any more, as it had until that moment, the choice I was about to make. It didn't seem like a series of hows and what ifs and buts to be weighed and solved, like that day in the furnace of the Grand Canyon – it felt like an urgency, a compulsion, a necessity.

I was tired, so tired of it all. I wanted it over.

I saw my hands rising from my side then, as Will peered over the drop, felt my feet begin to move, one two, one two, slow, steady – feet tired of pacing and following and stalking the streets all winter, heavy and desperate to rest.

I saw my hands, but not my hands, the hands of a girl who had once stood on the edge of a quarry and looked down, go out in front of me, the whirlwind in my head answering the thunder from the north. One step, two steps, three steps, staring at the back of Will's head, wondering what it would look like falling away from me . . .

That's when the man and woman appeared. By luck good or bad, who can say? But there they were, emerging from a hidden track on the right, from the parted curtain of trees, breaking the moment open, stopping me in my tracks.

'Hey guys,' the man waved, a blur of ginger ponytail and hipster beard, as I wiped my eyes with the back of my hand, realising there were tears there.

''Scuse us. Coming through,' checking his watch, breaking his stride for a second, assessing then heading for

138

the fallen trunk. 'Not far now, I reckon. Almost there, up to the top. It's beautiful up here, isn't it? Nature is a blessing and a wonder.'

The girl, a smaller blur of blonde hair and tanned legs, appeared a few steps behind him, grinning, adding, 'We're on honeymoon, best vacation ever, right!' reaching out to take his hand.

'It's bloody amazing,' said Will, grinning back, then pausing seeing my tear-blurred face.

'Hay fever is playing up,' I said embarrassed, pulling out a hanky and making a show of blowing my nose.

'It's a downer, all right, allergies,' said the girl. 'Here,' a packet of pills appearing from her shorts pocket. 'Try one of these. Work a treat for me,' popping a strip of antihistamines into my hand. 'Don't mix with alcohol though. Well, not too much, you know what I mean,' winking. 'Don't worry, I have two more packs in my backpack,' as I tried to protest with, 'Oh, no, I couldn't, really.'

'Well, see you at the top then,' said the guy, drawing her after him, making their escape across the trunk spanning the ravine where Will had stood two minutes before, so close to the edge, and I waited until the sound of their feet faded away before I let the great wrack of sobs out of me, hands knuckling my eyes like a child.

I couldn't stop, even when Will dashed over, clamping me in a hug saying, 'Liv, please. It's OK. Really it is. I know this is hard. But it's all right now. I love you, Liv. I'm so sorry for what I did to you. It's OK if you hate me. I deserve it. Anything you want to say to me, all the names you want to call me, they're all true. But I'll keep trying, I promise, to be someone worthy of you.'

Always the right thing to say. Always the thing I wanted to hear, pulling a Clif Bar out of his pocket, adding, 'Look, I saved one for you. Peanut butter too, your favourite,' sweet solace for a crying child.

Then he held out his hand to help me across the fallen trunk, grinning, 'Come on. Let's see this fabled grove of trees.'

Sure enough, the passing hipster guy was right. Despite the seeming remoteness of the location, less than five minutes later Will and I emerged from the dense trees into a glade dotted with damp tourists. John Galen's cabin sat in the centre, fringed by a shady brim of giant sequoias like a woodcut from a Grimms fairy tale. The fact the afternoon had darkened, a drum roll of thunder stalking the granite cliffs to the north, just added to the atmosphere, as I wandered away from Will for a moment, trying to catch my breath, slow my heart rate, putting the brook waving with grasses and chattering pebbles between us for a minute.

Pulling my anorak out of my rucksack I told myself to inhale gently, exhale slowly, while Will, on the cabin porch, wrestled his way into his stupid Little Red Riding Hood jacket. Watching him, oblivious, smiling, I wondered if he was thinking he'd had a narrow escape back on the road, congratulating himself that his secret was intact, and, whether, at any moment over the past months, it had occurred to him that I might have secrets of my own?

Sometimes I'd wished he'd be a little jealous. Occasionally, before I'd even slept with Gus, I had found myself telling him I was going somewhere with Bonnie or Pilar then leaving receipts for somewhere else almost in plain sight, like in my favourite cardigan pocket, hanging as always on the back of the chair by the dining table. I kept waiting for him to ask why I was at the Blue Otto Bar drinking Margaritas when I'd said I'd be at the Guggenheim or why I'd bought coffee in Times Square when I'd claimed I was in Greenwich Village.

I'd never messaged Gus on my own phone, I was more discreet than that, but I'd kept a few things from our encounters too, like a flyer for the grief group's annual bake sale. Later, I realised I hadn't even got rid of that note Gus had given me the night he had broken it off between us. I think a part of me wanted Will to find them, to get suspicious, ask questions, feel a flicker of doubt, and for the tables to be turned just once. But he'd never asked.

As the heavens opened and rattled down bullets of water onto the cabin roof, Will beckoned me back to him, grinning. In that second he was a boy enjoying the lightshow crackling across the sky, ducking in a knot of sheltering visitors under the rim of the cabin porch. And I almost envied him that trusting ignorance, a state I'd never known, a state of trust I'd never feel again.

The bearded, broad-bellied ranger in the doorway predicted, 'Don't worry, folks. It'll pass over in five minutes, you'll see. It's building up to a big one tonight, though. I can smell it. There'll be a grand blow before midnight. Hope you aren't under canvas.'

And I thought of them then, of the skank and Gus in their tent in Camp Curry, wishing myself a million miles away.

141

Fifteen

Yosemite Valley, California

It was later that afternoon, as I was buying snacks back at Pine Lodge's market shop, that I spotted Gus standing by the coffee machine, watching me intently. Startled by his sudden reappearance, his face pregnant with the promise of disaster, I dropped the blueberry muffin I was inspecting and watched it roll across the floor, giving him all the excuse he needed to come over, hand it back and say, 'Well, hi Olivia. *Long time, no see.* We must stop meeting like this.'

'What are you doing here, Gus?' I asked, ignoring the jibe and keeping my voice low in case the nearby cashier could hear us.

'I was about to ask you the same question, *Bonnie,*' selecting a squirt of hazelnut syrup from the six on offer for the coffee he was pouring from a pot on a hotplate.

'Look Gus, I'm sorry,' determined to get in first. 'I know you're hurt and you have every right to be. I can explain. I just . . . I needed some help for a while back there, in the city. Some comfort. Will and I have been going through some really tough times, even before we came over here for the new job, and I have no friends here. I needed someone to talk to. I made up a lie because I just wanted someone to listen, not to judge me.'

'I'm listening now,' said Gus, his face softening a fraction. 'I'm trying not to judge you but I'm still waiting for a proper explanation.'

'What do you want to know?' I sighed, in a way I hoped sounded defeated, handing over my authority to him. I knew how important that could be, in moments like that. I'd felt it myself when I was in his shoes and Will was in mine. It was easier than I'd expected, lying baldly to someone's face under pressure, not just for a lie's sake but when you know you're in the wrong and need desperately to hide it.

'Let's start with, I dunno, why you said your husband was dead?' said Gus.

'Because I was . . . I *am,* trying to decide if I need to leave him, if it's really over between us. My father died last year, Gus, but I couldn't talk about it then, couldn't process it. I wasn't ready for the grief, I suppose, I suppressed it. I'm still trying to work through it.'

That bit was true, about my father. My mother had told me on the phone two weeks before we'd left for New York. She'd found out after the funeral, about the testicular cancer, but by then I hadn't seen or spoken to him in twenty years and I'm not sure what good a graveside goodbye would have done, if I had even been welcome. Instead, using all of Angel's grief-group buzzwords to press my case, I pushed on as Gus's face softened further.

'I never meant to hurt you, Gus, or lie to you. I never expected to meet someone like you in the city. What I said in the group was true, about my father's cancer, I mean, the way it affected me. I just claimed it was my husband because I thought you'd all understand better, and Will and I were practically living separate lives, it was like he was gone too, it was almost like he was dead and I was practising for the day I'd be without him. I know that sounds messed up, but I only meant to go in that one time, and never see any of you again. But then everyone was so kind, and you helped me so much. You were the friend I needed when I needed it most. How could I tell you the truth, after I'd pretended to be someone else? After we'd become friends? It was too late.'

'I'm sorry about your dad,' said Gus, as I'd hoped he would. 'Was that all it was, between us, though? Just a friend and a counsellor thing? Was that a pity screw the other week?'

'No, I care for you, Gus. *You* broke it off with *me,* remember? You said you couldn't do it to Jenna and I respected that, though I was hurt, of course. I thought maybe . . .' I let it dangle there, the suggestion at the end of the sentence for him to fill in the blanks.

'I thought there was something between us too,' he nodded. There might have been a tear in his eye, or maybe it was just camp dust circulating through the store's air con. I glanced around at the cashier again, to see if she was looking but she was packing an elderly couple's brown bags.

'I thought, maybe, like, we were meant to find each other, to be each other's way out, way on . . .' said Gus, after an awkward silence, brushing away whatever was irritating his cornea with a finger.

'But how did you know I was here, Gus?' sidestepping the issue. 'You did know I was going to be here, didn't you? I mean, this isn't just a coincidence? You showing up here? It couldn't be.'

He looked sheepish then, guilty. 'Don't freak out, OK, but, well, I followed you once, maybe twice, back in spring. I was worried about you getting home after the group. I didn't know if you lived in a good neighbourhood. I wanted to be sure you were all right. I followed you to your apartment building then waited until I saw the light go on above the street and I knew you were on the ninth floor. It was just a way to check you were OK.'

'But . . .?'

'Then I came by again, to tell you I was missing you so much, about two weeks after I'd written you that dumb note. I wanted to tell you that things had changed and I was thinking of leaving Jenna, after this trip to San Francisco, maybe even going back there for a bit, a trial separation, spend some time with my folks.

'She's been so crazy these last few weeks, so paranoid. She's been like this before but never this bad. That's why I wanted to tell you. I was going to call it quits. But then that girl who lives on the ground floor in your block was outside smoking and she said she didn't know anyone called Bonnie. She said the woman in the almost top apartment was out of town, *with her husband*. What the fuck was I supposed to think then?'

'I'm sorry, Gus,' I said, thinking he could only mean Pilar, trying to look sympathetic while secretly horrified he'd come so close to my home, my life, without my realising it. It was, of course, a prime case of the pot calling the kettle black since he wasn't the worst stalker in the room but still . . .

'I felt like such a fool,' he carried on, reading my silence as contrition. 'I said I'd call by again on the weekend, asked her to take a message, but she said you were touring, that you'd be *halfway up El Capitan* by then, so I shouldn't waste my time. Well, when I heard that I just couldn't let it go, I started to drive myself crazy, I guess.

'We were supposed to be in San Francisco this weekend, anyway, and Jenna was always trying to get me to come up here for a few nights. I know her hotel has staff discounts at this lodge and I thought I'd pretend it was a last-minute thing and book to come up here for our anniversary. I guess I just thought I might bump into you by chance, sightseeing, and I could ask you what was going on. I know it was a long shot, but I couldn't bear to wait until the grief group when I didn't know if you'd ever be back or how long you were on vacation for.'

'Gus . . .' What was I supposed to say to all that? I'd thought I was obsessive, but he'd trumped me by several degrees. So I settled for, 'I'm sorry, Gus, for putting you through that. Thanks for not making a scene today, in front of Will.'

'I wanted to, when I saw you. But how could I? With Jenna right there? Just say, oh yeah, I've been having an affair with this woman, though I slept with her only once and she gave me a false name. Besides, I don't want to *hurt* you, Bonnie, *Livia*. I just wanted to know the truth. To know where I stand.'

146

Well, I knew how that felt. How someone might do almost anything to pin down answers, so I said, 'Gus, look. Can we talk about this back in New York? Please, I can't tell Will about all this here, not like this. He, well, he gets angry, he can get aggressive . . . I just want to finish this vacation and get back to the city before . . .'

I let that hang too, hoping Gus would draw his own conclusions, maybe want to be my knight in shining armour for a change. 'Look, I care about you too,' I said, reaching out and stroking the back of his hand for just a second. 'I had to work some things out. Can you forgive me? Can we start again? We'll be out of here tomorrow, off to Death Valley, then home. We can talk this through then, yes?'

I had no idea what that conversation would entail, or how I was going to talk myself out of it once we were back in SoHo, but I had to keep him quiet. A man who'd followed a woman who'd lied to him halfway across the country with his girlfriend in tow clearly needed to be handled carefully.

'Well, I did some pretty nuts stuff too, after Hallie died, my therapist could probably tell you a tale or two about that, so . . . I kind of get it. You lose your mind sometimes, for a while . . . you cling to anything, you look for something, someone . . .' He brushed his eye again, abruptly changing the subject. 'Well, we were lucky to get a last-minute cancellation here. It's a great place.'

'So you're staying here tonight, then?' I asked, as he nodded quietly. 'I thought you were camping?'

'Yeah, well, like I said, it was meant to be a surprise for Jenna, just as well since the forecast says heavy rain. This is stupid, though. I see that now. I wasn't thinking. I should go. We won't bother you tonight. I'll keep Jenna away. Her and Will aren't close colleagues, are they?'

'I don't think so,' I muttered. 'They just worked on a few projects when we first arrived, as far as I know.'

'OK, well that makes it easier. He won't suggest meeting up tonight, for dinner. I can't pretend I'm not hurt, Bonnie, *Livia*. But I'm fucked up too, I guess. I need to think too.'

'Sure. Thank you, Gus, for understanding. You've always been there for me. I like to think we could be there for each other again.'

I knew I was telling him what he wanted to hear but what choice did I have? Especially when Jenna popped her head around the coffee counter with, 'There you are, Gussy. Oh, hi Livia. Sorry to crash your romantic twosome with Will but Gus managed to surprise me. Hope you don't mind? Don't worry. We'll give you your privacy. You won't even know we're here.'

'No problem,' I smiled, moving with robotic awkwardness to the checkout with my muffin and a marshmallow thing called a Moon Pie Will had taken a shine to at our gas-station stops. Drawing out my dollars as quickly as possible, I spotted a small bottle of Jack Daniel's in the back of the glass cabinet and my heart screamed for some of the counselling only it could provide. 'And the Jack Daniel's please,' I added, showing my passport to the till girl before she could ask for the regulation proof of ID.

'Enjoy a birthday shot for me and say hi to Will,' said Jenna, behind me. 'I'll catch up with him next week, yeah?'

'Yeah, sure. See you,' was all I could manage as I walked, sick and sorry, towards our cabin, so eager to get inside and close the door I almost missed the young couple, striding at speed up the path behind me. Laden with their market brown bags I stepped aside to let them pass, but the girl gave a wave of her hand and a 'Hi again!'

It took me a moment to place them as the couple from the Mariposa trail, where the tree trunk had sat across the ravine.

'Coincidence, huh?' grinned the guy. 'You cabin or campground tonight?'

'Cabin,' I answered, caught off guard.

'Yeah, us too,' said the girl.

'Just as well, storm tonight,' said the guy.

'And the Mojitos are just awesome here, so that's a bonus. I'm Carrie, by the way,' said the girl, 'and this is Zach. Yeah, we're honeymooning on the open road,' so eager to tell me her news again, probably to tell anyone they'd encountered they were newlyweds, 'well on the shuttle bus actually, and then the train, road-tripping the West.'

'Yeah, we're "unplugging",' said Zach, 'you know, no phones, no TV, no internet. Hiking the old-fashioned way, backpacking and back to nature.'

'No rules about a great cocktail though,' grinned Carrie.

'It *is* our honeymoon after all,' grinned Zach. 'See you and your other half in the bar soon, then. They do great seared tuna here, the best I've ever had.'

He leaned down to kiss Carrie's nose then and I wanted to throw up in the face of their happiness. Instead I said, 'Well, I'm Livia. Congratulations to you both. My husband is Will.' *My husband*, the words ripping through me with unexpected violence before the glare of Carrie's artless smile, her hopeful faith in the future, from two words that used to mean so much, something solid, something contained.

My husband.

How could I not think of Jenna's words at the market counter, 'I'll catch up with him next week, yeah?' Innocent enough to anyone else, except she might have meant it and how could I allow that in any shape or form? Me. His *wife*.

The beast was there with me then, the one that had opened its throat on the roof of our apartment building in the January freeze, the one that had padded through the streets of New York with me for months, sniffing *her* trail. The wilderness call rang in my chest as I smiled at the couple and their 'see you laters', rage and regret rolling my fists into balls. I sniffed to hold back the tears, sure I could smell blood in the air, stopped on the cabin porch to rip the seal off the bottle of Jack and take several swigs.

I tried to ignore Jacky's whispers as the liquid fire warmed my throat, warnings that it would always be like this now, my life from that moment on, full of questions, full of anger, full of fear, until I did something about it.

So I leaned my head against the closed door, listening to the sound of Will moving around inside, eventually heading straight inside and to the bathroom to shower before he could smell the alcohol on me.

'You look very beautiful,' said Will an hour later, locking the cabin behind us. 'That blue dress really suits you,' draping my jacket around my shoulders against the faint chill in the wind.

Zach was at least right about the seared tuna, plump and pink and unlike anything that has ever been placed in a can, though I kept on drinking throughout our meal, just enough to help me tolerate the reality of my life, sipping wine but swigging from the bourbon bottle tucked in my handbag when I popped, more than once, to the toilet.

At the end of the meal, Will went to the bathroom while I tried to attract the attention of the waiter and put the bill on our room tab. A few minutes later, when I went outside, I saw Will standing at the end of the lamplit porch talking to *her*. Even in the gloom, against the almost dark outside, their body language looked easy and familiar, their heads bent too close for anyone other than lovers. She seemed wobbly, as if she'd also had a few drinks and was about to cry.

The image was too intimate to tolerate for even a split second as I found myself barrelling over to them, grabbing Will's hand, saying too loudly, 'Well, look who it is,' making no attempt not to sneer. Ignoring her startled smile and the waft of beer that came from her direction, I tried not to slur as I insisted, 'Excuse me, Jenna, is it? No shoptalk tonight. This is my birthday holiday, after all, and I'd like to spend some quality time with my husband, if you please? If it's all right by you?' pulling on his hand, drawing him away with a tug as she started to reply, 'Of course, of course, I didn't mean to . . . I just . . . sorry . . .'

'Jesus, Liv,' said Will, cheeks flushing as I practically dragged him towards the bar across the barbecue area. 'That was a bit rude. Was that necessary?'

'Rude?' I laughed. 'I'm *rude*? Doesn't that stupid bimbo understand the concept of privacy? What the fuck is she intruding for anyway? More importantly, why are you letting her?'

'I was just making small talk for two minutes, waiting for you.'

'Sure you fucking were,' I snapped, clinging to him as I turned on my sandal on the wood planked walkway, conscious I was sounding more than a little drunk.

'Jesus, Liv. I have to work with her. I have to be *polite* sometimes.'

'Good job I don't then, isn't it, or we'd be stuck with her mouth-breathing face half the bloody night? Good job I can say and do what the fuck I like, just like you have, dear Will, for the last year. And right now I'd like a drink with my *husband*.'

'Maybe you've had enough to drink already,' said Will, steering me around the side of the rustic saloon bar, bubbling with light and voices, towards the path leading off through the trees. 'Why don't we get a breath of air first, clear your head after those cocktails and the bottle of wine?'

He pulled my jacket collar up and fastened the top button before pulling on his own stupid red anorak. Ignoring my complaint that, 'I don't need you to bloody dress me,' he led me past the rec room and the deserted firepit square, towards the semi-lit woodland trail.

I don't really remember how it escalated, the inevitable row, only that I was spoiling for one, bristling and spitting for it. I wanted to goad Will into defending himself so I could tell him, yet again, what I had those months back, that he was a lying, faithless shit of a man who deserved to die alone and miserable. Of course, no one can apologise for ever. No one could have ignored the bait I was throwing out as we left the lights of the lower trail and headed up the looping path along the rim of the cliff.

Will kept trying not to rise to it, to conciliate me but eventually had to answer when I demanded yet again, 'Why her? For God's sake, why this Kath girl? What did she have that I didn't? Why was she so fucking special?'

I was close to telling him I knew who the skank was, but still held back for some reason as I demanded, 'Was it just for sex, for kicks? You never really gave me a good reason why you fucked me over for some whore. Why, Will?'

'You really want to know? You really want me to say this?'

'Damn right, say it. Be honest just for once.'

'Because she seemed to need me and I thought I could help her,' he yelled. 'Because you never really seemed to need me for anything, Liv, not back in Cardiff, not back in London. You're so damn self-sufficient, so capable, so independent and so bloody *angry* all the time.'

'What was I supposed to have been?' I yelled, shell-shocked by his accusation. 'One of those incapable women who can't entertain themselves for five minutes? The ones you said you always hated, until they dropped their knickers, obviously?' Hating the sound of my voice, nasal and high through snot and sobbing, I heard my mother again ordering, *Stop whining, Olivia, whining won't bring your father back. No one likes a cry-baby*, as Will sighed, his voice low again, trembling a little.

'No, of course not. But what was I *for* if you could do everything yourself? Find yourself jobs, manage your cash, entertain yourself, organise everything so perfectly I could never measure up? How was I supposed to be less than perfect in return? I've barely even met your mother, for Christ's sake, in case she somehow makes you look less than you are, when my bloody parents adore you! You're always in control.'

'Control.' I wanted to laugh at that.

'You bet you are. You wouldn't let me show you I was scared sometimes, you wouldn't let me in and relax so I could comfort you. I used to wish you'd just cry once in a while like a normal girl, instead of gritting your teeth and pressing on with that determined look on your face, like the world was against you.'

'But it was, it *is*. You know how hard I've had to pull myself up.'

'Yeah, and I never heard the end of how I've never had to, so I had no right to complain, right?' his voice rising again. 'Do you know how tiring that gets after a while? Constantly talking about how you wanted a different life, a better place, like I wasn't enough for you.'

'I wanted that for *us*.'

'But I was happy. I was happy with *you*. Wherever we were. But *you* wanted to come to New York. You made no secret of the fact that it was a wonderful opportunity, one *you'd* die for. Then you were stomping around like a New Yorker, so at home, and I hate that city, Liv. How could I tell you that and fail again in your eyes? How could I say I just wanted to go home? She just made me feel good about myself for a few minutes, like I had something to offer.'

'So this is my fault? I *made* you have an affair?' I snorted, too devastated to do anything but slip into defence mode. Backed into a corner, finally ready to bite and thrash,

I found myself snarling that, if that was the case, the trip was clearly a mistake and maybe he should just go back to his skank-whore, the real love of his life, since he'd thrown away a marriage and everything else for her.

'Grow up, Liv!' shot Will, finally snapping, halfway up the slope, the scudding clouds racing us to the vista point above. 'For the hundredth time, it wasn't like that. It wasn't anything like that. People get together for all sorts of reasons, bad, stupid, fucking selfish reasons, I admit, but then they come to their senses and get over it. Normal people make terrible mistakes. They have flings then move on and hope they can get their life back. I'm trying to put it behind me. I'm trying to show you I'm sorry, I can't say it any more times. Why can't you get past this?'

'Past this?' I sputtered. 'Past this? Past my life and my marriage and my husband being a strange and empty place I don't understand? Past not recognising the man I've loved for more than a decade? You could only say that if you'd never loved me as much as I loved you. Otherwise you'd know it was impossible.'

'Why are we here then? You're right. What is all this for? This bloody holiday? This trying to make it work? To move on and so forth, if you just want to rub my face in what a shit I've been?'

It was a fair question and how could I answer him? How could I say, it's for me to decide whether or not to destroy you now, because you've just failed the test I've set you for the last time. *Fail, fail, fail!* screamed the klaxon blaring, over and over again in my head, red lights flashing as I walked away – *three strikes and you're finally out! Game over!*

'Come on, Liv. I didn't mean it like that,' he said, trotting after me just a few steps. 'I just mean, get past asking me why all the time. Asking all these questions when you know I've given you all the answers I can and they'll never be good enough because I can never justify what I did.'

Then I was running, out along the track, through the crowding trees, into the darkness and the slow, spitting rain, ready to flee, to grab that go-bag of mine, to jump on the shuttle bus in the morning, escape out into the wild beyond, alone. It didn't matter where I went or for how long so long as I never had to look at him again.

And I wasn't just angry with Will, I was angry with myself, for allowing my life to come to that, for letting myself become that woman. For letting down the girl who'd dreamed of independence and adventure in that fucking damp pillbox. For clinging to this man and needing him so much. So being so afraid to be alone.

When I stopped running, drawing a shaky breath, I tasted blood in my mouth. I'd bitten my tongue but ignored the pain, standing for a few minutes, fighting off the panic attack stealing the breath from my body as the rain began to drum on the high wooden roof of the firepit square, echoing what was raging inside my skull, blood beating, hard, primal.

That's when I decided that I needed to tell Will everything, before I left for good; that I knew about him, that I knew about *her*, to throw everything in his face; the lies, the filthy video. I wanted him to know everything I'd done, about me and Gus and my stalking games in the city, how proud of it I'd been. Maybe then he'd look at me and see a stranger, the stranger I saw under the familiar skin and

156

bones of him every day, so he'd be surprised and horrified and know I was dangerous and wily, like the coyote, and could not be destroyed no matter how hard he fucking tried.

Then he'd know what I'd experienced over those months, because it's so much harder to be the one who has to find forgiveness than the one saying sorry.

So I swigged from the bottle of Jack in my bag, a long swallow of comfort, formulating how I'd parade my truth before Will, sharp and bright, drawing blood, turning back across the deserted quad, past the cold firepit, towards the viewpoint to confront him. But he wasn't there, nor was he back at our cabin sitting in darkness, nor was he in the bar when I checked through the window, stomping over, seeing no one but the Californians, gazing deeply into each other's eyes over a Mojito.

'Where the hell are you, Will?' I cursed, kicking the stumps of trees on the loop trail again so hard my feet would by purple by morning, checking my phone signal every few yards, just in case he'd messaged me, was pleading to talk it out, searching frantically for me somewhere on the site.

It was almost total darkness by the time I found myself striding towards the higher ground of the ridge, chasing reception in the thickening rain. Just a minute's walk from the lighted windows of the cabins and the twinkly, rustic charm of the bar, the dark of the wild was the dark of underground places, so thick and sticky I could taste it on my tongue.

Just when I realised I was wasting my time, and in danger of losing my footing in the inkiness, the squalls of rain quieted for a moment, parting for a roll of thunder rushing in from the west, booming across the peaks. A flash of lightning illuminated a figure on the edge of the canyon ahead, hood up, head down before hiding it in darkness.

A second flash confirmed it was Will in his stupid red coat, his back to me, right on the edge, the blue glow betraying he was on his phone screen, and I checked mine again, in case he was messaging, 'Where are you, Liv? I'm so sorry.' I caught a few bars of signal but my screen was dark, no notifications. *Is he messaging her, then?* demanded the voice in my head. *He must be. How could he think about her at a time like this when the world is exploding, falling around us in ruins and ash?*

I crept up quietly behind him, the wind covering my approach, my practised movements, aided by the squalls whipping through the pines and the patter of renewed rain, hiding me from him. I wanted so badly to know what he was typing, tasted it through the blood in my mouth, to look over his shoulder to see the words – to *know*.

And I knew I never would, not really, ever again, with the Jack Daniel's surging in my veins and my head singing. I'd never know he loved me enough, that I was the only one.

I couldn't see a moon up above through the night black, but I knew it was there, hiding its head, afraid to meet my eye. I wanted to howl at it, howl out the pain and betrayal and uncertainty. If not her, it might be someone else. If not today, tomorrow . . .

Even though I'd just vowed not to spend another minute of my life at his side, going through his pockets and checking his phone in secret, following him to work, doubting, I knew I'd still wonder, wherever I went out there in the world, if he'd got over me, given me up. I had no guts left for that; all my strength was gone.

Time was up. Time to flick the off switch.

Perhaps, in a confused way, blurred with bourbon, I was remembering James Scott too, the same betrayal close and familiar in my mouth, the heat and humiliation of his words that day so long before, 'Grow up, Liv. We're not ten years old any more,' echoed in Will's fifteen minutes before. Then I found myself running up the last few feet behind Will, my arms shooting out.

Will had no time to turn around and I was glad, because I didn't want to see his face as he loomed towards my fingers, shoving, hitting him square between the shoulders. That was all it took. One fierce shove then I was staring at the back of his head watching it fall, disappearing downwards in one swift swallow.

Then I opened my mouth and screamed silently to the hiding moon.

Sixteen

Yosemite Valley, California

That night, on the cliff edge, I didn't cry. For the first time in so long the riot of pain and fear was stilled, a circuit blown, my brain cool and empty. I felt nothing except a kind of cold, tight numbness. I'm not sure how long I stood there, air swimming out of me, rain washing under the collar of my jacket onto my bare head, a breathless baptism, a renewal.

After a while I willed myself to walk, one foot in front of the other, down the hill, along the walkway and back towards the cabin. When I passed along the back of the bar again, lights low, music drifting like water out through the open window, I heard laughter, the flow of words obscured by pattering rainfall, and imagined Zach and Carrie still wrapped in each other's gaze, hazy with mint rum and hope.

Once back in the cabin I sat on the bed, water puddling from my jacket and sandals as I looked at Will's shirt on the chair, his hiking boots, still muddy, by the door.

160

His smell was in the room with me. The weight of him carried with me. I wondered how long it would take to wane, to fade. I wondered if it ever would. But there was no going back.

Sitting there, in the stillness of aftermath, was a little like the night I'd returned to our council flat after James Scott's end, unsure then too whether to cry, run or both. No one was home that night either, a common occurrence except, for once, I was greeted by a note from my mother saying she was downstairs in Mae's, watching her new flatscreen HD TV. There was a birthday card in a pink envelope on the table with two parcels, one containing a makeup set with three eye shadows, blusher and a lipstick, the other a cheap set of curling tongs, methods of disguise I was then unfamiliar with; tools for a girl coming of age, turning sixteen.

'I waited for ages. Come join us downstairs,' the note read. 'Bet you thought I'd forgotten your birthday.'

After putting the card on the bedside table and the gifts in the bottom of the wardrobe I waited alone, waited for a knock on the door, for something to happen, because someone had surely seen us there together, in the wilderness behind the estate, in the long June evening, witnessed what I'd done. Someone who'd already run home yelling for their own mam and dad, for the police.

But no one came. Not all through that first night as I sat awake on my bed, listening, wondering if it was finally time to grab my go-bag, dash off into the night with my £43 and emergency supplies, go on the run, turn fugitive before someone could clap me in handcuffs. Yet somehow I didn't, couldn't move.

Through the floorboards between me and Mae's flat below, I remember hearing raised voices and laughter, a million miles away in another life. Later came the sound of a key in the door and a lager can popping, the microwave dinging, then my mother sticking her head into my room, voice wobbly saying, 'Happy birthday, Olive, love. We'll do Big Macs or whatever you want this weekend, yeah?' sidling in, kissing my forehead, moving away when I pretended to be asleep.

I must have dozed off about three o'clock, to the soundtrack of shouts from the flat above and running feet on the stairwell, because I dreamed of the soles of James's trainers, rising upwards in unison as he fell backwards.

The next day, at school, I was surprised to see how normal everything was, though there was no sign of James at biology, first lesson.

'James is taking a duvet day, then?' Mrs Parrish commented, marking the register with her usual resignation. 'Natalie? I'm talking to you. Where's your latest lovebird?'

'Dunno, miss,' Natalie replied, not her usual cocky self, no cheeky comeback. By two o'clock she was pale, her eyeliner smudged as if she'd been crying. By home time the rumour was circulating that James Scott was missing. Not just missing school, but capital 'M' Missing. At morning assembly, on day three, a policeman came to the school to say he needed our help.

'You're Olivia Compstock, yes?' he asked, when it was my turn, peering through his slightly comical wire-framed glasses and suppressing a yawn. 'We're speaking to all James's friends and I have to ask you where you were on Tuesday evening after 6 p.m. Did you see James that night?

Where did he like to go after school? Did you ever see him drinking alcohol or taking drugs? Do you know who his close friends are?'

My form teacher was there with me, in the staff room where the designated interviews, described as 'a bit of a chat', took place, but I couldn't tell him anything useful, I was just a kid and not a popular one.

On day five, a group of rock climbers on the western edge of the quarry spotted James's body. The news spread through the estate like a brushfire with people hanging over their balconies on the southern side of the tower block, watching the police trail in and out of 'the wilderness' with crime-scene tape and setting up a little white tent.

I waited longer. Still no one came for me and, after a while, I was glad I hadn't panicked and run. That I'd decided to hide in plain sight.

There were house-to-house, or flat-to-flat, enquires over the next few days but eventually, in the absence of any witnesses, the coroner concluded James had fallen to his death. There was cannabis in his system and some alcohol, apparently, enough to have impaired his judgement, to have led to a fatal accident.

And that was it. I couldn't believe it had been so simple. To end someone's life in an unintentional moment then watch the world hurry on without him. There was no righteous hand on my shoulder, no lightning bolt of justice to burn me up. He was broken and Natalie was broken too, no fight left in her after that, never returning to school after the summer break, taking a job in a bakery instead.

Meanwhile, my mother, shaken by the idea that my oldest friend had died, decided to clean herself up a bit, started cooking meals again, got a part-time job at the Spar. The school offered us counselling during the summer holidays for anyone struggling to cope with young James's tragic accident. Parents, even the ones who rarely rose before 11 a.m. and had a close relationship with daytime TV, roused themselves to complain that something had to be done, that they'd been saying 'the wilderness' was a magnet for bored kids to run wild in for years.

So the council distracted us with wholesome activities, such as street dance at the community centre and outward bound courses in the Brecon Beacons, which I immediately signed up for, to divert our attention from drugs and booze. Later, the wilderness was fenced off. I only snuck back into the pillbox once to rescue a handful of my favourite *National Geographics* and stash them at the flat.

The following summer I'd got my GCSEs, my A levels two years later, and made it to university. And, in a way, all that good stuff happened because of one moment of instinct. That bubbling up of something old and primal had become productive, good had come out of the bad because, without realising it, James had sacrificed himself to give me a fresh start.

Of course I felt guilty. But I hadn't done it on purpose. I still believed I wasn't a bad person, just one with a temper, and that's a different thing entirely. I wasn't the villain, I was the victim of circumstance, and turning myself in to the police wouldn't have changed anything, making my life so much worse when it had just started to get so much better.

Sitting in our Yosemite cabin that night, alone like that night years ago, my brain fused, body limp, part of me hoped some good might yet come of everything, as I fell into an adrenaline backlash sleep, roaring with rainfall, the sounds of the wind-lashed woods and dreams about being lost in the dark.

It was around sunrise, when the freshly washed sun began creeping through the cabin windows, that I heard someone scraping at the latch of the cabin door. Awake and alert in an instant, the reality of what I'd done poured back into me and panic started to crackle through every cell and muscle. Was it the police already? Were they about to burst in, guns blazing, and arrest me? Was there still time to get away?

I sat up, wondering if I should simply jump out of the bathroom window into the dense embrace of the woods. But I didn't have my go-bag ready, my travel stuff still strewn around the room, and, though I could probably have grabbed my passport, my purse, my jacket, then headed for the valley floor, I knew I'd never last out there, wouldn't make it more than a few miles on foot. There was no running now.

Plan B was to wait. To hide in plain sight once more.

In the milky grey hour between dawn and dreaming my mind had already started to play the scene of how, before breakfast, I'd knock on Gus and the skank's door, hair uncombed, asking if they'd seen Will, telling them he hadn't come back last night. Then I'd ask at the bar and the market shop, ask the Californians, if they were around eating breakfast, if they'd seen him anywhere.

By the time I approached the duty ranger at the registration hut, my wifely annoyance would have descended into twitchy fear, showing the first signs of panic as he patiently radioed around the campsite, reassuring me, 'Don't worry, ma'am. Your husband probably had a few beers and is sleeping it off somewhere. Happens all the time,' wise to the ways of city couples.

Somehow a sliver of me was invested in this story, almost as if it were the real truth. My actions already seemed to have been carried out by someone else, *something* else, carrying me along with its four-legged stride, riding my muscles, pushing my hands into Will's back. Another part of me just wanted to go home, to start clearing the mess up, join another grief-counselling group perhaps. Of course, before anything else could happen, whoever or whatever was outside the cabin, cranking the door handle, had to be dealt with.

Sitting up in the sheets, I prepared to meet my fate with dignity. Imagine my surprise when the door opened and Will was standing there, dishevelled, bleary-eyed, but very much alive.

I almost screamed, then, or perhaps it was almost a howl, thick with fear and confusion. How had he survived that fall? was my first thought. Had he caught himself on a branch perhaps? Landed on an unseen ledge? Climbed slowly back up to civilisation then called the police to tell them some unseen psychopath had tried to kill him? Is that where he'd been all night, making a statement?

Yet he was calm and clean and un-bloodied. Pretty dry, too, for someone who'd surely spent half the night dragging himself up a muddy cliff face in the rain. No, that wasn't possible, even my addled, hungover brain knew that. Then what? I'd imagined it? Hallucinated the whole thing like someone in a bad soap opera? Suffered a psychotic break?

Anything seemed possible by then. All bets were off that only one true reality could exist in my splintered head.

'Liv?' he whispered, clicking the door closed behind him, eyes adjusting to the cabin gloom. 'Are you awake? I'm so sorry,' pulling off his trainers, chinos and shirt, leaving them in a pile by the door. Frozen with a kind of existential terror I let him talk, expecting to wake up properly at any moment, to my reeking reality and clanging conscience. This was just the preamble, my subconscious mind preparing me for the new day to come.

'Where have you been, Will?' I asked, eventually, as he flopped down on the bed and stripped off his jeans and sweater, unresisting as he spooned up behind me and began stroking my hair.

'Liv, sweetheart, this is all my fault, not yours. I'm sorry for last night. I kipped down the rec room after . . . I know I was out of line. I should never have said those things. I hate myself. Look, if you think for one moment I don't feel terrible about what I've done, you're wrong. I hate myself every day for what I did. I know I might still lose you but I'm not giving up on us. We can go to counselling if that's what you need, move back to Britain, anything. It's just that, eventually, we'll need to find a way to stop asking why and ask if and how we can mend it. But if you're not ready now I will wait as long as it takes. You're the best part of me, Liv, you always were.'

He curled into me then, very much warm and breathing, taking my hand in his. 'I'll keep you safe from now on. I'll never hurt you again,' he whispered. Then he fell asleep.

After a few hours in bed we were up and packed by 9 a.m. Will seemed tired but determined to be solicitous and cheery. I avoided having to speak by nibbling the hangover-cure bacon roll he bought me from the market shop and, once the air con was on in the car, and I had a pint of hot tea inside me, I felt a little better.

It was our last day in Yosemite, our itinerary dictating we spin back down to stop off in Death Valley, more than 200 miles south-east of us, and what choice did I have but to simply go with the flow. As we crawled along the narrow track to the campground's exit gate, I spotted Gus standing on the porch of their cabin looking tired, giving a languid wave as he frowned at his watch. Their bags were on the porch already, side by side, waiting to be loaded into the car.

As we pulled past the lodge entrance hut we handed our parking badge to a ranger who barely looked up, nodding his receipt of the plastic tag with a phone crooked to his ear. As we pulled away, I could've sworn I heard the words 'a fight with his girlfriend' being spoken. And that's when I knew, as I craned around to look at the pile of jackets on the back seat of our rental car. That's when I asked, 'Where's your red anorak, Will?'

'I can't find it anywhere,' said Will ruefully. 'I've been everywhere looking for it, while you were in the shower. I thought I'd left it in the bar, after we'd argued last night but it wasn't there this morning.'

Of course it wasn't, I thought, because in that spilt second, I was 99 per cent sure it was at the bottom of the cliff.

'I filled in a slip for the lost and found,' he sighed, 'so they can post it on to me if someone finds it. Bet some backpacker nicked it. Still, we won't need it in Death Valley or Las Vegas, I suppose.'

I looked in the wing mirror then, chest tightening as I saw the ranger head out of his hut, up the track towards Gus's cabin. He could have been going anywhere of course, but he wasn't.

I knew where he was going and why. I also knew who I'd killed.

Seventeen

Death Valley, California

Time froze solid while Will steered us out of the park and southwards once more. There was very little phone coverage so we didn't see the first police report until we were eating breakfast, thirty hours later. Before that, every mile down from the Sierras, along the decline of the US 395, passed with the slow weight of a hundred and I barely registered the scenery as we threaded our way through the thinning trees, past the Inyo National Forest into the parched flatlands.

Sliding through the bone-white desert, I forced myself to swallow over and over, to stomach the turn of events and hundred emotions churning along 230 miles of that infernal landscape beginning to mirror the colour of my conscience. Because I was glad by then, so glad I hadn't actually murdered my husband; my husband who, with a pleased flourish, revealed he'd arranged a special birthday dinner for me that night at Death Valley's golden-stuccoed Furnace Creek Inn; my husband, who'd finally risen to the challenge and the occasion by requesting wine be left in our hotel room and then presenting me with a silver bracelet at dinner, engraved with my initials – the perfect romantic gesture, the perfect amount of pre-planning and spontaneity to ensure a sense of occasion.

'Happy birthday, Liv,' he said, raising his glass at our restaurant table that evening, toasting me with champagne and sealing a last-minute double pass on the test list. But of course it was too late – his ordeal was over and mine just beginning as I raised my glass, head bursting with the memory of Jenna's frail legs at the roadside in Mariposa Grove, her coldsore-cornered mouth, then the red anorak and the back of the hooded head wearing it, falling, falling.

I'd been scanning the Yosemite online alerts all night on the hotel wi-fi, under the guise of keeping up with traffic updates, so I had to say something when I spotted the National Park Service newsflash the next day in the morning sunshine, trying to eat huevos rancheros at a table with a blinding white tablecloth.

I didn't want to open the phone pop-up and utter the words 'Missing Woman' but think I managed to sound calm when I said, 'Oh my God. Look, Will!' holding the phone up towards him, exclaiming, 'That's that Gus bloke, isn't it?'

And there was Gus, asking the world if anyone had seen his girlfriend.

'Christ,' said Will, putting down his coffee cup, 'Jenna's missing?'

'Jennifer Parker, that's her,' I tapped my finger on the photo next to the appeal, one of the filtered 'I do yoga' shots pulled from social media. Will scanned the story, not that there was much to read, just a brief description of Jenna, a loose timeframe of her last movements and the words, *Last seen at Pine Lodge Campground, upper Yosemite, at around 9.30 p.m.*

As Will read I scrutinised his face, looking for anything more than simple shock, looking for grief, a sign that he'd loved her after all and was absorbing a great loss. I don't think it was there though, behind the furrowed brow, the tense jaw. I think it was an ordinary reaction to someone you knew being in trouble.

'Jesus Christ,' he said, nothing else, as the scent of jasmine drifted across the terrace and a jewelled hummingbird ghosted through the shrubs.

'Do you think we should call Gus or someone?' I asked, thinking proactivity would seem more normal and innocent than not.

'Yes, I suppose so,' said Will, taking a gulp of coffee. 'I mean, I guess we were there the night before last, when they say she was last seen. God, she's been missing for a day and a half already then. But . . . I don't know what we could tell them really. How would we get hold of that Gus anyway? He must be still at the lodge while they . . .'

Search, completing the sentence in my mind. I wanted to ask Will a million more questions then, but mainly, did you go to see her after you left me that night? I'd wanted to ask him that for forty-seven hours but hadn't been able to because I still hadn't told him I knew she was the *whore, the skank, the you-know-who.* Though it didn't seem appropriate to call her by those names any more, since the almost-certainty of her death had hit me like an Amtrak train. Since then I'd been thinking of her as Jenna for the first time.

Jenna Parker, twenty-six years old, PR executive from New York via San Francisco. The woman I'd killed.

By mistake, of course, my self-preservation instinct already insisting I hadn't meant to kill *anyone*, not even Will, not really. All that stuff about tests and fresh starts and decisive moments had been a fantasy, a defence mechanism born of despair – a moment while the balance of my mind was disturbed. Not that that would be a defence if I needed one, if anyone found out.

As I sipped my freshly squeezed orange juice to avoid meeting Will's eye, I knew that for the rest of that trip the tables had turned and I was now the one subject to a pass/fail, tick or cross exercise, in a fight for my own life. If I failed, failed to be contained and smart and careful, I would face society's 'contingency plans' for me, far more concrete than mine had ever been for Will, such as a little room of my own for the rest of my life, with bars on the windows.

But I was determined not to panic, acting carefully in order to cling on to the last pieces of the life that, just thirty-six hours ago, I'd sworn to leave behind.

'We saw her in the diner, after dinner that night,' I said, to say something, anything, to Will. 'You didn't see her after that, did you? After we fought? The night you said you spent in the rec room. You didn't see her and Gus?'

If it seemed an unusual question Will didn't notice. 'No, like I told you. I had a couple of drinks with that Californian couple, then took a beer to the rec room and pretty much passed out.'

I looked at the National Park Service appeal again, after he handed my phone back. It mentioned Jenna wearing a blue sweater, her not being equipped for the heavy weather that night when the bone-rattling storm had rolled over the valley. There was no mention of a red coat so I had to hold off on asking Will how, if he hadn't seen her during the time I'd spent searching for him, she'd ended up wearing it.

'Let's call them tonight then, the rangers at the park. Give it some time first,' said Will. 'See if we can help later. Hopefully she'll turn up today. Maybe they had a row or something. She's pretty highly strung, well, seems that way. Bit of a princess, you know.'

'Really? You mean at work?'

'Yeah, I mean . . . everyone in the office knows she's a bit of a drama queen.'

What more could I say, as we headed back to our room to get ready for our visit to Badwater Basin, our last excursion in California before heading to Las Vegas the next day, then flying home the day after? Though I was in no rush to return to New York, could have happily stayed out there for ever, in the vast white flatlands, the lowest point in North America. It suddenly seemed safer out there, in that moonscape brittle with salt and bleached centuries, no mobile signal, no wi-fi, no intrusion; no police. We could hide out like cowboys, me and Will, live off the land somehow, Butch-and-Sundance it, his Paul Newman to my Robert Redford. He could even wear his souvenir Stetson.

It would've been my penance too, to hermit myself away among the boulders and buzzards, away from civilisation, appropriate to spend what was left of my life wandering, lips parched, eyes slowly blinded by staring at the all-knowing sun, an outcast from a civilisation I was no longer part of.

As we gazed at the searing panorama from 'Dante's Viewpoint', I realised I was in a hell of my own making. A hell of waiting and wondering; of asking, What am I now? What will I be tomorrow? What will happen next? I'd sought certainty, yet I'd gained the exact opposite.

Will seemed preoccupied too, as the hours passed, hot, bright, relentless, wandering by my side, throwing me the odd smile, taking photographs. Neither of us really wanted to hike the trails in the shimmering heat and we were back at the hotel by three for a shower and, in my case, as much Jack D as I could discreetly inhale.

But, when we got the message at the front desk saying the Ranger Service had called, it was time to get into sober and concerned mode. I'd been expecting it since Gus must have told the authorities we'd met up, that we'd be heading towards Death Valley, for the next stage of our road trip like I'd told him. They must have rung each hotel in turn, until they found us. There was also a message on Will's mobile, from Sol in New York. A ranger had called the Lowbeck asking for his cell number, but there'd been no signal all day, out in the barrens. So we made the phone call to Officer Flores on speakerphone, placed on the table between us, in our suite.

'The queries are just routine, sir,' said Officer Flores, politely, his flat, slightly Spanish inflection becoming a little more formal as he reacted to Will's British accent. 'We're just speaking to anyone who was registered at the camp that night, in case there was anything amiss, or they saw Miss Parker that evening. Mr Gustavo Rodriguez says you worked with Miss Parker at the Lowbeck Hotel, in New York, is that correct, Mr Taylor? But you weren't travelling together as a group?'

'No, I'm travelling with my wife,' said Will calmly. 'We just bumped into Jenna and Gus by accident. The Pine Lodge camp offers staff discounts for our firm, quite a few employees go there on vacation, and our whole department has leave over these two weeks.'

'Yes, I see. And did you see Miss Parker on the evening of the thirteenth?'

'Only after dinner, as we were leaving the dining room. That was at around nine-thirty p.m.'

'And Mr Gustavo Rodriguez? Did you see him later in the evening?'

'No, not at all, not since we'd met that afternoon, for the first time. I mean, Mr Rodriguez and I met for the first time.'

'So what did you do after dinner?'

'Liv and I, my wife Olivia, went for a walk then back to our cabin, around ten, I think. The weather was terrible, the storm was picking up. Oh, I had one drink first, with a couple we met at the lodge, two newlyweds, Zach and . . . sorry, I forget her name.'

'Ah, yes. Mr and Mrs Benedict, from LA. Yes, we are looking for them. They appear to be on an extended honeymoon, travelling the parks, hopping on and off the shuttle buses. They're "digitally detoxing" apparently,' he sounded weary, tired of monied city dwellers and their affected foibles, 'so aren't carrying cell phones. But we'll track them down soon enough. Do you work closely with Miss Parker, sir?'

'No, not really, we're just colleagues who work on the same accounts from time to time.'

'I see. Did she seem her usual self to you when you bumped into her?'

'Yes, I think so.'

'Nothing unusual?'

'No, I don't think so. I mean, she was a bit stressed. She'd had some trouble at work. She mentioned that. Nothing serious I don't think, you know, deadlines and so forth.'

'What would *and so forth* be, Mr Taylor?'

'I'm sorry?'

'You said, deadlines *and so forth*? Would that be problems with other staff?'

'No, I don't think so. You'd have to speak to Gus or our boss.'

'Yes, I see. Do you have any reason to think she might have, how should I put this? Decided to leave Mr Rodriguez at the camp, leave with someone else perhaps, or on her own?'

'What do you mean?'

'I just mean, couples argue sometimes and people need time to cool off. We understand her family lives in San Francisco. We're speaking to them right now.'

'No, I can't help you. I don't know her that well.'

'Yes. I see.'

I was relieved for once, that Will's lies were so convincing, hoping mine would be equally straightforward. Luckily Flores asked me almost exactly the same questions in the same order, *Where were you? What did you see? What do you do?* So I told the appropriate lies then we ended the call with confirmation that we'd be back in New York in two days' time, promising to keep checking our phones until then.

We drove on to Las Vegas the next morning, tired and subdued, then dutifully strolled the gleaming casino halls and watched the dancing fountains perform. But there was something anti-climactic in our final champagne toast at dinner that night. Jenna was still missing but I knew it was surely only a matter of time before they found her, and I wasn't oblivious to the fact that, once they did, there could be awkward questions coming our way.

If, for instance, they started looking into her life, looking for reasons for her death, at her phone, how far back would they look? Would they then find the text messages I'd sent her? The nasty, dirty sext messages? The last sent just two weeks before? Would they find the explicit photos in her desk drawer too? In this new light, all my games, my little tricks, so harmless surely, so playful, started to look sinister. Laughing leads to crying, as my mother had always said, and suddenly I wasn't laughing any more.

And if they found any of those things would they start looking further? Further in, further back. Would they find out about Will's affair? About mine? When might they start suspecting something amiss, suspecting foul play?

But I was jumping the gun, overloading with the variables of panic and possibility. I took a deep breath, snapped a final photo of Will against the glittering backdrop of the Bellagio, reminding myself to play it cool.

Eighteen

New York City

The first thing I did, when we fell tired and hungry through the doors of our New York apartment, was to get rid of the pay-as-you-go phone I'd used to send the taunting messages. I was fairly confident no one would find out it existed, let alone who'd bought it and where, but I couldn't risk having it anywhere near me. So, while Will crashed out on the sofa, asleep in five seconds flat, I popped out for groceries, casually strolled eight blocks down Canal Street and threw the phone, plus the flash drive with the sex video on it, into the Hudson River.

Watching the water send the evidence of my guilt swirling out of harm's way, I felt a little better. Until I thought about Gus, the life-sized chunk of guilt still in Yosemite while the search for Jenna continued. Of course, he'd want to be on hand there, for any developments, but it also meant I couldn't gauge how he was feeling or what he might say about us, under pressure, now the police were

179

involved. He'd already proven to be more needy and persistent than I'd anticipated. What else might he do?

The police always look at the partner first; when a woman goes missing, everyone knows the husband, the boyfriend, is always the first suspect. So, as the days passed with no phone call, no 'Sorry, Mom, I'm taking some time out,' voice message from Jenna, no 'See you in the city' text to Gus, they'd surely start looking towards him as a suspect. Upset, feeling persecuted, perhaps guilty for our little fling, would he tell the police about our affair? Even worse, about the whole grief-counselling situation? I really hoped not. From anyone else's point of view, lying about a dead husband and your own name to conduct an affair did not sound like the behaviour of a stable person.

It was certainly an unholy mess but, grabbing a carton of milk and bag of buns from the corner market, I reminded myself that if Jenna's body was found quickly it still might all go away. The police might assume it was an accident and I'd still be simply one of four people who knew each other a little and had been in the same place when a terrible tragedy occurred. In the meantime, I had to speak to Pilar, the only person who could actually connect me, and our apartment in New York, to Gus.

Luckily she was out front as I headed home, smoking a cigarette at the propped-open door of the apartment foyer in a fug of turps and paint thinner. I smiled widely as I waved a bag of cinnamon buns at her, like it was a happy coincidence, asking, 'Fancy making me coffee?'

'So how was your road trip?' she demanded, as she hugged me and called me inside. 'Filled with *On the Road*,

Kerouac-inspired craziness or terribly, terribly British with barely a good cup of tea for miles?'

'The terrible latter, of course,' I hammed, in an over the top 'British' accent, as she set the espresso pot on the stove and flicked on the gas, waiting until she'd poured me a corrosive cup before I slid in my questions.

'Pilar? You know after Will and I left for Arizona last week? Did a guy come by, asking for me?'

'Oh yeah,' she nodded, stirring three sugars into her tiny cup, 'I meant to tell you about that. Good job you reminded me. A guy did come by, asking about you, a day or so after you left. He wanted to know which apartment you were in. I didn't tell him, right, because he said, "Bonnie, yeah? In the top but one apartment?" As if I'd fall for that old scam and just tell him your name! So I said, there's no Bonnie here any more. Well, he insisted he was a friend and wanted to go up and put a note through your door, until I told him that's what the mailbox is for, hun.

'He got a bit antsy then and asked if you'd be back soon so I said you were on vacation. So he said, "Upstate, right?" And I was getting a bit creeped out, cos he was pretty intense, so I said, no actually, in Yosemite, *with her husband*, halfway up El Capitan by now. I guess he finally got the hint when I said *husband*. You know him, then? Hispanic guy, skinny? He hassling you? If he is, I'll set Beau on his ass.'

'No, I mean, he's not hassling me,' I improvised. 'He's just someone I met through Will's work. Someone said he'd asked for me a couple of times at the Lowbeck but I didn't think he knew where I lived.'

'Yeah, well, that's how he knew where to find you, then. Figured it out.'

'What?'

'I thought he looked familiar. He lived here for a short time, back around eighteen months ago. His girlfriend worked for Will's hotel too. A skinny redhead? Super smiley but you could just tell she was a major pain in the ass. Course me and Beau were going through our "exploratory" period then, testing some high-quality import products, if you know what I mean. It was a very "creative" time for me, but, well, the troughs weren't worth the peaks, know what I'm saying?'

'They lived here?' I started. 'I mean, this guy and his girlfriend?'

'Yeah, well Piper-Dewey put up a lot of their new out-of-town employees here while they settle in. There were two Lowbeck guys before that too, though they were pretty cool. Her name was Bonnie, now I think about it. The guy, Wally, or something, asked me to put forward some of my paintings for the hotel but they went with all that minimalist skyscraper shit from the Mark Bright gallery.'

Well, that actually made sense. Gus had seen me go into the apartment, assumed I worked for Piper-Dewey, known they had Pine Lodge discounts because of Jenna, and gambled 'halfway up Yosemite' meant there was a good chance I'd be there. Not such a coincidence after all.

'Have you seen him here before?' I asked. 'I mean, before he came around this time?'

'Don't think so. Sure I got a whiff of the old weed from him though. Come to think of it, he was always trailing the aroma of cannabis. Those West Coast dudes do like a toke. I asked him for some once, back then, just a spliff, but he was all, like, I don't do that shit, and I was like, yeah right, if you say so.'

'Look, Pilar. If anyone comes around asking, could you maybe not tell anyone about him looking for me?'

'Who'd ask, sweet thing?' she said with a smile. 'Jealous girlfriend?' Clearly a joke so I laughed.

'No, well, maybe. You're right, he has a bit of a thing for me and I don't want Will to know, especially if he's, like, a pothead or something. I've told him to back off.'

'Yeah, you've got to shut that stalker shit down. I know his type. Can't take no for an answer. Thinks persistence is a virtue.'

'Yeah, and it could mess up our visa if anyone in authority got wind of it and thought we were, you know, hanging out together and there were any sort of drugs involved.'

'No problem,' nodded Pilar. 'My lips are sealed.'

Shame it's too late now, I thought.

When I got back upstairs Will had woken from his nap and taken a shower. As I carried my brown bag into the kitchen he was standing at the window, wrapped in a towel. When he turned to face me, the phone was still in his hand but his eyes were far away.

'Bonnie called,' he said. 'Jenna's dead.'

Just like that, flat and matter of fact.

'Yeah,' continued Will, pulling out a chair and sitting down, 'I can't quite believe it. It seems the rangers found her body at the bottom of a cliff, not far from the lodge. They don't really know what happened. The helicopter search spotted her. Guess it was an accident.'

'Bonnie called?' I asked, steadying myself against the kitchen table. 'The police didn't call to tell you?'

'No,' his eyes were still far away somewhere and I hoped he wasn't recalling the feel of her skin under his hands, though that was certainly better than imagining her cold and smashed limbs like I was. 'Apparently they called the Lowbeck, the police, I mean. They spoke to Olly. Jesus, I don't believe it.'

'They're sure?' I managed, trying to make my caught breath climb down from my throat. 'I mean, they're sure it's her?'

'They must be, mustn't they? They must have identified her. There's a statement on the NPS site, gone up in the last few minutes. It says they found her early this morning.'

'Oh God, that's awful,' and I really did feel it was awful and getting more awful by the minute. I pulled out a chair and sat down next to him.

'Yeah. Bonnie was really upset. She wants to talk to you, by the way. She asked me to ask you to call her. She was kind of hysterical, actually.'

'Why? I mean, were they that close?'

'I don't think so. It's just a shock, isn't it? You don't expect something like this to happen.'

'No. Should we call someone? Do we need to do anything?'

'I don't know. I suppose the police might want to talk to us again, until they work out what's happened.'

'But she must have fallen, right? It was an accident? She was pretty drunk when we saw her in the bar that night and that was quite early. I guess she must have just . . .'

'Yeah, I guess. Unless . . .'

'What?'

'Unless the police think there's something suspicious about it.'

'Like what?' Like your jealous and unhinged wife killed her? Though I obviously didn't say that.

'I don't know. I suppose they just cover all the possibilities in these cases, don't they? Check who was around that night, probably check out the boyfriend, other *associations* . . .'

'What are you trying to say?' I asked slowly, though I knew what he was trying to say – associations like you, my love, my husband. Has that thought only just occurred to you? But to play along I asked, 'You don't mean Gus?'

'No, I don't know. I just mean, I suppose they look into people's backgrounds in a case like this. Who they were involved with.'

'Yes, I suppose they would do that, to see if there were any . . . red flags . . . Why, Will? What's wrong?' and if I hadn't already known what he was about to say I would've been scared, because that look on his face was the one I'd seen the night I'd sat him down on the sofa and coaxed a full confession from him.

The feeling from that night rushed back, that sick, desperate sensation that the truth was hurtling towards me and I wouldn't like it when it arrived, that I might not survive the impact as he said, 'Liv, I've got something to tell you. I think I should tell you now, before we speak to the police. I wouldn't want you to find out from someone else.'

'Will, for God's sake. What are you talking about? You're starting to scare me,' saying lines that sounded like they'd come from some clichéd cop film, as he took my hand across the table, held it tightly and closed his eyes.

'I didn't want to ever have to bring this up again,' he said, swallowing, 'but it was her. Jenna was the woman I had the fling with.'

Hearing him say the actual words I felt the gut punch all over again. Though it was old news it was easy to slide into character, embody the surprised and outraged wife of six months ago, on discovery of yet another lie. It felt just as real.

'You told me her name was Kath,' I said quietly, pulling my hand from his.

'I know I did. I just, I didn't want you to know. I thought it would make it worse. I thought you might . . . do something, if you knew who she was. If you knew she was here in the city.'

'Do something like what?' I snorted, alarmed by the mania in my own voice but relieved to be saying it at last. 'Like make a scene at the hotel? What do you think I am? So she's been here in the city this whole time? She wasn't visiting on a conference?'

'No. I thought if I came clean you wouldn't believe it was over, not after that stupid . . . after you caught me out that second time. It's been over since then, I swear, not that she wants to accept it. She's kept on trying to be friends, at work, bumping into me. Hell, it's been awkward but I just stayed cool and kept repeating *it's over*, hoping she'd get it into her head eventually.'

'Why are you feeling this urge to be honest now?'

'Because . . . she's dead, Liv. If they look into her life, her relationships, they might find a connection to me. And I couldn't let you learn it from some police officer, or that Gus guy. If he finds out, I mean. That's assuming he doesn't know already. He was looking at me pretty weirdly when we saw them in Mariposa Grove.'

'Can they find out? The police, I mean?' steering the

subject away from that awkward roadside confrontation.
'If you haven't been in touch with her for months? You got
a new phone in March, remember? You smashed the old
one to bits right here.'

'Yes, but I don't know. I suppose it depends on how far
back they feel they need to search her records. There
probably is stuff, in the iCloud or whatever, from before.
I turned mine off but I don't really know if she was . . .
careful. What might be archived. What stuff she kept.'

'What sort of stuff?'

'You know what sort of stuff, Liv. You read it. Some of
it. The texts.'

'And you'll be in her phone contacts too, I'm guessing.'

'Yes, I suppose so. But, that'd be under my old number
and I don't think she had me in there as "Will" anyway.'

'Just like you had her contact in your phone under
"Sol"?'

He nodded, shamefaced.

'Well, let's hope it doesn't come to that,' thinking of how
her phone was at the bottom of that cliff, probably
smashed, even if they'd retrieved it. But that wouldn't
necessarily erase what was on it from existence, hoping the
police would never need to download anything archived in
the iCloud, floating there like a bloody axe, waiting to fall.

We were both silent then, sitting next to each other, not
touching, not speaking, not acknowledging the third party
hovering there with us. Me, because I was wondering how
to proceed, and Will, because he was waiting to get to the
request he needed to make. The real reason he'd confessed.

'Look, Liv. I don't know what happened with Jenna up
at the lodge, but I told the ranger, that Flores chap, I was

with you in the cabin all night, remember? On the phone from Death Valley? Can you make sure you say the same thing if they ask again? I mean, they're bound to ask now, aren't they, for a formal statement?'

'You mean . . .?' I pretended to let what he was saying sink in, then to find the words unfamiliar on my tongue. 'Like, to give you *an alibi*?'

'No, I mean . . .' he sighed, running his hands through his hair. 'OK, yes, I suppose so. I mean they'll want to ask where we were that night. You just have to say I was in the cabin with you until morning. It's easy enough. It's just, if we change our story now it might look suspicious, like an inconsistency, and it's not suspicious. The fact I spent the night in the rec room alone is nothing to do with Jenna going missing.'

'Isn't it, Will?' I pounced, as I suppose any wife who hadn't killed the person in question would. 'It's nothing to do with this? You weren't by any chance with her that evening, were you? After we had the fight? You didn't rekindle your little seedy relationship behind the firepit or something? Because if you did, now's the time to come clean, not when New York's finest are knocking on the door.'

'No! Shit, Liv, no!'

'You're sure? Don't lie to me. You didn't see her at all?'

He sighed. 'She came into the rec room, a few minutes after you walked off. I was looking for you and she was in there, crying. She was pretty drunk and said she'd had a row with Gus, that he thought there was something going on at work, that she was cheating on him but he didn't know with whom and wanted her to tell him. He'd got a bit rough with her, shoved her around, she said.'

'Seems like all her boyfriends like to shove her around – wasn't that the line she used to get you into bed?' I snapped. 'Was that supposed to be Gus, or some other slap-happy guy she'd driven to distraction?'

I could see him thinking then, about the lies she must have told him in addition to not mentioning she had a boyfriend. I felt a little spurt of triumph as I allowed Will to say, 'Look, it's the truth, Liv, I swear. She started saying she missed me and wanted there to be something between us again but I told her it was over. I stayed about two minutes, that's all, trying to calm her down. She seemed a bit unbalanced, going on about how she thought someone had been following her around, stalking her. She thought maybe it was Gus; that he'd seen us together during the autumn and was trying to get her to confess.'

'Do you think any of that's true or was she just trying to make you feel sorry for her again?'

'I don't know. She seemed very agitated and I just wanted her to be quiet and not kick up a fuss with you so nearby. I didn't help her, I just left her there crying, told her it wasn't my problem. I left her in that state and then . . .well . . . that was the last I saw her. Maybe if I'd . . . maybe I could've . . .'

Oh Will, I thought, my do-right kinda guy, it's too late for that now, to wish you'd done the right thing. Instead, let's hope to God no one saw you with her or this could get even messier than you think it is. 'Well, you can't tell any of that to the police, for God's sake!' I sighed. 'Do you even know how that sounds, how it might look to an outsider?'

'Of course I know, Liv,' he shot back, slamming the palm of his hand down on the table. 'That's precisely my point.'

'Did anyone else see you together?'

'No, we were on our own. I only stayed a minute or so. I went back out to look for you. When I didn't find you I came back to the cabin and saw the light was on, so I knew you were there, but I thought I'd give you some space. I went for a drink with those two Californian kids. That's it, I swear. I spent the night alone on the rec room sofa.'

'That's it? OK then, if the police ask I'll just say we went back to the room together after dinner.'

'That's for the best, Liv. No need to get involved in this more than we need to.'

He must have mistaken the look on my face for doubt because he said, 'You believe me don't you, Liv? I wouldn't jeopardise this chance you've given me. I made a terrible mistake before. I don't even recognise myself now, when I look back. I don't even know what I saw in her. She was never anything to me. Not in the way you are. I learned that soon enough and even back then I was so sorry I'd ever started something so stupid with a girl so . . .'

'So like everything you said you hated?'

'So unlike everything we had that mattered.'

'I believe that part,' I said. 'There's not something else you're lying about is there, Will? You didn't lose your temper that night because she wouldn't back off . . . you didn't . . .?' I let the sentence trail off for him to work out my meaning. I mean, I had to ask. Only a guilty person wouldn't have asked, right?

'Jesus, Liv. You can't think . . . I didn't have anything to do with this. I'm not capable of . . . how could you think that?'

'There were lots of things I once thought you incapable of and look where that got me,' I muttered, before I let him take my hand then pull me into a hug.

190

'This is a new start for us,' he said. 'We get a chance at a new life and I want that life with you.'

So we sat there for a while, holding each other, listening to the sounds of the city through the open window. When I could bear it no longer, the weight of his sincerity and the weight of my actions, I got up to make us some supper. As I buttered the brioche deli rolls and unwrapped the artisan salami, he looked at me like he used to when we first met, with warmth, with love, with gratitude. And I wanted him to keep looking at me like that, like I was a good person, a good wife, not a monster with something dark crouched inside her. I could never let him find out, let him see it, not if I wanted to keep him. And I did. I really did.

So, as I added mustard to the sandwich I set my story straight in my head, preparing my statement for the police, each moment expecting them to call.

Nineteen

New York City

The next morning I found myself in an alarmingly trendy vegan coffee shop in Tribeca wondering if I could stomach a charcoal cortado or turmeric latte if Bonnie was paying. I'd called her after dinner as Will had asked, and, though she said she couldn't talk on the phone, had suggested we meet somewhere before work.

I assumed she simply wanted to rake over how awful it all was, Jenna dying so tragically, but seeing her stumble in through the doors in crumpled sweatpants, with crayon-purple crescents under her eyes, I knew it was more than just the 'shock' of a vacation tragedy. I'd seen that bereft look before, on my own face, every morning I'd looked in the mirror for the last six months. Seeing it on the usually pristine and perfectly groomed Bonnie could only mean trouble.

'Thanks for coming, Liv,' she sniffed. 'I just had to talk to someone. Someone who would understand and not just . . .'

Judge, I thought, on instinct, judge while telling you everything's going to be all right.

'What's wrong, Bonnie?' I whispered, as she slid into the retro-futuristic plastic scoop of a seat next to me, waving away the waiter eager to say a bright good morning and tell us about the immunity-boosting specials.

'It's so awful, Livia,' she snuffled into a paper hanky, balling it up, unwrapping it again. 'I don't know where to start.'

'Just say it, honey, that's best. Is it Jenna's accident?'

'Hah! That fucking bitch! I'm glad she went over a fucking cliff. I'd have pushed her myself given the chance,' the words out of her mouth ricocheting around the white tiled walls, causing a momentary hush in the morning chatter.

'Bonnie, hon,' I whispered, still British enough to be embarrassed by public displays of emotion, 'let's walk outside, shall we? Where there's more privacy.'

Gathering her bag and jacket, I led her to the door, steering her across the street to a green space with a bench under a tree. Once seated, I said, 'OK, Bonnie. Spill the beans, sweetie.'

'It's Olly. It's Olly and Jenna,' as if expelling the words physically hurt her, bursting into proper tears. When I eventually calmed her down she told me that, while Will and I had been on vacation, a police officer had called at their apartment asking to speak to Olly in private.

'Well, we were in the middle of dinner, so of course Olly said, anything you want to say you can say in front of my wife,' explained Bonnie, 'until this detective says, "I'm not sure that's a good idea, Mr Sheldon." So then *I* said, "I definitely want to hear this!" That's when he told us, that they were "informing a number of people" that they're investigating a case of voyeurism, that there's video footage, taken at the Lowbeck, videos of an *intimate* nature.'

She laughed then, mirthless and harsh, a sound I'd made so many times since November, a bark of shame and pain. 'I was so fucking slow, Liv. I actually said to him, "*Intimate*, you mean, like sex? But we've never had sex at the Lowbeck." And then he looked so sorry for me and said, "Perhaps you should discuss that with your husband after I leave."

'So there I was, being pitied by a fucking fifteen-year-old detective in a suit that cost more than my Smeg refrigerator, and it took so long to dawn on me I didn't even process that he was asking Olly about Jenna, how well he knew her. It was only as he left he had the decency to tell us she'd gone missing, out in California.

'Then yesterday afternoon he came back. Of course, by then I'd kicked that lying piece of shit that used to be my husband out of the house. So I tell him Olly's not there but he says it's vital he speaks to me then asks me how well I knew Jenna and if she ever spoke about her boyfriend. Had she ever mentioned anything about him being violent or controlling? Did I think someone else could have found out about the *indiscretion* with Oliver?

'That's what he said, *the indiscretion*, like getting a blowjob from that tramp is like accidentally using someone's first wife's name on a guest list instead of their second, and I give two shits if she's lost on a mountaintop somewhere after what she's done.'

I had to interrupt her spillage of misery to say, 'Bonnie, slow down. I don't understand. What footage are you talking about, at the hotel?'

'I don't know exactly, the detective, Van Allen, said it was still under investigation but there's a video of Olly and Jenna, believed to have been recorded at the Lowbeck. And it's not the only one. There're more, over a period of a few weeks, in the guest suites. Not with Jenna, I mean, of other guests who stayed there.

'Olly came clean before I kicked him out, said it happened the night I told you about, after the German reception. He helped her, when she was drunk. Since she was adamant that he shouldn't call Gustavo, he took her back to the Lowbeck, to one of the empty suites, to let her sleep it off. But she asked him to stay a little while. Then the skank came on to him, apparently, stripped off her clothes and somehow his dick just fell into her mouth.'

'Jesus, Bonnie, honey,' I muttered, trying to process what I was hearing, 'I'm so sorry.'

'The worst part is, I never suspected a thing. I never in a million years thought he'd be that kind of guy, you know the type, the nail-it-if-it-moves type, who can't keep his dick in his pants. I feel so stupid. He came home to me that night like nothing had happened. How could he do that? He lied to my face and I never even knew it.'

Join the club, I thought. I wanted to tell her, I know how you feel, that I, of all people, understand. That it was probably partly my fault, for spiking Jenna's drink with the pills, freaking her out so she did what seemed to be a pattern, turned to a married man for desperate attention.

'I'm so sorry, cariad,' I muttered, the Welsh endearment my mother had used with me when I was a child, as I put my arm around her.

'I'm sorry too,' she wept. 'There goes my fucking marriage, after barely twelve months!'

'It's OK, Bonnie,' I soothed, while the sobs wracked her body. I admired her in a way, her ability to share her pain with me, so un-British, being so vulnerable. Maybe letting it out instead of holding it inside, where it could turn into poison, would stop her from ever turning into me. I was glad, though, that I'd never confided in her about me and Will. That was still my only protection. No one knew about the affair.

But who else might be captured on this 'mystery footage' the police were talking about? Could it be Room 717 where Will and I, and Will and Jenna, had had sex? Was there more than one room? How far back did these 'intimate' videos go?

'Listen, Bonnie,' I said, pushing her snot-streaked face up from my shoulder, 'listen to me. You don't have to let this ruin everything with Olly. You don't have to decide anything while you feel like this. I know he's done a shitty thing but what does he say about it all?'

'All the right things,' she said, calmer, the ocean of rage released, 'that he's *so* sorry. That he loves me. That it was a mistake. But how can I believe anything he says now?'

'So it was a one-off thing?'

'Yes, I think he's telling the truth about that at least.'

'And they can't think that it has anything to do with Jenna going missing, surely?'

She looked baffled for a moment, 'No, I don't think so. I mean, Jenna didn't know about the videos. The police hadn't had a chance to tell her before she left to see her folks in San Francisco, I guess. Then she went missing. This detective just wanted to ask me how she'd seemed over the last few weeks, because we'd worked on a few projects together, I suppose.'

'Well, what did you tell him?'

'Only that she'd said once that she was getting odd messages on her phone, dirty messages, you know. And once she said she thought someone might have been following her around. But she was always a bit of a drama queen, liked the attention. I didn't take much notice. Maybe I should have.'

'You told the policeman this?'

'Yes, it wasn't really anything useful though. He seemed more interested in Gustavo, asked again if Jenna had ever seemed afraid of him or if he has a temper. I said I don't know him beyond a quick "hi" at the concierge desk. I guess they always look at the partner, don't they? Though if this is the way she carried on I wouldn't blame him for wanting to kill the little bitch. You know, two days after she sucked my husband's dick she asked me out for coffee, to talk about her fucking problems, because she was sure someone had spiked her drink at the German party. Like we didn't know she'd just got wasted and high. She wanted me to help her get some better PR ratings to impress Toby and make sure her contract was renewed in August. And I actually said I'd help her out.'

'But Gustavo?' I couldn't let it go. 'Did she say he was, you know, violent or something?'

'Not exactly, but you don't know what goes on inside people's relationships, right? Ha, even my own. She said he had a temper once, said he was super-jealous, thinking she was seeing other guys. Guess he was on to her. Poor bastard.'

'So what will you do now? About Olly, if you think he was telling the truth, it was just a one-time thing?'

'I don't know, I think so. I mean, that cop must have felt sorry for me because, as he was leaving, just after he told me they'd found Jenna's body, he said, "For what it's worth we found messages on Miss Parker's phone records from a number that corresponds to your husband's. He sent her two messages the evening she went missing, telling her it was a mistake and that he loved you." What was I supposed to say to that? "Thanks for nothing, Officer. It still won't change what he did."'

So they'd already started looking at Jenna's phone records, I thought, taking Bonnie's hand and squeezing it. I thought of Jenna that night, standing at the edge of the cliff, the glow from her phone screen making me wonder if Will was texting her, or she him, the rage it had inspired and what had come next. Had she actually been reading a message from Olly about another marriage she'd helped wreck? Did that make a difference to what I'd done?

We sat there for a while, since there wasn't much else to say. I mean, there were a million things to say but no way to say them.

'Guess we just wait and see what the investigation turns up,' said Bonnie, blowing her nose. 'God knows what the deal is with this pervert video thing. The creepiest thing is that it must be someone at the hotel, mustn't it? Someone we work with, someone who bugged the rooms with cameras.'

'It could've been a guest though, I suppose. How did the police find out in the first place?'

'They wouldn't say. They're being "discreet" and Van Allen said there's no need for anyone to know the identities of the victims. *Victims*, he said. Olly wasn't a fucking victim. He went willingly.'

'I suppose they mean guests though, people on holiday or business, violation of privacy and so forth.' Couples having affairs even, which could be very embarrassing to Piper-Dewey's wealthy clientele.

'Yes, I know. But really, what's wrong with people, Liv? When did things get so seedy and empty?'

'Well, give yourself time now, Bonnie hon,' I said, as she got to her feet. 'If you love him, don't rush into anything. Everyone makes mistakes.'

I actually meant it then, as I of all people should know that. Perhaps Olly was a weak person, not a bad one. And me? The jury was still out on that one.

'Thanks, Liv,' said Bonnie. 'I knew you wouldn't judge us. You're a good person, you know that.'

And she held me in a grateful hug, both of us swallowing down tears until she released me back into the city and what was waiting for me in my apartment.

Bonnie was right about Detective Van Allen, sitting on my sofa, drinking coffee when I got home. He looked only about eighteen, though must have been older. Something about him annoyed me from the minute he opened his mouth, stood up, introduced himself and had the gall to ask me if I'd care to sit down.

His own accent was clearly cultured East Coast and, coupled with his slick fair hair and elegant suit, I wondered if he was the slumming-it son of some Ivy League alumnus, determined to do a public service with his blue-collar colleagues. For a moment he looked slightly familiar, or maybe it was just his type that was familiar, so I tried to keep my face neutral.

Will had beaten me back to the apartment so if the boy-detective was about to reveal the existence of an 'intimate' video of my husband and the dead woman, I'd had no time to warn him. Instead, I sat down next to Will and readied myself for the first real part of my own pass/fail test.

'Mrs Taylor,' said Van Allen, 'your husband tells me you're already aware that we found Ms Jenna Parker's body yesterday morning, near the Pine Lodge campground. If we can skip the preliminaries then, I need to follow up with some questions, if that's all right?'

'Certainly, I mean, yes anything we can do to help, Detective. It's so terribly sad, such an awful accident. I suppose we city people forget it can be a dangerous environment out there.'

'We haven't yet determined a cause of death, Mrs Taylor,' said the boy, eyeing me coolly.

'Oh, I'm sorry. I thought she fell from one of the cliffs?'

'We found the body at the base of a cliff, yes. That doesn't mean she fell now, does it? We wouldn't be doing our job if we made assumptions like that, would we?'

'No, of course not, I just meant . . . do you think something else happened?' trying not to think of how the brutality of the words 'her body' finally made it all real.

'Why don't you let me ask the questions, Mrs Taylor, and we'll see how we get on?'

Arrogant little shit, I thought, smiling, nodding.

'You told Ranger . . .' he stopped to consult his notes, 'Flores, that you bumped into Ms Parker and her boyfriend by accident, at Mariposa Grove, the day she went missing. Bit of a coincidence that, isn't it? Just running into each other in the high Sierras?'

'Yes, I suppose so,' I replied, 'though Pine Lodge has discount rates for Piper staff and the whole department was on vacation that week. Jenna and her boyfriend had apparently driven up from San Francisco for their anniversary.'

'Yes, that's what your husband said, and is pretty much exactly what you told Ranger Flores when he called you while you were staying in Death Valley.'

'Yes, that's right.' He'd obviously seen a transcript of our first phone conversation with Flores.

He waited for me to speak and when I didn't, asked, 'What time did you see Ms Parker at the lodge diner the night she disappeared?'

'At around nine-thirty.'

'Then you and Mr Taylor went back to your cabin?'

'Yes.'

'Well, I had a drink with the young couple,' Will interrupted, 'remember, while you were settling down?'

'Oh, yes. Yes, that's right.' I'd forgotten that part.

'So you *didn't* go back to your cabin together right away?' said Van Allen, as if used to wrangling people with the inability to be precise.

'No, I suppose not, though, it wasn't very long though, from me getting back to the cabin and Will coming back.'

'How long is not very long?'

I made a slight show of trying to think back. 'I got undressed, got ready for bed and so forth, opened some wine, then Will was back.'

'How long was that?'

'Twenty minutes, there or thereabouts, I think.'

'There or thereabouts? You think?'

Damn, I hadn't asked Will about this, how long he and I were supposed to have been out of each other's sight while he was with the Californians. It was important because if I was his alibi, he was also mine.

'Yes, I guess it was about that,' I said, pretending to think back. 'I didn't look at my watch. Didn't know I'd need to remember the time.' I smiled, but Van Allen didn't.

'I was with that guy Zach and his wife,' said Will, stepping in, looking at him. 'They'll tell you how long I was with them. We just chatted for a bit, swapped holiday tips and so forth, small talk, you know.'

'Ah, yes,' said Van Allen, 'the newlyweds,' pretending to check their names in his notebook, though I was starting to suspect there was very little wrong with his memory or attention to detail. 'We're still trying to reach them. Most people don't really mean it when they say they're going "off the grid" for a few weeks, can't last two days without their cell phones, but the Benedicts are on a "loose schedule" and have no smartphones, just a pay-as-you-go relic for emergencies, according to her mom.

'Their car was registered at Zion National Park yesterday but they're camping out. Due in Salt Lake City in a week's time apparently, to meet an uncle of his. So, when they pop up in the land of the Mormons, they'll tell us you were with them for twenty minutes "there or thereabouts"?' tossing my phrase back at me with a slight British inflection.

I knew then that he didn't like me. I just hoped it was

because he wanted to pull the high hand with the British toffs and not because he suspected I was actually lying. Swallowing hard, I held his gaze.

'So, is there anything else you'd like to tell me? Anything you think is pertinent?'

Will and I waited, both looking straight at him in what we hoped was a way that said, nothing's coming to mind.

'What about Mr Rodriguez, Ms Parker's boyfriend? How did he seem to you that day, Mrs Taylor, and the night before Ms Parker went missing?'

'We barely spoke to him,' I answered. 'That was the first time we'd met,' cringing inside at the outright lie.

'But you worked with her, Mr Taylor. Did she ever mention Mr Rodriguez to you? Did you get any idea of the sort of relationship they had?'

'Relationship?' said Will, stiffening slightly with what I hoped passed for distaste at the personal question and not his feelings about the fact Jenna had hidden Gus's existence from him.

'Yes, you know,' prompted Van Allen, 'was it a happy one? Did they fight a lot? That sort of thing?'

'No, she never talked about a boyfriend,' said Will. 'We weren't close.'

Van Allen made a slight purse of his mouth, suggesting that was hardly what he'd asked, and that you don't have to be close to someone to hear them moaning about their other halves in workplaces across the country every day of the year.

'Mr Taylor,' changing tack, 'is it correct that you reported losing an outdoor jacket at Pine Lodge on 14 June, the night before Miss Parker was reported missing?'

'Yes, that's right,' replied Will, confused for a second. 'I told the "lost and found" woman.'

'A distinctive red Fjord Extreme anorak, yes? Norwegian import, 345 dollars, retail.'

'Yes, I bought it in a half-price sale. Why, did someone find it?'

'You could say that, Mr Taylor, but I'm not in the business of returning lost property. It so happens that Ms Parker was wearing a red Fjord Extreme anorak when we found her. When we found her body, I mean. It was lucky really, that she was wearing such a bright colour or the helicopter crew and mountain rescue team might never have spotted her at all.'

Will's face flickered with horror, as Van Allen had no doubt intended, continuing, 'Can you think of a reason why she might have been wearing your coat, Mr Taylor? If you didn't see her that evening, after dinner, after the "quick drink" with the AWOL Californians and you weren't *close*? It was raining that night, wasn't it? Didn't you think you'd need a coat yourself?'

'Yes, I did. I mean. I took it to dinner with me. I think I was carrying it when we left the diner, but it hadn't started raining then and it wasn't that cold. I only realised I didn't have it when I left the bar and it was raining.'

'And you didn't go back to look for it? An expensive jacket like that?'

'Well, yes I did. I checked the bar then ran back to the diner but it wasn't there. I thought maybe Liv had picked it up and I was getting soaked, so I just ran back to the cabin.'

'Hmm, then next morning you reported it missing.'

'Yes, when we were packing. I thought it would still turn up so I checked around a few places just in case I'd put it down somewhere, you know.'

'After you'd *chatted and had a few drinks*?' he smiled, reading Will's words back from his notepad. 'How many drinks exactly?'

'I'm not sure,' said Will. 'A couple of beers and a couple of glasses of wine.'

'And two whiskeys, neat, with the Benedicts. I asked the barman who looked at the bar receipts. That's quite a lot, isn't it? No wonder you lost your jacket.'

'I certainly wasn't drunk, if that's what you mean,' said Will, affronted, getting a little bit more British with every sentence.

'But you'd had *quite a few drinks*. You too, Mrs Taylor? Your bar tab shows a bottle of wine at dinner and three cocktails, alongside the two beers. I'm assuming you shared the wine and you drank the cocktails.'

'Yes, but . . .' I hadn't expected them to go into so much detail, so soon, checking what we'd drunk.

'And the woman at the market store remembered you buying a fifth of Jack Daniel's that afternoon, $11.50. That's a lot of booze, isn't it? Even for the Brits?'

Well, what was I supposed to say to that? That I'd been putting away half a bottle of Jack a few nights a week for months and my tolerance was high? I could see where he was going with it, the next step he was guiding us towards.

'Well, we were on vacation,' I said. 'I didn't feel that drunk. The Jack Daniel's was to take with us, not to drink that night.'

'So you weren't *that drunk* – you were sober enough to be sure of your movements and your husband's *and so forth*. You didn't doze off in the cabin perhaps, waiting for him, lose track of time? Having a teensy Jack D nightcap?'

'What are you . . .?'

'You wouldn't have been too drunk to wake up if Mr Taylor had left the cabin after you went to sleep?'

Before I could answer, he turned to Will. 'Mr Taylor, you didn't bump into Ms Parker that night after your drink with the Benedicts, did you? You haven't maybe forgotten about running into her somewhere and for some reason, some chivalric urge perhaps, in the rain, offering her your coat?'

'No,' said Will, doing a better job than I was of not rising to the challenge in Van Allen's voice. 'I already told you. I did not see Jenna, Ms Parker, that night after she left the diner.'

'So how did she get hold of your coat, Mr Taylor?'

'I don't know. I guess she must have picked it up somewhere, realised it was mine, meant to give it back to me when she saw me.'

'And decided to wear it?'

'Maybe she just got caught in the rain without a coat.'

'Perhaps. Mr Rodriguez said she left their cabin at nine-twenty p.m. They'd had *a disagreement* and she was wearing only her blue sweater at that time. She didn't return to the cabin after that. He'd also had a drink, says he went for a walk in the rain, searched for her when he'd calmed down, fell asleep in the cabin. He reported her absence to the duty ranger after he woke up at around two a.m.'

There was nothing to say to that, as Van Allen held my gaze for just a moment too long.

'Why didn't she bring your coat to your cabin, do you think?'

'She probably didn't know which cabin we were in,' Will replied.

'But she could have asked at the reception, or messaged you to say she had it. She must have your contact number, since you work together?'

'Maybe,' said Will. 'Perhaps she didn't want to disturb us. We weren't there together, Detective, as a group. I was on vacation for some alone time *with my wife.*'

'Yes . . .?'

The question implied a 'but' but neither one of us intended to fill in the blanks.

'OK then. Thank you, Mr and Mrs Taylor, for your time,' said Van Allen, getting to his feet, suddenly all sunshine smile and handshakes. 'I will probably be in touch again soon. Don't leave town for now,' he added, with a nod, as if to underline a joke.

As we followed him to the door he turned and asked, 'Did you like it out there? In nature?'

'Excuse me?' asked Will.

'Did you like it out there, in the wilderness?'

'It's very beautiful,' I chipped in.

'Yes, it is. I've been up there camping myself. Majestic. Scary too, though, don't you think? People don't respect it, the wilderness. People are careless. They don't think of the consequences and do silly things they wouldn't do at home, like on all vacations I suspect. But the rules apply there like everywhere else. People forget that.'

As I closed the door on his narrow back, I wasn't sure if he was talking about Jenna and her 'accident' or about us, and I wasn't sure I wanted to find out. My first real encounter with the law felt like a fail and somehow I suspected Van Allen would be back.

Twenty

New York

I forgot all about Bonnie until after dinner, when Will had fallen asleep on the sofa, so I resolved to tell him the next morning. But he left for work early, after leaning over and planting a kiss on my forehead, leaving a note in the kitchen that said, 'Thought I'd better go in and get this over with.'

After a poached egg on toast, I occupied myself by finishing the vacation washing, taking one load out and shoving more shorts and T-shirts, still grimed with Monument Valley red dust and Grand Canyon salt patches, into the basement washer, anything to distract myself from what was going on – it was easier to fold what was flapping around my head in half, then into quarters like the clothes, tuck it into a pocket inside me and leave it undisturbed for as long as possible.

While the washer spun I went downstairs to check the two weeks of mail in our foyer box, not surprised to hear a 'Hey, Mrs T, how was the grand vacation?' and find smiling Mr Luigi, just back from walking Poppet, offering me a little bow of greeting. I'd told him we were taking a trip and he, in turn, had spent a good fifteen minutes telling me about his youth hitchhiking from the East to the West Coast that sounded suspiciously like a section from Jack Kerouac's *On the Road*. After a renewed discussion on the merits of the desert climate, he said, 'Sad thing, about that little girl dying, isn't it? The one who worked at your husband's hotel.'

'You know about that?' surprised he'd found out so quickly. Jenna's death hadn't made any newspapers or online sites yet, certainly not in New York. I'd been checking every hour.

'Pilar told me. You know, she used to live up there, the girl,' gesturing up to our apartment. 'Yes, we saw Pilar on our way out for walkies, didn't we, Poppet?' He nodded. 'She said the Five-0 came by today, real early, asking her about the girl. Asking about her time living here, her *relationships*,' my skin suddenly crawling at the thought of the police, probably that little shit Van Allen, creeping about eight floors beneath my feet while I'd slept.

'Oh yes, very sad,' I mumbled. 'Did you know her then, Mr L?'

'Not really. They weren't a nice couple like you and William, an odd pair. Kind of *modern*. They weren't *married*. Though that's common enough these days. She didn't like Poppet much. She said she had *allergies*. Seems like everyone has allergies these days, milk, gluten, nuts. But who doesn't like Poppet?' And, as if in support of his statement, Poppet jumped up to lick my hand. 'See! Poppet is a good judge of character. Anyone who doesn't like Poppet is no friend of mine. Like I said, she was a strange girl.'

'Strange how?'

So Mr Luigi told me how he'd found Gus and Jenna on the roof of the building one night, arguing. How the position of his bedroom, on the top floor against the inner stairwell, means he can hear the rooftop door squeaking 'all to hell' if anyone opens it. It'd been happening for a few weeks, waking him up late at night, and he'd wanted to see who was up and down there all the damn time. He'd meant to get on to the Super about oiling the hinges or locking it for good.

'She was just standing there, up on the wall above the street, arms out like she was flying,' he said, shaking his head, 'like in that *Titanic* movie. No way you'd catch me up on there, that's for sure, but she was laughing like it was a big joke, like she was drunk. He couldn't get her to come down. Strange girl, like I said, a little bit crazy, like all these young girls who don't eat enough because they want to be a size two or whatever, the lack of sugar in their bloodstream.

'I'm not sure *he* was a very nice guy either, you know what I'm saying? He was shouting at her, calling her not nice names to call a lady. Well, he stopped when he saw me and she jumped down like it was all a big hoot, but I heard him some nights, yelling at her, *not this again*, and *you promised me*, that sort of thing.

'I think maybe she had an eye for the fellas.' He touched his nose at the side, an Italian gangster flourish straight from a Scorsese movie. 'That doesn't mean he did anything to her though, does it? Couples fight all the time. I always fought with my Vera, cat and dog, we were. It's part of the game, as long as you make up, eh? The making up's the best part!' giving me a wink.

'Did you tell the police this, Mr L? Seems like they might want to know about it.'

'Nah, Mrs T,' making a face as if he'd just detected a bad smell, 'they haven't got around to talking to an old fool like me yet. What could I know, right? And it's not my business, is it?'

He tipped his little homburg saying, 'You take care now, Mrs T. Gonna be a hot day today, I think,' leading Poppet back towards the elevator. I decided to knock on Pilar's door across the hall, ask her what exactly she'd said to the police. The thought of Van Allen making a note in his book about Gus's unexpected call, asking for Bonnie, made me feel nauseous.

'You didn't say anything to the police this morning, did you?' I asked, the moment she answered the door, still apparently dressed from a late-night party, in red silk and black leather with sleep-smudgy eyes, 'About what we talked about the other day? About the guy who called here for me?'

'Slow down, girlfriend,' she yawned, 'let a lady come around before the interrogation. You're as bad as that cop. Rude son of a bitch woke me from my beauty sleep at eight a.m., banging on my door. I'm surprised he didn't ask to see my *immigration papers*.'

'Sorry, Pil,' I said, as she waved me inside. 'I was just surprised to hear he was in the building, talking to people.'

'Yeah, well. He's a dick. So you know that girl's dead then? The one who used to live up in your place?'

'Yeah, we just found out. He came to see us last night.

We saw them up in Yosemite actually, the day she went missing, Jenna Parker.'

'Shit, girl, that's creepy,' she yawned, rummaging in the fridge for orange juice. 'So Mr Stalker tracked you down after all, then? That's him, right? Her boyfriend, the one who was looking for you? Oh Jesus, I told him where you were up there.'

'No,' I corrected, quickly, 'I mean, yes, but he wasn't up there for me. They'd been to see her folks in San Francisco and were up there for their anniversary. Just a coincidence.'

'No such thing in this life, sweet thing. I bet that one wanted to *bump into* you all right. I should've kept my mouth shut, right? You didn't say she'd gone missing though, when you asked me about him coming around the other day.'

'I didn't want you to worry about it. I thought maybe they'd just had a fight.'

'So, she's dead and they think he's a suspicious dude, I bet.' She nodded, drinking from the carton. 'He seems like the type. Told you I never liked him. Dramatic, isn't it? A mystery in our midst. Bet they had a lover's tiff and he tipped her over the cliff, bet that's what the police think or they wouldn't have come here nosing around. Want coffee?'

'No thanks. But did the cop ask about Gustavo? I mean, I didn't know he had a girlfriend before we met up there, before I spoke to you about him. I'd already told him I was married. Told him I wasn't interested. I don't want to get involved in any of this, you know.'

'Not to worry. I'm no fan of the cops. You know me, girl. Silent as the grave, well, from now on, right,' she smiled.

'Right, thanks, Pilar. Sorry to disturb your beauty sleep. I just didn't want Will to think there was something up. This is nothing to do with us.'

'Quite right, that little shit Rip Van Winkle or whatever can go harass someone else.'

'Thanks, Pilar.'

'Any time. Guggenheim next Tuesday, for the new exhibition?'

'Sure,' I smiled, glad to flee back to my apartment with my churning thoughts.

By the time Will got home that night I was grateful to see him, if just to remind myself what all this was for. He was white-faced though. He'd had a rough day too, because his manager had taken him into his office that morning for a quick chat.

'Toby said there's a police investigation, Liv. Some sex videos have been found at the hotel, can you believe it? The police won't say who's on the films exactly, because they're "intimate", but there's a member of staff on there as well as some guests, and as team leader he thought I should be in the loop.'

He collapsed heavily into the armchair, beer in hand like an American for once, draining half the bottle in one swallow before saying, 'It could be me, couldn't it, Liv? What if it's me on the tape? What if that Detective Van Allen knows already and that's what all those snide remarks were about yesterday?'

'I know,' I said, forgetting I wasn't supposed to have seen his homemade romp with Jenna at the hotel. 'I know about the sex tapes.'

'You know, how?'

So I told him about Bonnie and Olly and Jenna, and our meeting at the Tribeca coffee shop.

'Jesus! Why the hell didn't you tell me last night?' he glared, though it was too late to explain.

'I forgot and you left early this morning.'

'Jesus, Jenna gave Olly . . .' he broke off, blushed fuchsia, unable to say the word blowjob in front of me, little old delicate and refined me. Then he broke off because what he meant was, she sucked him off too? She made a play for him too? All at once Will wasn't feeling so special any more.

'Well, it could just be Olly and Jenna on the videos, couldn't it? I mean, surely they'd have said something by now, if you were actually on video, screwing her?' Then, catching up with my own supposed naivety, I added, 'You mean you did it at the hotel, Will? Really? You had to do it at the Lowbeck? With a million hotels in this city, you couldn't have been more discreet?'

'I know,' he said. 'It was fucking stupid. It was her idea. She said she wanted to talk in private and then . . . up in the room . . .'

'Which room was it?'

'Does it matter?'

'Answer the bloody question!'

'It was 717.'

'You mean, the suite where we . . .?'

'I know, it wasn't my idea. She called me up there. She was already, you know, undressed . . . then . . .'

Then she whipped out a video camera? I wanted to ask. It was quite a little double party evidently, amateur movie night times two, but it hardly mattered by then, what mattered was where we stood with the police.

'Perhaps I should come clean now,' Will sighed, finishing the beer and poking in the fridge for a second. 'I mean, it's better to be upfront, surely, than to keep lying and still have them find out?'

'We lied already. We lied last night to that prick Van Allen when we insisted you were just colleagues and we spent all night together. Besides, did Toby say it was 717, where these videos were made?'

'No actually, he said he couldn't say which rooms.'

'Rooms? So it could be another one then, nothing to do with us?'

'Perhaps, but maybe I should just admit the fling – I could say I wanted to protect you, not say anything in front of you. That it had nothing to do with what happened in Yosemite. I mean, this is getting more and more serious, Liv. Keeping us out of it, up there at the cabin, seemed like common sense but this is another investigation entirely, and maybe it's perverting the course of justice or something. We should do the right thing while we can.'

There he was, my Will, my good old chap, my Jimmy Stewart. From his point of view it made sense; why dig yourself into a hole even harder to get out of? But he should have thought of that before he lied in the first place. I couldn't let him admit to anything that gave the police an excuse to dig into his relationship with Jenna and therefore into *me*, uncovering a potential chain reaction of stalking and harassment that could lead to . . . to consequences.

And I wasn't ready for those, or to hear my justifications dissected in the cold light of day by unsympathetic officers of the law. There was no way I could ever hold my hand up to them in court, then bow my head in prison, sitting inside

a concrete cage where I'd see the sky once a week. I'd
rather take things into my own hands, climb to my rooftop
eyrie and fly away to freedom, arms flung wide, all the way
to the concrete.

But we weren't there yet, I told myself, ordering myself
to breathe, use my brain, hold tight.

'Did Toby call you into his office alone or all the team
leaders at once?' I asked.

'What? All of us, separately.'

'Well then, it's best if we don't blow it and sit tight for
now.'

When Will looked at me, uncomprehendingly, I said,
'Because he hasn't singled you out. Because Bonnie seems
to think the footage is recent. You must have had sex with
her back in the autumn, right? Not since then? So maybe
you're in the clear. That's right, isn't it, Will? It's been over
since then?'

'Yes, I swear. I promise you, Liv.'

'So, this shouldn't involve us. Let's sit tight. You don't
want this to turn into a scandal, do you, Will?' I asked,
suddenly inspired. 'You don't want people to know you
had an affair with a girl like that? What would they think?
Because it'll get out, if you tell the police. The company
will know, everyone at Piper-Dewey; it'll get back to
London probably, to people who know you there. What
would your old team think? What would your mother and
father think when they hear it?'

It was my trump card because I knew it would sway
him, the thought of everyone who liked him and believed
he was such a decent guy looking at him with new eyes;
then would come the wither of his mother's disapproval,

his father's disgusted frown. I watched his face fold into despair as he saw how it would play out – his gentleman's veneer cracking away for good.

'Look, this Van Allen is just trying to rattle us for some reason,' I said, placing my hand on his arm, giving it a reassuring squeeze. 'The best thing we can do is keep to business as usual. After all, you haven't really done anything wrong. Not legally. You haven't actually hurt anyone.'

He knew what I meant, and I knew he was trying to convince himself I was right, even though he knew he was responsible for enough hurt of his own.

Twenty-One

New York

My next problem, with Will back on board, was Gus. Now that Jenna's body had been found I half hoped the police wouldn't let him return to New York any time soon. I didn't want him coming to the apartment again, no doubt trying to speak to me, where Will or someone else might see him. I was dreading the sight of his haunted eyes, searching for pity, but I knew it had to happen sooner or later and, like Will, I needed to reassure him and convince him to stay silent.

As it happened, he called me the next morning, the phone beeping me out of staring through the living-room window, hoping to see a solution etched on the sky between the gleaming buildings elegantly scraping it. The sound of the words, 'Hi, it's Gus,' triggered the urge to flee but somehow, someone using my voice managed to say, 'Oh, hello Gus. Are you all right? How did you get this number?'

'I got in touch with Bonnie Sheldon, the PR girl who did our meet-and-greet last year. Seemed the easiest way since

Will works at the Lowbeck. Guess I know where you got your other name from now. She gave me your number. I told her I wanted to talk to you about Jenna, to thank you and Will for your help with the investigation. She was very upset. She burst into tears. I guess Jenna was well-liked, huh?'

'Gus, I'm so sorry,' I offered, despite the flashback to Bonnie's words, *I'm glad she went over a fucking cliff. I'd have pushed her myself given the chance.* 'What's happening now? Where are you? Where's Jenna? I mean . . .' I couldn't quite bring myself to ask, where's her body?

'She's somewhere in a mortuary in Mariposa. They won't let me look at her. They say it won't do any good, because of the injuries from the fall. They're still waiting for the ID from dental records but it's her, I know it is. They showed me her clothes, her watch, a photo of her butterfly tattoo. They're taking her to San Francisco. They say, because we're not married, I'm not her next of kin. Her parents are her next of kin. I'm nothing, apparently.'

'Gus, I'm so sorry. Where are you?'

'I'm coming back to New York tomorrow. The rangers have said I can. They're being quite difficult about it all, though. I think they think I might have had something to do with it. But I couldn't hurt Jenna. She must have fallen. At least, I hope that's what happened. I hope she fell and didn't . . . She was prone to . . . she'd tried suicide before, remember I told you, with the overdose?'

There was a long silence then, stretching time into a void between us that I had no words to fill.

'We had a fight that night,' he said eventually, his voice thick, 'and I said a whole bunch of mean things to her.

I should've gone after her. I should've *run* after her and brought her back, but I didn't. I kept drinking and then I fell asleep, and while I was acting like a fucking child, she died. I mean, I guess I was going to leave her after the vacation, I knew that in my heart, but not like this . . .'

I still had no idea what to say. The conversation was unreal and I was not having it, merely watching someone else, a woman, pale and tense, holding a phone.

'I'll be back tomorrow,' said Gus and I knew what was coming next. 'Can we meet up, Bonnie, sorry, Livia? I'm still not used to that. Can we talk? I need to talk to someone and there's no one else in the city. I know you probably don't want to, but please? I can't do this alone.'

I suppose he assumed the strangled note in my voice was sadness as I said, 'Of course, of course,' trying to breathe. It was against my better judgement but what could I do? I didn't want him to come to the apartment, already half-wondering if the police might be following him, but no, that was just paranoia. They couldn't honestly have any reason to suspect Gus, just like they had no reason to suspect me or Will.

'What if we met in the park, by the boats?' I offered, eager to cut the conversation short. If I met Gus somewhere public it could easily be written off as a condolence gesture, comforting the bereaved man whose husband had worked with his girlfriend.

'That'd be great, Livia, thank you. Thank you so much. It all seems so stupid now, doesn't it? So pointless? Not the way I feel about you, I don't mean that. I mean, all the sneaking around we do, all the hurting each other, and for what? When someone can be snatched away in moments?'

'I'll see you there at four tomorrow, Gus,' I said. 'Try and get some sleep.'

The next part of my test suddenly had a definite time and a date.

Gus's words followed me around for the rest of the day, nipping at my heels, making me edgy. 'So pointless,' he'd said, 'all the hurting each other', and he wasn't wrong. Though what scratched at me most, made me itch and fidget, was what he'd said in the middle that wasn't pointless – 'the way I feel about you'.

What would he expect from me now? I wondered. Nothing I could give, certainly. I wasn't looking forward to the answer as we sat in Central Park the next day, a little way from the boating lake, polite acquaintances or office colleagues with coffees in hand, taking a break on a bench, not quite touching.

While I waited for Gus to speak I found myself recalling that first hopeful summer when Will and I had arrived in the city, just twelve months before, discovering the beginning of our new life in the new world, where anything was possible. If I could make it there, I'd make it anywhere, I'd promised myself. I'd been right about that but not in any way I'd expected, or wanted.

Sipping coffee next to the man I'd cheated on Will with, I realised it probably couldn't have happened anywhere else, if Will had had an affair at home in dreary and normal London. There was something about New York, that cinematic winter, that had made me bold and abandoned, made it easier to slip away from reality and from myself.

Towards something else entirely. But I was back now, in my body, in my head, and I had to keep it that way.

'So what are the police saying?' I asked Gus eventually, when my own bloody conscience and the silence between us threatened to snap me in half.

'Nothing new,' already sounding defeated. 'What is there to say? I thought about it a lot on the flight home. Jenna either fell or she jumped. It's as simple as that. Either way, it's my fault.'

I remembered Mr Luigi, his story of the strange girl standing on the roof, arms flung wide, hovering over the precipice. 'Do you really think she'd do that, Gus? Do you actually think she'd kill herself?'

'I don't know. She always claimed the overdose thing, just before we met, was an accident. Too much booze and pills, coming out of a bad break-up with her college boyfriend, so I can't really say, but she hadn't been very good the last few months, in a good place I mean. She'd started taking her anti-anxiety tablets again. She was taking them before, in San Francisco, stopped for a while, then something triggered her again.

'This thing with the German guys really messed her up. She was convinced someone had spiked her drink. Nothing to do with the fact she weighed a hundred and ten pounds, ate six hundred calories a day and had knocked back a bunch of Manhattans. She actually accused me of following her around too, stalking her, tracking her movements.'

I thought of the nights and afternoons I'd trailed her along the winter streets of Manhattan, carefully bundled in my coat and hat, night pulled in around me; the spring afternoons I'd done something similar in sunglasses and a sundress, sipping a cool drink, hiding in plain sight. Had she sensed something, perhaps? A shadow in the corner of her eye? An old instinct of prey in the presence of a predator?

'*Were* you following her?' I asked, because I wouldn't have put it past Gus, after he'd followed me. 'I mean, it'd be OK if you were, Gus, if you'd just wanted to reassure yourself things were all right. I guess we've all done that once in a while.'

'No, I wasn't following her. Well, maybe once or twice, when she said she was working late and I wanted to make damn sure she was telling the truth. I just had this feeling that maybe she was seeing someone else. I know I sound like a hypocrite, with what happened between us, but . . . that was different. It was something I didn't go looking for.

'With Jenna, I don't think it was the first time. I think she was seeing someone back in San Francisco too, but when we moved out here I convinced myself it was a fresh start. That she'd chosen to give it a go with me. You never knew with her, though. She got off on the attention. Away from it, she was, well . . . she never knew how to deal with just being herself, by herself, you know. She didn't know how to be alone for even a minute. I thought I could help her with that, mend her in some way. What a fool I was.'

'But still, suicide?'

'Maybe . . . I was kind of a prick to her lately. I told her I knew something was going on. She was deleting stuff on her phone all the time. She wouldn't show me. I was angry with you. I felt like a fucking fool and I couldn't take it out on you so I took it out on her. I called her a pathetic whore that night, up at the lodge. I told her I wasn't going to be the dumb boyfriend she was fucking around on, that I was going to go back to San Francisco if my old job would have me back and she'd have to fucking get a life on her own. I think that scared her more than anything. I drove her out into the storm that night and . . .'

'Did you tell the police? I mean about the fight?'

'Some of it. I mean, it's private, isn't it, and fucking humiliating. I'm not proud of myself.'

'Did you tell them about us?'

'Jesus, no, Livia. I'm not proud of that either, and with my girlfriend missing why would I want them to know I'm a massive asshole who cheated on her?'

'And you didn't tell Jenna?'

'No, that least of all.'

I was relieved. I mean, it would, perhaps, have given the police a good insight into Jenna's state of mind, a reason for a distraught suicide, but the rest of it would be too complicated to explain.

'So what happens now, Gus?'

'I don't know. I went back to our apartment last night, for the first time without her. For the first time it seemed real. The whole time out there, in the mountains, it seemed like a bad dream, some movie I was in. Then I was back here, her stuff everywhere, her smell. I don't know. I can't stay there. Maybe I'll go back to San Francisco for a while, to my folks' place. Unless . . .'

'Unless what?'

'Unless there's a reason for me to stay? I don't mean right away. Not today or next week, but maybe in the months to come, when you've had a chance to think about things, about you and Will.'

It was all I could do to stop my mouth dropping open as it dawned on me that Gus meant he might stay in New York *for me*, that we could be together. In that second I felt angry and sick, thinking of his wife Hallie, dead only a few months in that car crash before Jenna had installed herself in his apartment, wanting to feel outrage on behalf of all women so easily replaced by men, but I hardly had the right.

Instead, I found myself panicking, jumping to my feet, empty coffee cup bouncing onto the floor, saying, 'Gus, please . . . don't, just don't!'

He'd been expecting it, his hand shooting out to grab mine, already apologising, 'I'm sorry. I'm sorry. I know it's too soon. I don't mean . . .' and suddenly I was conscious of how we might look, to anyone watching. To that rollerblader weaving among the glacial boulders, to that man in the suit standing by the tree across the green drinking his own coffee, to the old lady walking her ugly pug in the clearing – like two lovers in the middle of a spat.

I felt revulsion then, for myself as much as Gus, for my failure to maintain self-control. I sat back down, managing to let my hand sit in his as I said, 'Gus, it's . . . Jenna's dead . . . I can't think about that now. I just can't.'

'I know, but I care about you, Liv, and if I thought there'd be a chance, just a chance, a month from now, six months or a year, I'd stay. You don't love Will any more, do you? You've already made up your mind to leave him. You just need the courage to make the break and I could help you through that. You don't have to be on your own. We could help each other.'

226

I'd never wanted to be alone as much as I did in that moment, never so much longed to escape the searing heat of the secret burning me away to my bones, because Gus couldn't have been more wrong. I wanted *Will*. I wanted that clean slate, that fresh start I'd bought at so high a price, to build backwards to what we'd once had, not perfect but near enough, something kind and close and real, even if we'd got so much of it wrong. Even *I'd* got so much of it wrong.

I'd deliberately avoided thinking about Will's side of things, after the night on that Yosemite cliff when he'd finally told me the truth – that I'd made him feel I didn't really need him, that I was never able to let my guard down, never let him drop his. That, without realising it, I'd made him almost as unhappy with my battle against the world as he'd made me.

So Will's behaviour was a choice, mine was unintentional, but perhaps I had some amends of my own to make to him, to my marriage. If I didn't have Will, didn't get the chance to show him I needed him more than anything in the world, what was it all for?

Ignoring my phone, suddenly ringing in my handbag, I found myself pleading, 'Jesus, Gus, please. You won't tell him, will you? You won't tell Will about us?'

'Of course not. I told you I wouldn't ever hurt you, Livia. I care about you too much.'

'Then just let me go, give me time to think about everything. I need to sort my head out.'

'I know. I do too. I'm sorry. I shouldn't have said that. I'm just desperate, out of my mind. I don't know how to cope with any of this.'

'All right, Gus, it's all right,' I said. 'No one knows how to deal with something like this. No one is ever ready. You'll be OK. Go home and get some rest and we'll talk again. You *will* get through this. At least when the police wind up the investigation you'll be able to think about what you want to do next.'

'You're right. We can't even set a date for a funeral yet. Jenna's parents won't discuss it. I think they blame me. As they probably should.'

'Nonsense,' I said, 'you didn't kill her. It's not your fault,' the only truly honest thing I'd said to him in months.

As we walked to the edge of the park and parted without an embrace, I watched him as he joined the crowd, head down, shoulders slumped. He waved at me from the crosswalk as he melted into the sea of tourists as the lights changed, and though it was a pointless thought, I found myself praying I would never see him again.

Twenty-Two

New York

When I heard Van Allen's voice, calling, 'Hey, Mrs Taylor,' as I reached the doorstep of my building, it was all I could do not to run in the opposite direction. He came up from behind me, slightly breathless, as if he'd been running, asking, 'Do you have a few minutes?'

'Is it news about Miss Parker?' I asked, as he followed me through the foyer door, once more propped open by Pilar with a wedge of paper to vent her paint fumes.

'Not precisely,' puffed Van Allen, as we climbed the stairs to the ninth floor. 'You should be careful with that street door, you know. Leaving it open like that. There are some dubious characters about, opportunists. Thieves. Don't you use the elevator?'

'I don't like them. And I like the exercise.'

While I made coffee, he stood at the kitchen window pretending to admire the view, clearly dragging out telling me the purpose of his visit, making small talk, commenting, 'Nice spot up here. A few blocks north and people are paying more than a million bucks for this sort of apartment now. I suppose it's only a matter of time until this block follows. You should keep this window closed though, Mrs Taylor, wouldn't want any opportunists sneaking in while you're out – these old fire escapes are a thief magnet in a building like this.'

'Well, I'm grateful for the security advice, Detective,' I smiled, putting two mugs down on the table with milk and sugar. 'Help yourself, but please, I assume you didn't just pop in for more of Will's Colombian roast coffee?'

'Sadly no,' he smiled, still standing, taking an approving sip. 'I'm here because I want to talk to you about some video footage from the Lowbeck, an investigation we're conducting,' a theatrical pause, 'but you know that already, don't you, Mrs Taylor? Bonnie Sheldon told you I'd been to see her. She told me you're aware of what happened with her husband Oliver, too, when I visited her again this morning.'

I was taken off guard but there was no point in trying to be clever so I just pulled out a chair, sat down and said, 'Yes, yes I did. It's terribly bad for poor Bonnie, as you can imagine, Detective. She's in pieces over it.'

'You knew about it the afternoon I first called here, didn't you? Yet you didn't ask me about the videos, Mrs Taylor. The voyeurism?'

'No, I, well you were here about Miss Parker's death, and I wasn't sure if Bonnie was supposed to have told me anything. It's a very private matter.'

'Yes I see,' excessively patient and letting me know it. 'But now that you *do* know? Don't you want to ask me anything? Do you want to ask me if you're on those tapes?

You and your husband I mean, being *intimate*. I thought you might have asked . . . after all, private or not, most people would want to know that.'

'I'm not sure I . . .'

'Solomon Adler, the night manager at the Lowbeck, gave us a list of all the people who've stayed in the rooms under investigation over the last year. *Unofficial* visits as well as official guests as they have to keep a record for fire safety and security, you understand. It shows you and your husband stayed in one of them not long after you arrived in the city. I'm assuming you weren't just admiring the view or enjoying the rainfall shower?'

'Which room?' I asked as innocently as I could.

'Room 717,' and my heart sank as he pretended to check his notebook, 'the week you arrived, June sixth, last year. A little romantic liaison, I'm assuming.'

'Yes, I mean, we did stay in that room, but I didn't know that was the room in question until now. Bonnie didn't say, she didn't know many details. I assumed if we were part of that disgusting breach of trust, you'd have spoken to us already.'

'That's pretty much what your husband said.'

'So you've spoken to him first?'

'Yes, half an hour ago.'

I remembered my phone ringing in my bag while I'd talked with Gus. I'd forgotten to check my messages. Had Will called to warn me? But about what? Where was New York's finest going with this?

'So, are we? One of the couples on the tapes?' I asked, when Van Allen's silence stretched out for my reply.

'No, you're not one of the couples on the tapes, Mrs Taylor.'

'Thank God,' I muttered, 'I mean, you just don't expect that, do you, at a top hotel? What is wrong with people these days? Do you know who's responsible? Bonnie didn't know much about how all this has actually come to light. It's got everyone wondering if it's, well, you know, someone on the staff. '

'Indeed,' he deflected, sitting down on the chair next to me, pulling it closer than I would've liked, as he asked, 'Did you ever gossip with Mrs Sheldon about Ms Parker?'

'No, I didn't know Ms Parker. I already told you that. We hadn't met until that afternoon in the Mariposa Grove.'

'But girls like to gossip, don't they?' leaning in a little closer again, trying for a conspiratorial tone. 'To talk about what everyone's up to?'

'Well, not really . . .' Close up, I noticed that, while his suit was expensive, the collar of his shirt looked like he'd been wearing it for a few days, and while his aftershave had an elegant note his breath was coffee-sour.

'Bonnie Sheldon seemed to think someone might have been following Jenna Parker. She said Ms Parker mentioned it to her. I'm sure Mrs Sheldon has formed an opinion of Ms Parker, in light of what happened, and I can't blame her. "Drama queen" is one of the phrases she used, one of the polite ones. But did she ever mention to you about Jenna and a stalker, someone carrying out spiteful pranks, or about Ms Parker and other men? You know, office gossip. Did Jenna have a, how can I put it, *a reputation*? Did your husband mention it, perhaps?'

'No,' I replied, a little frostily, trying to edge away. 'Will wouldn't indulge in petty smut like that about colleagues.'

'Not to you, you mean? Not about the pretty ones anyway,' he gave a wry grin that made me want to slide off the chair or smash his face in with my coffee mug. I dug my nails into my palms to avoid giving him the advantage of either, asking, 'What exactly is that supposed to mean?'

'Nothing, *exactly*. Only that Jenna, Ms Parker, mentioned her stalking fears to her partner Gustavo too. He knows about the Lowbeck tapes now. In light of them, he seemed to imply that Jenna might have been having an affair with someone, perhaps Oliver Sheldon, but Mr Sheldon insists otherwise. You haven't heard anything to the contrary?'

'No, look. I don't socialise with Will's colleagues very often. I haven't heard any gossip about Oliver and Jenna or Jenna and anyone else.'

'You're sure? Because Solomon Adler said he thought Ms Parker had used that hotel suite before, with another man. He was discreet, of course, as all good night managers should be. Actually, he said it was one of the laundry staff who saw her, Ms Parker, coming out of room 717 one night when the room should've been empty, looking a little "unfixed up" was her phrase. Mr Adler confirmed the woman had mentioned it to him because she'd had to change the sheets twice that day, but he couldn't be sure who the man was as the woman has since left the hotel's employ.'

'I'm sure I wouldn't know anything about that, either. Look, I'm sorry, Detective,' I said, getting to my feet, 'I still don't see what this has to do with what happened in Yosemite and what any of it has to do with me and Will.'

'Well, neither do I, Mrs Taylor. But in my experience cause and effect can be a complicated thing. We keep our minds open. Consider all the possibilities.'

'Such as?'

'Such as, perhaps someone had a grudge against Ms Parker and acted on it. Someone with reason to dislike her.'

'Well, are you checking with the other staff at the hotel?'

'Oh, we are. Thing is, we asked around at all the places she told Mr Rodriguez strange things had happened to her, like the Blackbird Gym where her yoga kit and clothes were stolen. The manager said she'd seen a woman hanging around the gym that day, not a member.'

'I'm not sure I'm following you.'

'Really? Hmm, I'm not sure there's something to follow yet either. Only, well, hell hath no fury and all that.'

'Yes, I suppose so. You mean it could be someone from work then?'

'I don't mean anyone at this stage. Well, thank you for your time.'

He got to his feet but, instead of heading straight to the door, idled in a slow lap around the living room on his way, taking everything in, brushing his fingertips against this and that.

'Nice pictures,' he smiled, pointing to the black-and-white print of the Brecon Beacons above the mantel, Pen y Fan shrouded in diffuse sunlight, a shot I'd taken myself at the end of one of our walks. 'That's beautiful. Is it England?'

'It's Wales, actually. We're Welsh.'

'Really? You sound English, especially your husband. He sounds *terribly* English, in fact.'

'He's from the border. He went to school in England. Wales is the bit on the left side of England.'

'I know Wales,' he smiled, 'I know *of* it I mean. Dylan Thomas, Anthony Hopkins, Tom Jones – land of passion and song. The green, grass of home. I'd like to go there one day. I'd like to see the castles. You have amazing castles. We have a lot of great history in this land of ours but nothing like that. That's Dylan Thomas's boathouse, right, in Lough – harn?' stumbling over the pronunciation as he picked up a framed photo.

'Laugharne,' I corrected, looking at the snap of Will and I, in the mists of Carmarthenshire, taken on our first anniversary. Will had it developed and put it in a cheap, wooden frame for me. Neither of us were really fans of Dylan Thomas, but the rare gesture had touched me so much it was one of the few things that made it over in our luggage instead of into storage at his mum's house.

I tried not to wince as Van Allen picked it up and traced his finger across the word Caru, craved on the bottom of the frame.

'Caroo?' he offered.

'Car*ee*.' I tried to smile. 'It means love.'

'Ah yes, love. Makes the world go round, apparently.'

'I thought that was money, according to the song at least.'

'That too.'

He looked sad then and I realised just how uncomfortable the whole conversation was, also how pointless. I doubted he'd really wanted to ask me anything about the videos or Jenna. It was more as if he'd wanted to tell me what he suspected. Watching him leave, the more his questions prickled my skin – they'd been far too focused on Jenna's sexual habits and her 'reputation', surely. Hardly appropriate when a girl had just died?

Obviously he'd been trying to imply that some jealous lover, or a slighted woman, had been playing dirty tricks on her. He was bang on the mark, of course, but why raise that with me? Unless, God forbid, there was something on those tapes he wasn't telling me about.

'You're not one of the *couples* on the tapes,' he'd said. Did that mean that Will and Jenna were on there after all? And he knew I had a reason to hate her?

For some reason I couldn't put my finger on, the second encounter with Van Allen felt like a fail too, my second of the day since the awkward encounter with Gus. I was already raking up far too many crosses and not enough ticks – I couldn't let it get to three strikes, or who knew what might happen? That's why I pounced on Will as soon as I heard his key in the door.

'Did that Van Allen detective come and see you today?' I demanded, as soon as he was barely inside.

'Of course he did,' closing the door before speaking. 'Didn't you get my message? That's why I'm here now. I nipped out for an hour. He came to the hotel, asking me all sorts of odd questions. I wanted to give you the heads-up. Did he come here too?'

'You just missed him.'

'Jesus, that smarmy little shit. What's his problem? I think I managed to keep everything in hand but I'm pretty sure he was trying to bait me, make me lose my temper, making snide remarks, *insinuating* things. Asking me about my relationship with Jenna, if we were *close* friends and that I could be honest now that you weren't there to hear. Liv, I couldn't help wondering if, maybe, me and Jenna are on those tapes and he's sniffing around trying to make something of it.'

'Like what? What's there to make of it?'

'I don't know. Unless, like I said before, they think there's something odd about Jenna's death. If there's a connection to New York.'

'What connection could there be? She was halfway up a mountain in the middle of nowhere.'

'He asked me about Gus again. If I'd ever seen him hanging around the hotel, if I saw him that night at the lodge. I think they think maybe something isn't right about him or his story. That maybe Gus . . .'

'That's nuts, Will. I doubt he had anything to do with Jenna's death. I mean, accidents happen all the time. You remember how dark it was that night. I can't think why Gus would . . .'

'Well, maybe if he knew about Olly and her? Had found out Olly wasn't the only one? Maybe Gus had suspicions about me. Up there, seeing us, perhaps they had a fight. That's a motive in the eyes of the police, right?'

'No, that's a hell of a lot of maybes. And, surely, if Gus knew about you and her he wouldn't have behaved like that, at the side of the road, so polite, so civil. He'd have punched your lights out.'

'I know, it's all so odd, the more I think about it, them being there in the first place and then this happening. The police obviously think something is off.'

'It's a bit dramatic, isn't it?'

'Perhaps, though maybe we should just explain everything while we still can.'

'Seriously? How would that look now? We'd be putting a question mark against ourselves for no reason. Nothing will come of this, Will, it's all just procedure and one cop with a thing for dead redheads and who they liked to screw. Van Allen is probably getting off on this, that's all. Jenna's bloody gone and good riddance. Poor little girl with a bad boyfriend needing to be rescued. Jesus Christ, what a cliché. You fell hook, line and sinker for that one, didn't you? But what goes around comes around. Maybe if she hadn't whored around and treated people like accessories, she wouldn't be dead.'

The outburst seemed to explode from my tongue out of nowhere, and by then I only half felt what I said, half-believed it, but it had the right effect, reminding Will he was an agent of all this too, in his own way.

'If it makes you feel any better, I don't feel good about myself, Liv. I feel even more like a fool now than I did before.'

'Because you thought you were using her and she was using you?'

'Because it was all lies, from the start, a game, and I let myself risk everything for it, even though I knew it was nothing real.'

Twenty-Three

New York City

So, while Will went to work, I spent the next few mornings pacing the apartment and the corridors of my brain, trying to anticipate and avoid the next set of pitfalls in front of me. In the afternoons I forced myself to keep busy, sweating my way through a couple of Kim Lae's cross-fit classes, but steering well clear of Jenna's neighbourhood and all the places I'd once haunted as her shadow.

The memory of that hollow-eyed stalker I had once been, collar up, hat pulled down, frightened me in the bright light of day. I'd certainly turn away if I saw her on the street, her tight jaw and tighter fists, instinctively recoiling from the sense of something waiting to lash out, from the sort of person you move away from on the Subway or cross the street to avoid.

As children clattered up and down the SoHo sidewalks, and the hipsters met for iced coffees, I tried to reclaim the sunlight and shade-dappled sidewalks of the end of June with everyday tasks such as grocery shopping and dry cleaning. Then, once darkness fell, climbed to the apartment rooftop once more, trying to stay sober for a change, knowing my wits needed to be fully un-addled in case of a sudden ambush.

Inhaling the heating summer on the wind, I tried, without success, to thread the past months through the eye of the needle in my head, one that focused on that ridge in the Sierras and the hood of a red coat, trying to stitch some sense into them. I tried not to think of Gus and what he was doing sixteen blocks north, in an apartment singing with his girlfriend's absence.

Then, four days after Van Allen's visit, I found Gus waiting for me outside my exercise class and my worst fears were confirmed.

'I'm sorry, I had to see you,' he said, bounding across the leafy street to greet me. 'And I didn't want to call you on your cell again.'

'Gus, how's it going?' I asked, trying to smile, hiding my alarm at how much weight he already seemed to have lost and how much his little goatee was starting to annoy me.

'It's awful. I had to talk to someone, Liv,' as we set off down the street towards the Subway. 'I've been going through Jenna's things and, Jesus, it's like unearthing a corpse. She had stuff saved in shoeboxes going back years, letters from high-school sweethearts, birthday cards. Remember when people used to write letters?'

'Barely.'

'All that stuff we hang on to, all that childhood nostalgia. It made me cry to think of her, young and hopeful, thinking the world could be a good place.'

'Yes, that's always sad,' I muttered, hoping he wasn't

going to go on about delightful, innocent young Jenna for too long because I simply couldn't bear it.

'And her parents are being total douche bags, by the way,' he added, trotting to keep up with my pace. 'They want me out of the apartment. Nice eh? Not even a funeral held and they're kicking me out and washing their hands.'

'Well, they can't actually do that, can they?' I asked, as we headed swiftly down the steps into the gloom of the Subway, looking for a bench. I could tell from the pitch of his voice that Gus was building himself into something of a frenzy and I was too tired to cope with that standing up.

'Well, they can, actually,' he continued, pacing back and forth. 'It's her apartment, Jenna's, not mine. Her parents helped pay for it. That was the thing about Jenna. She was such a child in some ways. She always said money didn't matter to her, that she wanted to work her way up on her own merits, all that jazz, but then, when she needed something, she'd just take a hand-out from mommy and daddy and the trust fund.

'Don't get me wrong,' he emphasised, waving his arms in a way that made him look exactly like the sort of person to avoid on Subway platforms, 'I encouraged her to let them help. We could never have afforded to live in Manhattan otherwise, not even to rent. But now the Parkers want me out of the way. They've wanted it for years, now they have the perfect excuse.'

'Gus,' I warned, 'come and sit down. Come back from the edge a bit,' the metallic scream of the tracks yelling that a carriage was coming. 'I don't understand. Why don't you sit down for a minute?'

'You know her parents are the Parkers of Parker-Swiss, right?' When I looked blank, he shook his head, 'The tech giant, the original Silicon Valley start-up? Worth millions? As you can imagine, they had plans for their princess that didn't involve the older, gold-digging Puerto Rican boyfriend from Sausalito rehab.'

He laughed bitterly. 'Irony was, I didn't even know Jenna was rich until after Hallie died, after she moved in with *me* in *my* cheap apartment. It wouldn't have mattered if I had. But now, well, it's not my name on the lease. They got me my job here too, so guess what? In the light of what's happened, my boss has given me notice. Says they're *downsizing*. Guess the bluebloods are closing ranks and pulling some strings, cleaning house.'

'Gus? I think you might be reading too much into it. They're probably just upset.'

'Yeah, upset enough to kick me out at the end of the month. Fuck it, I guess. Back to the one-bed in Sausalito and see if my old firm will have me back. That's if the police let me go, leave me alone.'

He looked exhausted all of a sudden, finally sitting down as a train blew in with a dragon breath of hot oil. It was going towards my stop but I ignored it, thinking it was better to let Gus burn himself out where we were.

'I've been called down to the precinct and the police have been to the apartment,' he sighed. 'They're giving me a hard time, courtesy of the silver-spoon gang no doubt, and a little word with the mayor or the commissioner or whatever the fuck they call themselves.'

'Gus . . .'

'I guess it moves things along now though, doesn't it? It

gives you three weeks, Liv. Three weeks to decide, until I'm on the street.'

'Decide what?'

'If you want to come with me, of course.'

Grabbing his arm, shouting over the leaving Subway car, I said, 'Gus! Stop! Back up a bit. What are the police saying? They can't think you had anything to do with this? You didn't do anything.'

'I know, but the more I talk the more it seems like I'm tying myself up in knots. This detective, Rawlins, he's been asking about Jenna and this stalking business she was going on about. And guess what? There's some scandal thing they're hushing up at the Lowbeck. Some videotapes of guests in *compromising situations* and Jenna is on there, sucking some guy's dick. Just a couple of weeks ago.'

'This Rawlins told you that?'

'Yeah, well he said, "performing a sex act", so what else could that mean? That was a nice little surprise. He was very embarrassed and all, "I'm very sorry Mr Rodriguez but we wouldn't want you to find out from some other source".'

'Rawlins? That's the cop's name? Not Van Allen?'

'Van Allen? No. Who's Van Allen?'

'The cop who came to speak to me and Will about the night at the lodge.'

'Van Allen, really? Wait,' he paused, frowning, as if searching for a name, before sighing and asking, 'was it by any chance a Charles Van Allen?'

'I think so.'

'Fuck, that explains it then. I should've known. They have fucking tendrils everywhere, don't they, in the old boy network? Jesus, I think I'm screwed, Liv. Maybe I should flee to Mexico. Fancy a trip to Tijuana? Great weather all year and my brown little face will fit right in. You might have to get the fake tan going though.'

'Gus, you're not making any sense,' I snapped, his eyes roaming the next train releasing its passengers as if he expected to see someone watching, waiting with handcuffs even. He was sweating heavily, wearing what I suspected were yesterday's clothes. I wondered how much cannabis he was smoking to get him through the nights – there was no ignoring the fact that he reeked of it.

'Well, it can't be a coincidence that Jenna dated a Charlie Van Allen at college, at New York State, can it?' he muttered. 'I found some of his old letters in one of Jenna's boxes last night. She'd mentioned him to me before, years back. I'd just forgotten. His mother and her mother had been old Harvard or Yale buddies, or something, and he and Jenna had known each other since they were kids – summers in the Hamptons, winters in Santa Catalina, fall up the Sierras, you get the picture.

'He was the *right sort*, I guess, blue chip, rather than blue collar. Jenna said it was just a young crush and she'd called it off after she graduated, letting mommy and daddy down by ditching the golden beau and refusing to join the family firm. He didn't take it well, this Van Allen. He kept calling her up, even after we started dating that summer, over a year after they'd broken up. Judging by the letters I read, the man was half crazy for her and I think Jenna liked the idea of having her little rich boy on the hook, dangling there if she ever changed her mind.

'She mentioned once that her ex had joined the NYPD.

Just another rich kid wanting to piss off mom and dad for a few years, but I didn't think anything of it. You don't think, when we came here last year, it was because . . . do you think she came for him?'

'I don't know, but I doubt it,' I said, as calmly as I could, *not for him.*

'Well, either way, if this Van Allen is in on this investigation it's because the Parkers are gunning for me and I need to watch my back. They must have asked him to get involved and that isn't going to work out well for me, is it?'

'We don't know that, Gus,' speaking quietly, not wanting to agitate him any further. 'This guy certainly seems like an arsehole but he can't do anything to you because you didn't do anything wrong. If he comes to speak to you, just stay calm and tell the truth about that night. Don't give him any reason to think anything is amiss. And please, remember we haven't spoken about this because we don't know each other. Don't give him any reason to get suspicious or think that we're hiding anything, OK?'

With that, more metal shrieking announced another train and I gave in to the urge to flee Gus's contagious panic. Patting his arm, getting to my feet, I said briskly, 'Right then. I'm going this way. Go home and get something to eat. You'll feel better tomorrow. And maybe leave off the weed for a bit, I can smell it from ten paces and that won't look good to the police.'

As he nodded reluctantly, I felt a twinge of pity, adding, 'This will all sort itself out, Gus. I promise. It'll be over soon,' throwing him a smile then heading to the train as the leaving alarm sounded.

'Don't forget, Liv,' he smiled, 'three weeks. Three weeks

to decide,' his hopefulness cutting me in half as he waved at the closing doors.

Rattling along in the pulsing tunnel I tried to process what Gus had said about Jenna and Van Allen. It would certainly explain his unnatural interest in her – if he was still carrying a torch as high as the Statue of Liberty. A cop, jealous as all hell and determined to find the answers, was very bad indeed. But what in God's name, I wondered, was it about that girl that seemed to make men gravitate towards her?

Though, barrelling through the bowels of the city in the hot, rattling darkness, I already knew the answer, because it was nothing to do with her really, not who or what she was. It was what she represented that had mattered. Like trophy wives or Victoria's Secret models, the illusion of desirability is everything. She'd known that and used it, known that men rarely like you for who you are, instead turning a mirror to face them so they'd see in her what they wanted to see in themselves – who she could make them.

She'd ignored the danger though, when the shine comes off, when reality returns and you're barefaced at 7 a.m. on a Monday morning in your saggy pyjamas. Whoever Jenna Parker had been under the skin of all those filtered selfies, she'd paid the price – she'd vanished long before that cliff top in Yosemite. In some ways she'd never really existed at all.

Twenty-Four

New York City

By the time I got home Will was curled on the sofa, fast asleep. He stirred when he saw me, calling me into the crook of his arm so we ended up spooning like we used to in the flat in London, when we'd fall asleep in front of *The Maltese Falcon* or *True Grit* on a Sunday afternoon.

Curled against his hip, his breath fuzzy in my ear, I was wracked by the sudden urge to tell him everything. Not like before, like the night on the cliff, not to hurt him, but to hear him say it would be all right, that, even when he knew the truth, we could start again. But I knew we never could, *he* never could, so I stayed silent, shaking him awake ten minutes later, asking, 'So who gets the benefit of your charms tonight?'

'Six fat men from Minnesota,' he smiled, stretching, pulling himself to his feet. 'Help me choose a tie, will you? I'd rather stay here, though. I could make us cheese on toast and we could watch *Vertigo* again, or *Rope*, for a change.'

Rope, where good old Jimmy Stewart sniffs out a murder under his very nose – thank God he didn't mean it, because the client dinner was inescapable. Instead I picked out a green tie while he dressed and then ran some polish over his shoes. When he eventually left, dusk gathering, the evening cooling, I was alone. Leaning out of the open kitchen window, I waited until I saw the top of his head crossing the street below before pulling on my comfort cardigan, checking no one was watching, then climbing my iron escape ladder to the stars.

As the faded denim of the sky deepened I watched the once magical lights of Manhattan flicker into life to the north, tossing back a Jack from my bottle stashed up there to loosen my mind a little. The sounds of children playing, their voices reflecting off warm stone, travelling on the breeze, reminded me of the afternoon with Will on the Central Park boating lake, a lifetime ago. How happy he'd seemed then, splashing along, oars in hand, just like he had at uni when I'd watched him train from the bank, one of six pairs of strong arms flexing, flying along the wide ribbon of water.

He'd missed his rows on the Wye so much, after we'd moved to Kensington, missed the water, never any time to get onto the choked Thames. He'd really wanted to get out onto the rapids in the Grand Canyon too, to raft the Colorado River, but my itinerary hadn't allowed for it. My itineraries rarely did. Just as my life itinerary hadn't for one minute included looking into the opening for a leisure manager at a new resort in West Wales instead of jobs in London.

'No one moves to Pembrokeshire if they can move to the city, surely?' I'd laughed, vetoing it immediately, thinking it was a victory when, after a curt discussion, Will gave in with the words, *I'm happy if you are, my love* – the biggest lie in any marriage.

Surprised to find myself crying, I fished an old tissue out of the clutch of hankies and bits and bobs in my pocket, a summer's worth of receipts and 'infidelity' evidence I'd once hoped Will would find. When my phone rang I hoped it was Will. I wanted to tell him that I'd been thinking through what he'd said up in Yosemite, that I could've done some things differently and would try to from then on. That I understood he'd shown me he loved me in his own way, even if it wasn't the way I'd craved. But it wasn't Will on the line.

'I'm coming over,' said Gus's voice, bristling into my ear, 'I need to talk to you now.'

'You can't,' I said, not in the mood for him then, certainly not at home. 'I don't want anyone to see us together while things aren't sorted out. You said I had three weeks to decide. Not three hours! You're pressuring me, Gus.'

'Yes, but things have changed. That's why I need to see you, Liv. Now!'

'I'm not at home,' I lied, 'I'm on my way out with Pilar.'

'No, you're not. I saw you climb up the fire escape. I've been waiting out here under the tree for Will to leave, to make sure you were alone. Waiting for that painter girl and her boyfriend to go inside.'

'You're outside, right now?'

'Not for long.'

Sure enough, peering over the wall, I saw the top of his curly hair heading for the foyer and warned, 'Don't buzz the door, Gus. I won't answer. It's late and this isn't a good time. We can meet tomorrow.'

'It can't wait and I don't need to buzz. She's left the door on the wedge again,' as he vanished into the porch below.

With each second I counted his imagined steps from the door to the elevator, or moving upwards through the floors below, throwing back another shot of Jack for courage, hoping I could talk him down from whatever new crisis was brewing. But I knew my chances weren't good the minute he emerged from the stairwell door, sweaty and wired.

'What is it then? What's so important?' trying to keep the challenge out of my voice. I was nowhere near drunk, only the two Jacks in my bloodstream, but my patience was already fraying, even more so as I struggled to make sense of what he was saying.

'Liv, they're trying to get me. The police, Jenna's parents. They want to frame me up for it, for murder. They're going to do it. I think it's really happening.'

'OK, sit down, take a drink, why don't you?' I ordered, holding my bottle of Jack towards him, sitting down with my back against the low wall out of the neighbourhood's eyeline. I scanned around, evening dark settling over the retail spaces, pale moon cresting the horizon. Each window was unlit as usual but I didn't want to take any chances.

Gus looked like he was about to resist but then relented, 'Thanks, but I came with my own supply,' pulling a fifth-size bottle of liquor out of his jacket and slumping down next to me. As he did, I caught a fair dose of the scent of Wild Turkey, the bottle in his hand, on his breath.

'So, I'm guessing you didn't just come up here to party?' I said, trying for a smile as he raised his bottle, swigged and wiped his mouth with the back of his hand. 'Come on, Gus, what's bothering you now?'

'It's this Van Allen guy, Liv. He's saying all sorts of crazy shit.'

Of course he is, I thought. In his mind you're the guy Jenna replaced him with and he wants to think you're guilty of something, anything, to make you pay. I was annoyed with Gus, then, for being so weak-minded when I had a real secret to hide and wasn't falling apart. Inside I might have been stitched and hammered together with razor wire and nails but outside I was calm and rational, not drunk and rambling, glazed with bourbon.

'I really think he thinks I hurt Jenna,' Gus continued, swigging again, following his swallow with a theatrical coughing fit, 'and the Parkers, those bastards, they must be goading him on. Mrs Parker rang after we spoke earlier and called me all the names under the sun. She had the nerve to bring up Hallie, for fuck's sake. That cast-iron bitch said she was going to send me to the electric chair because I'd killed their daughter just like I'd killed my own wife. Can you believe the nerve?

'She must have been talking to this Van Allen because he came around to my place, not half an hour later, in his thousand-dollar suit, asking all this stuff about Hallie and then if I'd ever hit Jenna or sent her dirty pictures. He practically accused me of losing it and pushing her off the cliff, telling me to confess, to get it off my chest before I don't have a choice and have to tell it to a jury.'

'Jesus, Gus. What are you talking about? And what does Hallie have to do with anything?'

'Nothing! He's just saying that because of how she died. I mean, I lied to you, Liv, when I told you about the car wreck, because I felt like a fucking asshole. She didn't die

251

when the airbag failed. She jumped from the Oakland Bridge and killed herself.'

The blood began to pump in my ears then, drowning out caution as I let my face fall into a horrified O.

'We'd had a fight that night, downtown,' continued Gus, 'and she walked away from me, then drove to the bridge and jumped into the Bay. I found out later that the cancer was back but that wasn't why she did it. She accused me of having an affair, found some of the texts from Jenna in my phone. Even though it was innocent then, I swear that, I think she saw through me, knew I wanted it to be more. She said I was just waiting for her to die and maybe she was right about that, so she decided to save me the trouble.

'At the time the police asked a lot of questions but it was ruled a suicide, goddammit, because it was. Now they're dragging that up, that Parker bitch and the cop, and I see what it looks like. One woman falling to her death is an accident, two is starting to look like carelessness, right?'

He swigged from the bottle again and this time I swigged from mine, deep and long, needing the fire and clarity to carry me above everything, show me which path to take. *Hi honey*, said Jack's gravelly voice in the back of my head as my throat and stomach singed with the third shot, *nice to see you again.*

'Yeah, OK,' said Gus, reading the look on my face, 'I'm a total prick but I didn't hurt Jenna and I'm not letting them do this to me. With all their cash and their lawyers the Parkers can buy the bloody NYPD. But I think I know what happened and it's not me the cops need to be looking at.'

He reached out then, gripping my chin, raising my eyes to his. With the Jack swirling through my brain I wanted to yell don't ever touch me again! You're ruining all this, making it complicated, making them suspicious, but I clenched my hands, struggling for calm.

'Olivia, I know what happened that night in Yosemite and you have to be strong now, to help me make this right.'

Seeing his earnest face, the stare he was giving me, I felt a flare of fear. He really does know after all, screamed my head for just one second. Somehow he's found out about Jenna and Will, about what I did to her in the city. He's found something in her things, in her laptop, her desk, the pictures I sent, put two and two together and made it add up to a murder.

Tread carefully now, darling, warned Jack, as Gus raced on with, 'You see, Liv, those two Californians who were staying at the Lodge that night have finally been tracked down. They've told the police they *think* Will was with them until ten o'clock, then you said he was with you all night. Van Allen made it clear when he came over, cool as can be, that I'm the only one with no alibi.

'Though that's not really true, is it? If those guys were too drunk to really know the time and it was ten-thirty or ten-fifteen that means there's time he was alone. And I think maybe he wasn't with you the whole time, was he? I remembered something today. The first morning I was looking for Jenna, two of the housekeeping staff told me they saw someone asleep on the rec room sofa around seven a.m. I thought it might have been her but they said it was a big lump under the throw rugs, too big for a woman.

'I didn't think any more of it then but, well, was it him, Liv? Was Will really with you that whole night? If he wasn't, if he was back late, or went out, even for an hour, he could have done it, couldn't he? He could have met her, done something to her? Pushed her?'

'Gus,' I managed, relieved and horrified at the same time, a pulse of panic starting in my temple. 'But why? Why would he want to hurt her?'

'Because she wasn't depressed. She wasn't stupid either, stupid enough to fall off a cliff. She hiked all the time. She knew the dangers. They were having a thing, weren't they? Her and Will? It makes sense now, how weird she was that day we met on the road in Mariposa Grove. Had he been stalking her? Is that it? Is he the one who did that stuff at the gym then spiked her drink? Did she want to end it and he wouldn't take no for an answer? Poor Jenna, she wasn't imagining it, was she?'

'What are you talking about?'

'I think they had an affair. Maybe he followed her to the cliff that night and lost his temper. You told me he could be aggressive. Maybe he didn't mean to, maybe it was an accident, but still,' he put a hand on my arm, 'I don't want to hurt you, Liv, but maybe you don't know the man you're married to.'

'An affair? What the hell makes you think they were having an affair? Don't be absurd, Gus.'

'Because she talked about him all the time, back then, last fall, for a good while. I remember now. Will, the new guy, Will this and Will that. Then she just stopped.'

'So?' I burst out laughing. 'That's it? That's your big evidence?'

'There was this sudden interest she had in Wales, too. I saw her looking stuff up on her laptop all the time.'

'But they worked together, Gus. Maybe she just wanted

to know more about the country. Some people like to travel, you know.'

'It wasn't just the places, Liv. She was looking up words, poetry, Welsh words, writing them down.'

'So?'

'So I found something in her stuff. A pendant.'

And as he pulled it out I remembered, all those months back, the receipt in Will's emails for the silver pendant. As Gus offered it to me I almost expected him to click open a hidden recess on the front, to reveal a photo of Will or a lock of his hair, something gothic and melodramatic, incriminating. But in a way it was worse.

'This was in a box at the bottom of a drawer,' said Gus, turning it over to show me something engraved on the back. 'Does this mean anything to you?'

It did. It was one word, in Welsh, *Caru*, engraved on the back in flowing script. *Love*. The one word I'd hoped Will had never said to anyone but me.

Will, you stupid, selfish, faithless fucker, spat the rage in my mouth, Jack D snickering. It took everything not to bare my teeth and snarl at Gus then, to rip his throat out, slash the concern off him. How dare he show me this? Make me see it in the scalpel-cool silver of all its betrayal? My fists clenched tighter, even as I tried to dismiss him, and it, with a laugh.

'You think, because she had a pendant with a Welsh word on it, she was fucking my husband? Jesus, Gus, don't you think this is just transference? Your guilt about us is making you think Jenna and Will must be involved? It's nothing, it's bullshit, it's your imagination.'

'Is it, Liv? I think it's worth a few questions and some

answers. That's why I have to tell that cop. I have to make him realise that I had no reason to kill Jenna but someone else might have. Even the Parkers aren't so vicious that they want the wrong guy on the hook for this – they want the truth. We have a chance to find it. Why don't you just ask him, if you think it's so dumb, then see if you believe him? Ask him if they had an affair.'

'I can't do that.'

'Sure you can. Or I can. And the police can.'

'This is pure jealousy,' I yelled, getting to my feet, swigging the Jack again, long and scalding, because I had to move, away from his touch, as he leaped up after me and grabbed me tight by the shoulders. His bony fingers were sharp, making my muscles clench as he gave me a hard shake, shouting, 'It's not just jealousy, Liv, you fool. Don't you see? It's not just me I'm worried about. If he hurt Jenna, then who's next? You said he could be violent. How long might it take for you to piss him off? Do you know the man you're married to? What he's capable of?'

Of course not, I wanted to say. No one knows anyone, ever. We just live on trust and hope. That cuts both ways.

'He's my husband,' I said.

He looked at me, letting me go. 'You really didn't know? You didn't suspect even a bit? If you think back maybe you had an instinct. That's why you reached out to me.'

And I wanted to laugh then. If it had hit the air it would have been a sound more frightening than a howl, from a black part of my heart. How could he think, even for a minute that I'd reached out to him for anything but revenge?

I bought time by staring at the pendant he pressed into my hand, not having to try too hard to feign breaking beneath his words because I was starting to cry, my whole body burning at the thought of her, on that video, asking, 'Do you love me, Will?'

I turned away then, cupping the pendant in my hand, feeling something crackle as I slid it into my cardigan pocket. I knew it made sense to Gus, what he was saying, because his version of events had its own internal, ticking logic, just with the wrong perpetrator. It was what I'd dreaded, someone taking the little threads of circumstantial detail and pulling them together into a crime story.

A pendant alone was hardly evidence, but it was interesting. And I remembered the look on Van Allen's face as he'd gazed at the photo of the Brecon Beacons, then lifted the photo on the mantel, trying to say the unfamiliar word 'Caroo'. If Gus told him what he'd told me, Van Allen would listen, look into her phone records, her movements, and Will's. It could all lead to the truth of the affair, then I'd have not just means and opportunity, but motive to kill – the unholy trinity, the unlucky charm.

If that happened, I'd have to choose whether to plead ignorance and stick to the story we'd told, or confess. If they actually suspected Will, I might remain free but then I'd have to watch him go to jail. Either way it would be over, because Gus would tell Van Allen about us. Will would know about the fling, the grief group, the lies, what I'd done to torment Jenna, and I'd lose him anyway.

The thought was enough to make something break inside, one last link, the final inch of chain that had held me in check, held me in the world, worn through with struggle and thrashing. I didn't feel broken though. I felt free. I felt in control for the first time since Will had let his midlife crisis dick do the thinking for him, perhaps for longer than that. For the first time ever.

So I found myself saying, 'Of course I didn't know, Gus,' my mind already looking at the bourbon bottle he'd set down on the low wall, fingering the pendant in my pocket and one particular scrap of paper I realised was still rustling there that I should have destroyed. Then I was away from his grasp, stepping back, muscles flooding with heat, insisting, 'It's not true, any of this. It's just not true.'

'OK. Let's allow the cops to decide,' said Gus, dropping his outstretched hands, losing patience. 'Let's get the cops to look at his phone records. You'll see I'm right, when you're calm enough to think about it. You're just upset right now and I don't blame you.'

'You don't know what I am or what I feel,' I laughed, feeling the hairs on my spine rise up, my neck stiffen, 'and if you tell the police I can only assume you intend to tell them about us?'

'Yes. I know it's a bad situation. I'm sorry but it's for the best.'

Please let it go, Gus! I was saying in my own head, just stop talking. Leave and go back to your apartment and sit with the uncertainty and the guilt and the questions that are driving you crazy. Stay calm, wait for this to pass.

'I have to do this,' said Gus. 'Please help me. I owe her that much, Jenna, I mean, and I also have to keep you safe because I failed her.'

That's when I knew that I had to do it, the howl pouring out of my mouth at last, though only I could hear it, smoking, steaming out into the sky above. When the wild inside called, the wild outside answered, and it wasn't afraid.

Gus leaned back then, no doubt startled by the look on my face as I stepped towards him. *One, two, three,* said Jack's voice, or the voice of the thing in my head, *easy does it, swift and silent.*

Never taking my eyes from his, I gripped the collar of his denim jacket with one hand, the front bulge of his suddenly stupid, baggy hipster jeans, far too young for a man of his age. I realised Jenna had probably bought them for him. Then I tensed my thighs and core muscles, just like Kim Lae had taught me.

Gus was confused for a second, perhaps thinking my sudden grip was some sexual thing, a passionate moment, a lustful need on my part to be saved from Will and from myself; an acknowledgement I would be his, would leave on a jet plane with him in three weeks' time, after falling into his arms on that very roof under the moonlight.

He was half right, there was passion in me, as I braced my back leg and lifted him just enough to put him off balance, pushing back, using the low wall behind him as a pivot point. His upper body weight was against him as I shoved with the collar hand and lifted higher with the other, thinking again that he was quite slight really, under his city clothes. It wasn't brute strength, it was surprise, balance and simple physics, and it happened in the space of a moment. He went over the wall without a sound, falling as I released my grip, soles of his shoes dipping out of view a fraction of a second after his soundless scream.

Twenty-Five

New York City

Not wanting to watch him go, to see him plummet towards the asphalt all those feet below, slipping past my apartment windows on the way down, I stepped back as Jack D counted – *One-one thousand, two-one thousand, three-one thousand . . .*

I heard the thump a few seconds later, ten storeys being quite a few less than the fall that had killed Jenna but more than enough. Then I lifted my face to the moon, to the vacant windows watching and the velvet sky, a paw to the ground, a sniff of the air, head cocked, listening.

I didn't check over the wall. I knew someone might look up and I was not there when it happened, when this terrible thing occurred. I arrived too late, in time only to see the Wild Turkey bottle on the wall, to look down and gasp a note of high-pitched horror.

It took me just a few seconds to pull the scrap of paper out of my cardigan pocket, smooth it off and wedge it under the bottle Gus had left on the low wall. There was no more time to worry about whether or not I'd done the right thing, passed or failed the final test – tick or cross, it hardly mattered any more. It was done.

So I hurried away, knowing there'd be sirens soon, using the rooftop door to get back to my apartment since I couldn't creep down the fire escape in full view of the people gathering on the street. I took my bottle of Jack with me into the stairwell, careful to avoid making any noise or creaking the door hinges as I crept down past Mr Luigi's door and opened my own.

When I heard his open door above me I ducked back inside, putting the Jack bottle down, then making as if I was stepping out onto the landing instead of going in. Mr Luigi, peering down in a red silk dressing gown that would have looked at home on Cary Grant in a different age, said, 'Hey Mrs T, did you see something just then?'

'Oh hi, Mr L,' I smiled. 'I'm just going to get some milk. Do you want anything?' then, 'See something? Like what?'

His face furrowed into a frown. 'I was looking out my window, getting some brandy and I thought . . .' shushing Poppet, jumping at his dressing-gown cord, and, as if on cue the open rooftop door creaked in the wind somewhere above us.

'Do you think someone's up there?' I asked. 'I think that door's open again. Better close it, or you'll never get any shut-eye tonight.'

Seeing him pulling his dressing gown tighter, pushing Poppet back inside as if to go and check, I said, 'I'll go, Mr L. You go back to bed,' knowing his elderly chivalry wouldn't allow it.

So we went up together, the roof empty, of course, but the sound of stirring voices already rising from the street.

'Kids probably,' I said, looking around. 'There's no one up here. What a beautiful night, though. I had no idea there was such a view from this rooftop.'

That's when I pretended to see the bottle of Wild Turkey on the roof ledge, walked over to it, adding, 'Look, kids, little buggers,' in an indulgent, *remember what it was like to be young* way.

'Oh, well, at least they have good taste,' said Mr Luigi, picking up the bottle and the note wedged under it.

I'd meant to leave it a few minutes before knocking on his door, then asking him to come up to the roof with me, claiming I'd heard a sound, but it had worked out better than I'd intended. Like that night in Yosemite, a cool calm had descended after the explosion and I knew I needed a witness, since my fingerprints were on the note I'd wedged under the bourbon bottle.

'Is this a note?' Mr Luigi asked, unfolding the paper as I'd planned. 'I can't see without my glasses, not in this light,' handing it to me as I'd hoped, so his prints were on it too.

'I'm sorry. I can't do this again. I have to end it,' I read, keeping my voice light until I reached the end of the message Gus had written, just over three weeks and a lifetime ago when breaking up with me. As the words sank in, I made a show of frowning and reading it again. Then we looked at each other for a second, just as a woman's guttural scream rose up from the street.

Out of instinct we both leaned over to see the source and I spotted what I thought was Pilar's topknot of dark hair, her bare shoulders in her painting dungarees white against the gloom. About a dozen people had already joined the commotion and a woman seemed to be crying.

'Holy Mary,' said Mr Luigi, too weak-eyed to see exactly what was going on below but taking a good guess. 'Did someone fall? I thought I saw a . . . saw something, passing the window. Poppet barked like crazy.'

'Jesus,' I said, feigning shock. 'I think there's a body down there.'

'Put that back, honey,' he muttered, nodding at the note. 'We shouldn't touch anything now. The police . . . We shouldn't have touched anything at all. Oh dear, oh dear.'

'You mean? No, oh no. Oh God,' leaning into him as if I was about faint.

'Come on, honey,' he said, ever the gentleman. 'It'll be OK. We need to go down now. Come with me. I could do with that brandy and so could you.'

With that we heard a siren approaching in the distance, thin and high, as I allowed Mr Luigi to guide me downstairs, sit me down in his immaculate apartment and pour me a tot of Courvoisier. *Traitor*, whispered Jack's voice, *turning your back on an old friend*, as I chugged back the liquor, but I shushed him, harsh and finally. I didn't want to hear his voice ever again. What could we possibly have to say to each other after what we'd shared? We'd outgrown our friendship and never spoke again after that night – to this day even the smell of Jack Daniel's makes me want to vomit.

The police were on the roof for a long time. We heard them trudging up the stairwell, the faint clop of their heavy boots overhead, above Mr Luigi's kitchen, back and fore, back and fore. Eventually Mr Luigi corralled Poppet in her playpen and we headed downstairs to speak to the officer on the door, the foyer and street choked with residents and passers-by intrigued by the street scene and flashing lights. The block was still closed an hour later when Will arrived home asking, 'Jesus, what happened? Was it a mugging or something? Are you OK?'

'I'm fine,' I insisted calmly, though I was anything but, gratefully inhaling the safe smell and warmth of him as he pulled me into a hug.

'Someone jumped, we think,' said Mr Luigi, tipping his chin upwards, 'I saw someone fall. We went up to the roof and there was a note.'

'Christ. How terrible,' muttered Will as I pulled back, offering him a brave smile. Then Pilar was there, pulling me into a violent hug too.

'Jesus, thank God you're all right,' she said, adding, 'I think it was that guy, Liv,' whispering into my ear so Will wouldn't hear. 'You know, the one who used to live here? Your stalker guy? I saw him hanging around outside earlier. He was wearing a denim jacket and sneakers just like that. For a minute I thought . . . Did he come to harass you, Liv? I should never have left that damn door open. This is my fault. That must be how he got inside.'

'It's OK, Pil,' I insisted loudly, then whispering back, 'I don't know why he was here. He didn't come up to see me. I'm fine, honestly.'

There was no need to explain further because, luckily, Beau arrived, looking impatient, glancing up at the roof saying, 'Goddamn police. Come on, sweet thing, I don't want to be involved in all this,' drawing her back inside as the officers started to take statements. The uniformed sergeant wasn't very pleased when Mr Luigi told him how we'd picked up the note and the liquor bottle on the roof, making a note in his book and sighing in a way that said a great deal about his opinion of old people and foreigners with upscale accents.

Later, after the cordon tape was unwrapped from the lampposts, the police cars crawled off behind the mortuary van to wherever New York suicides spend the night. Back in our apartment I didn't say anything to Will about who'd fallen from the roof. I didn't think it would help to speculate, and obviously I hadn't seen the body before it fell, before the face had been rearranged by its speedy meeting with the sidewalk. We stayed up for a while afterwards, sipping Scotch on the sofa, because it seemed the thing to do to calm our nerves after a cup of cure-all strong tea.

'They've offered me another year at the Lowbeck,' said Will, almost as an afterthought, as we climbed into bed later, clicking off the light, listening to the city never quite sleeping. 'Toby told me tonight. They've offered me sector leader, if I want it.'

'Do you want it?' I asked, in the darkness.

'We can talk about it in the morning,' he said, kissing my neck.

Listening to him snore, I spent the night staring sightlessly into the dark.

When I bumped into Mr Luigi at the mailboxes the following afternoon, he seemed bright eyed and already recovered from our little adventure. There was even a hint of gossipy excitement in his voice as he asked, 'Are you OK today, Mrs T? What do you make of all this then?'

'I'm OK, Mr L. Though it's horrible, isn't it? You don't expect something like this to happen.'

'Well, yes and no, Mrs T. I mean, I don't want to sound heartless, but I've lived in this city a long time, seen some pretty bad things; like the time old Mrs Stanetti fell down the stairs and broke her neck on fifth, before that when young Danny Biltmore got hit by that milk truck. Life's dangerous at the best of times so death ain't no stranger here. Still, wish I'd gone up there though, when I first heard the door creak. Wish I'd gone to look right away. Maybe then I could've talked him out of it. Talked him down.'

'You think he jumped then?'

'Well there was no one else up there, honey. I didn't hear anyone come down. I told the police that this morning. They finally sent a lieutenant to talk to me.'

'Really?' wondering why a lieutenant hadn't come to talk to me. 'Do they know who it is yet? I mean, it's not a resident, right? Or we'd have heard?'

'Oh no, it's not a resident. Pilar thinks it's the boyfriend of that girl who died up in the Sierras, in Yosemite Park, you know, the one they were asking about. I saw P this morning and she said she saw him, the boyfriend, hanging around outside only yesterday.'

'Really?'

'Yeah. I told you he was an odd man, that one. Maybe he finally snapped – weak men do sometimes. Weak men make mistakes – they are human and frail.'

He was talking straight to me then, and I wondered for a moment, as he'd obviously heard Jenna and Gus arguing when they'd lived beneath him, had he also heard me and Will on those terrible nights of revelation? If anyone knew the secrets of our building, it would be him. As if half reading my thoughts, he said, 'I mind my own business, of course, though when this big, black cop came today I told him about them both fighting, back before. About *her*.

'He didn't say it, of course, the officer. He reminded me of a guy I used to box with back in the day, face like a sad bear, but he didn't name the man, just asked about the Parker girl. I think they think he did something to her up there, in the mountains, her boyfriend. Maybe he couldn't face it and came back here to – well – weak men sometimes take the easy way out.'

I was relieved to hear him say that, that the evidence was pointing at Gus. It was hardly fair to him but it was too late to worry about his legacy now no one could prove or disprove what had happened to Jenna.

'Or maybe he just couldn't live without her,' I offered, because it seemed like the thing to do, to say a word on his behalf. 'Maybe he didn't hurt her but still blamed himself for her death. Or maybe he just loved her too much.'

Mr Luigi smiled indulgently. 'You're a romantic, Mrs T. Take my advice, stay romantic. It's a rare quality these days.'

It wasn't until the following afternoon that Lieutenant Rawlins finally called on us. Filling the big armchair to overflowing, he did indeed look like a sad bear, heavy set and heavy-eyed, wearing a cheap suit and carrying the weight of the world on his thick shoulders.

'I regret to inform you that the body we found on the sidewalk two nights ago is that of Mr Gustavo Rodriguez,' he said. 'I believe you knew him slightly and his deceased partner Jenna Parker.'

Will frowned while I tried to make my face into an approximation of shock and Rawlins explained how he'd discovered that Mr Rodriguez and Ms Parker had lived in this apartment when they'd first moved to New York. Miss Pilar Baptiste had confirmed that, on the night of the incident, she'd propped the street door open to vent her paint fumes, a dangerous habit, that must have given Mr Rodriguez access to the building rooftop.

'But why would he come here, even if he'd once lived here? I don't understand,' asked Will, white and tight and no doubt genuinely confused.

'Well, that's what we're trying to determine,' sighed Rawlins. 'Did he call on either of you, Mr Taylor? Mrs Taylor? I mean, I know you said you weren't friends but you were at the lodge in Yosemite that night when . . . when Ms Parker met with her accident.'

Accident, I thought, he's finally said the magic word. Accident. A simple, no-one-to-blame explanation to place on a death certificate, in a dangerous place where there are great heights to fall from and things that want to bite and eat you and many clumsy and unlucky people end up in body bags.

'No,' said Will. 'We've not spoken since that day at Yosemite. Had you, Liv? Spoken to him?'

'No,' I said, carefully, 'I mean, yes,' conscious it was better not to lie outright, just in case anyone ever felt it necessary to check Gus's phone records. 'He phoned me, after they found Jenna, to ask if we would come to the funeral. He said he'd got my number from Bonnie Sheldon. Actually, I remember now, he did call me that evening too. He sounded upset but that seemed natural. He just said he was very sorry and he hoped we'd go to Jenna's memorial service if we could.'

'That was it? You didn't tell this to the police who attended on the night?'

'About the phone call? Well, no . . . I didn't know it was Mr Rodriguez who'd fallen, did I . . . I mean, you only just told us.'

'Yes, of course. So when he called, Mr Rodriguez didn't suggest meeting up?'

'No, the call was very brief. It didn't make a lot of sense actually.'

'He didn't come over that night, then? Ring your apartment bell, or come straight up here, since the foyer door was open?'

'No, why would he?'

'Well, it seems he hadn't really made many friends in the city. We were able to ID him, provisionally, from his wallet, but his father had to come in from Sausalito today to officially identify his effects.'

'His effects?' said Will.

'Yes, because of the damage sustained . . .'

'Of course,' blushed Will, for being slow.

'And to confirm his handwriting on the note, since it wasn't signed. So he didn't visit that night? After he called?'

'No, I was in the shower for a bit then I had my earbuds in, working. If he did ring, I didn't hear him. I was just going out for milk when I saw Mr Luigi come out of his apartment and say he'd heard something from the roof.'

'Yes, we've spoken to Mr Luigi. He said he heard the door to the roof creak open a short time before he decided to get himself a nightcap and well, you know the rest. He says he's heard people messing about on the roof from time to time.'

'You think Gustavo might have been here before, up to the roof?' Will asked, still looked perplexed.

'Well, Mr Luigi told us him and Ms Parker used to go up there sometimes. That he once saw them up on the roof and she looked like maybe, well, she was standing on the wall over the street, maybe threatening to jump. They were fighting.'

'But . . .' began Will.

'There's also the small matter of the cannabis we found up there.'

'Cannabis?' I asked, my surprise genuine this time. 'You mean those plants in the pallets?'

'Not exactly. We carried out a search of the scene and found, um, well, in the air conditioning outlet, the brick chimney, we found twenty-two bags of cannabis, plastic baggies and some rubber bands. Someone had quite a little business enterprise going up there. Any idea who that might have been? Have you been up to the roof much, either of you?'

And I thought of the evening I'd encountered Beau in the stairwell on his way to Pilar's, a brown bag full of goods including Twinkies and what I'd thought was herbal tea. I remembered his anxious face in the street, the night Gus died, his eagerness to be away.

'No,' I said, quietly. 'I can't think of anyone.'

'No, indeed,' said Will, startled. 'Do we seem like drug addicts to you, Detective? Like we'd know drug *dealers*?' a little on his public school honour.

It worked on Rawlins like it hadn't on Van Allen, and he

assured us, 'No, no, of course not. Mr Rodriguez actually had a minor conviction for possession of cannabis some years ago and had been in rehab. We think he was probably using the roof to grow the cannabis since the time he lived here. I just have to ask you certain routine questions.'

'I must say,' continued Will, 'I'm not sure that you and your colleagues' *routine questions*, and frankly, your handling of all this, hasn't been bordering on harassment from the start. I mean, visiting me and my wife at home, insinuating things about Jenna, about Ms Parker and her love life, implying Mr Rodriguez might have been involved. Are you trying to say once and for all that you suspect us of something?'

This is it, I thought, this is the moment.

'Quite the opposite,' said Rawlins. 'It seems clear to us now that Ms Parker either suffered an accident, a fall in the darkness in a distressed state or, well, perhaps she took her own life. I shouldn't really be telling you this but, under the circumstances, she had a history of depression and had over-dosed once before. She was taking some strong medication.'

'Well, that's very sad,' I said. 'We had no idea.'

'Why though? Why would she kill herself?' insisted Will. 'What reason would she have to do something like that?'

'I'm not sure it's for me to say, Mr Taylor. She and Rodriguez had fought that night. It seems she was convinced she was about to lose her job after some incidents at work. She'd told Mr Rodriguez her parents had threatened to cut her off if there was a scandal, that they wanted her to come back home and work in the family business... Well, they're a prominent family. A very *rich* family. But it's not for me to say. Sometimes you can never really know if someone is in great pain and what that might make them do.'

Will didn't look satisfied but, to head him off, I asked, 'But what about Mr Rodriguez? You think he killed himself too?'

Rawlins sighed. 'Well, with the note we found on the roof, the fact he had a lot of alcohol in his system and rather a lot of cannabis, I think it's fairly clear. Perhaps he wasn't able to deal with the loss of Miss Parker. And his first wife committed suicide, you know. That must have dredged up some painful memories . . .'

'Well, that's terribly sad,' said Will. Good old do-right Will who actually blushed at the idea he'd had an affair with such a damaged girl and cheated with the girlfriend of a man with such a sad history of his own. I knew he felt like a prick and perhaps he deserved to, though not as much as me.

'Yes,' continued Rawlins, as Will composed himself. 'This must have been very traumatic for Mr Rodriguez, which brings me to another matter . . .'

He cleared his throat and for a second I thought I wasn't free and clear after all, that there was a penance pending and the bill due in full, but in the next breath he asked, in an official manner, if we wanted to make a complaint of harassment against Detective Charles Van Allen. It took him a few minutes of carefully phrased, legal language to explain why – to admit that, as far as the department was concerned, Charles Van Allen had 'exceeded his official role' in the investigation 'by some degree'.

Apparently the investigation into Jenna's death had been given to a senior colleague of Van Allen, to make some enquiries on behalf of the National Park Service, as she was a New York resident, but Van Allen had taken it upon himself to carry out some enquiries of his own. That had included visiting us and Bonnie and Oliver Sheldon. It had soon come to Rawlins's attention that he might have been 'overzealously pursuing' some 'unauthorised lines of enquiry' linking two ongoing cases.

'He had a personal connection to Miss Parker, I'm afraid,' frowned Rawlins. 'It seems they were college sweethearts and, well, that may have clouded his professional judgement and made him see criminal intent where there was none. At no point were his views and opinions the official opinions of the New York Police Department and I apologise unreservedly for any distress caused.'

I heard the clear plea then, the *please don't get a lawyer and sue us for one guy's mistakes* plea, as he continued, 'It also seems Mr Rodriguez left a message on my office phone two days ago, complaining that Detective Van Allen had called on him, made ranting allegations about his wife's and Ms Parker's death. Honestly, Mrs Taylor, Mr Taylor, this is something of a hot mess and I would have followed it up with Mr Rodriguez *personally* if . . . But later that night, well, he . . . he came here, and . . .'

He paused, folding his heavy hands in his lap as if he didn't trust them not to give away secrets. 'I can't say what would have happened if Detective Van Allen hadn't become so *overly involved* but the matter is under investigation now and will be looked into under great scrutiny. There are procedures to follow and that's why I have to ask if you wish to make a complaint because of the treatment you've received? I will be asking Mr and Mrs Sheldon the same question later today.'

Will and I looked at each other, surprised but clearly very much of the same mind. *Let's be done with this. Just let it go.*

'Well,' said Will, 'I think it's something we're prepared to overlook. He seems like a promising young detective. I'm sure your internal procedures will serve the purpose.'

I saw relief on Rawlins's face then, the sad bear almost smiling for a moment. It didn't take a leap of the imagination to know that it would look very bad if anyone suggested Van Allen's allegations might have played a part in making Gus feel persecuted and subsequently, a part in his 'suicide'.

'I'm very grateful to you both,' said Rawlins, as if the weight of ten years had lifted from him. 'Lives are messy, God knows! A turbulent relationship isn't a cause for unfounded allegations but, well, we're all human when it comes to the people we care about ... I'm sorry you and your husband were involved in this. Some people just get obsessed. They never understand that things end. People move on.'

He was talking about Van Allen, and I tried not to read anything more into it as he got to his feet and said, 'I give you my personal assurance you won't be bothered by Detective Van Allen again.'

Closing the door behind him, Will and I raised our eyebrows then spent the next hour talking through the whole bizarre drama we'd found ourselves in.

'I still can't believe Jenna would kill herself, though,' said Will, shaking his head. 'Well, I suppose the firm will make arrangements for a memorial service or something now the investigation is over. Jesus, that'll be a nightmare but I suppose I should go though, for appearances' sake,' eyeing me carefully.

'Fine, we probably both should. It would look strange not to.'

'Well, at least everything is over and done with at last,' said Will. 'As far as Rawlins is concerned, it's over. I knew there was something up with that Van Allen. At least he's off our backs now.'

Twenty-Six

New York City

The next day I finally got around to tidying up the apartment, catching up on all the chores I'd let slide over the weeks. No one really wants to scrub the kitchen sink or wipe the gooey drips out of the icebox slot when they're worried about being clapped in handcuffs, but there was something reassuring about doing something functional for once, with no consequence beyond making things clean and neat once more.

July was infernally hot and all the apartment windows were pushed wide open, the circling breeze, carrying the scent of faraway green making me wish I was on a country hilltop somewhere instead of staring out at the sun-bleached city. As I wiped and scrubbed, I tried to chafe away the last vestiges of Gus's hollow-mouthed face as he'd fallen away from me, knowing the image, after-burned on my retina, would never leave me, that none of it would – not the flash of James Scott's trainer soles or the back of Jenna's hooded head. I just had to find a way to fade them down to a manageable level. If I could do that then things might actually return to a semblance of normality, allow me to say the words, *it's over*.

So I felt remarkably calm until Van Allen's face appeared at the kitchen window. I didn't scream or drop the jug I was drying as he hovered outside, nine storeys up, floating in the air like the cinematic ghost of misdeeds past. Unshaven, sandy hair flopping over one eye, he tapped on the window frame.

'Surprise!' he called, in that elegant East Coast accent of his, the only remnant of the immaculate officer who'd sat at my kitchen table days before now grinning the sort of grin you see on people about to do something very unwise.

'Jesus, Detective . . . what are you . . .? How did you . . .? Why are you . . .' I began, before words failed me.

'What am I doing on your fire escape, how did I get here and why?' he completed. 'That's what I like about you, Mrs Taylor. You get straight to the point. You're nothing if not practical. And you don't startle easily. I bet you're quick on your feet when surprised, too. Are you surprised now, Mrs Taylor? Go on, admit it, you are. Surprised to see me again when you've been told I'm out of the picture and all's well that ends well?'

'I don't know what . . .'

'To answer your first question, I pulled down the street level section of your fire escape with the help of a very fat but very obliging trashman called Joe. That section slides down from the first floor, you know, for security, then I climbed up. It was really quite easy.'

'OK, but why? Do you need to talk to me? Wouldn't it be easier to . . .'

'Why indeed! You see, Olivia. Can I call you Olivia? Because I feel we have a lot in common. You know, of course, that Gustavo Rodriguez is as flat as a pancake after nose-diving off your roof and that my colleagues think it was suicide, probably because there's what passes for a note in the evidence file and they're simple folk who don't always see the full nature of cause and effect.

'You see,' he leaned in through the open window, one arm up against the sash, gaze fixed on mine, 'your neighbour, the comical Italian guy upstairs, told the uniforms that there was no one else on the roof that night. No one passed his door, or at least, no one he heard. And your downstairs neighbour, the pretty but petulant Pilar, didn't see or hear anyone pulling the fire escape ladder down past her kitchen window. Indeed, according to the report, it was still bolted in place, in the raised position, when the officers arrived at the scene.

'So, if no one went up the inside stairs and no one went up this fire escape, then good old Gustavo was on his own on the roof when he jumped. Right? Except . . .' his smile faded, 'this is why I'm here . . . My esteemed colleagues don't seem to have considered the possibility that someone could have gone up to the roof from one of the lower floors. Someone who could climb a flight of steps easily, if they had the nerve. What do you think, Olivia?'

'I think this isn't a good place for a conversation,' I said, already wishing I could back away, put the kitchen table between us instead of behind me without making it look obvious. 'I think you should call again this evening, when my husband is home.'

He lunged at me then, still outside, grabbing my left

wrist and pulling me towards him against the windowsill. It was so sudden a move I was too startled to pull away, the jug in my left hand smashing, leaving a jag of blood across my palm as I threw my hand against the frame to stop myself being hauled out.

'I thought you might say that,' smiled Van Allen. 'That you might not invite me in after what they've told you about me, that son of a bitch Rawlins for one. I was right. You have fast reactions, Olivia. Not quite fast enough because I surprised you, and surprise is everything, isn't it, especially for a woman? You're not as strong as me but you could have done the same thing with timing and guts. You have those things, don't you, Olivia? Timing and guts?'

'Detective, let me go. You're hurting me,' I yelled, struggling to pull against his fingers, vice-like on my lower arm.

'You don't like this, do you, Olivia? You don't like it because you're not in control right now, I am,' giving a little heave so I could feel his strength. 'It's tiring though, isn't it, being so calm, so controlled all the time, thinking, thinking, thinking, never letting go? Wouldn't you like to do that, Olivia, come outside right now and let go?'

Without taking his eyes from mine he cocked his head towards the grille of railing, the street below, and my mind screamed, thinking he meant to pull me out and throw me over.

'Oh, I don't want you to fall, Olivia,' he continued, reading my expression, 'not just yet, anyway. I think, given the option, you might have a confession to make first, something to get off your chest?'

'Are you insane?' I winced, my hand braced against the window frame running slick with blood, my feet losing their purchase on the floor, tipping towards him, half demanding, half asking, 'Please let me go, I don't understand.'

'Understand? Neither do I but I think you can explain it to me. I know what it means to be hurt and rejected and what that can make you do. I know what it's like to suspect and to fear but never to *know*, to understand you might never actually know the truth.

'Jenna was the love of my life from the time we were just kids. Then, when college was done, she threw me over for that fucking computer-nerd welfare case. But love doesn't just stop, does it? Though I had a rough time when she refused to see me, stopped answering my calls, I knew I had to try and look after her, keep an eye on her, that one day she'd want me back.

'I knew Señor Gustavo wasn't good enough for her, especially after I followed them to Muir Woods one day above San Francisco, where we used to go, me and Jenna. It was our special place, our hideaway, which made it even worse, seeing them there. Do you think I could ever unsee what I saw that afternoon? Watching them fucking under the trees like apes? After she'd promised *yet again* that there was no other guy, she wasn't cheating on me, it was just *over* for us. *We'd grown apart.*

'Seeing something like that might make you do something unkind, mightn't it? Something like, say, sending certain photos you'd taken to the bastard's wife so she could see the sort of man she was married to? OK, if that woman then decided to, well, jump off the Oakland Bridge, for example, rather than live with it, that would be beyond your control, right? Unexpected cause and effect, unavoidable collateral damage.

'But it made me think, when she came to me back in April, Jenna, I mean, because she did come to me, as soon as she needed me. She tracked me down at the precinct, showed me some photos a nasty little person had sent her, intimate photos of her naked and doing things with a man. You couldn't see who the man was, only that he was there and it wasn't that Puerto Rican piece of shit, it was a white guy and a white dick.

'That hurt, of course, but I knew it was only a fling because she was unhappy. She thought she was being stalked and needed me to protect her, and once that was over she'd come back to me. Then this Lowbeck Hotel and the Oliver Sheldon stuff came up. Well, it seemed too much of a coincidence, and Bonnie Sheldon being such a nice woman, I couldn't imagine her doing anything like that . . . but . . . she probably wasn't the only wife or girlfriend who had a reason to hate Jenna . . .'

He paused then, staring right into my eyes, the stare of obsession I'd glimpsed time and time again in the mirror, before his eyes drifted away behind me. I realised why there'd seemed something familiar about him the day he'd first spoken to us. I'd recognised myself even then, on an instinctive level, I'd recognised one of my own.

The narrow windowsill was still biting into my leg as I tried to keep upright, my arm braced on the window, but I didn't interrupt him, hoping he'd loosen his grip just enough for me to get my leg up on the sill and lever myself backwards. If I could do that then the pieces of broken jug on the floor behind me would make a good weapon . . . one shard into the meat of his bicep . . .

'Then I found out she was dead,' said Van Allen suddenly,

snapping back into focus. 'No one told me, though. No one broke the news gently. I saw the file on my lieutenant's desk, *Jenna Parker, deceased*, and wondered if maybe she'd just taken the easy way out at last, ended it all. I only wanted to talk to the people who were with her that night, her *friend*s, you understand. But then there you were, Olivia, you and your oh-so-English husband,' he nodded, like it was already a foregone conclusion. 'I came to see you and something just seemed familiar, in your face, in the way you told your careful story.

'I realised it wasn't the first time I'd seen you. That was a few weeks before in the Greenwich Regal lobby, when you were reading from a portfolio or something, done up like a proper businesswoman in a dirt cheap but smart suit and perfect pink lipstick, looking like you had every right to be there.

'Jenna was there too and I was watching over her, looking out for anyone shady hanging around, looking for her stalker I assumed was a man. But I never saw anyone watching her except you, so cool, so pretty, so composed. I remembered how you never spoke to her, never even acknowledged her, yet you never once took your eyes off her, left when she left and followed her to the Lowbeck.

'So I followed *you* once or twice, afterwards. I saw you at your workout classes. I watched you attack those bags and mannequins – punch – kick – punch – so much rage. Then I saw you in the park with good old Gus after the *accident* and that's when it really started making sense – the nip, nip, nip, on the back of my neck – the two of you on that bench, fighting like you knew each other so well, fighting like *lovers*.'

282

The man with the coffee, I recalled, that day in the park – the rollerblader, the pug lady and the man standing under the trees when I'd told myself, hairs prickling on my neck, not to be paranoid, that no one was watching us.

'I thought maybe you were hiding something,' grinned Van Allen, 'but what? Was your mistake as simple as mine? Were you the sender of the dirty photos, maybe with unexpected consequences? But how would you have gotten hold of them? And why would she matter so much to you that you'd want to torture and humiliate her?

'You wouldn't have done it because of Gus, that's for sure! You couldn't have really wanted him when you're way out of his league, just like she was. So if it wasn't because you wanted him, then . . . You see, alibi or no alibi, I couldn't really imagine Gus hurting her like I pretended to the day he died, making him think I thought he'd killed her in a jealous rage. Jesus, he'd have to grow a pair first.

'You, on the other hand . . . I think you have a big pair of your own, Olivia. I think you might have the balls, the opportunity and the motive to find a moment on a high cliff and . . .

'Then, just two weeks later, good old Gussy himself takes a high dive from *your* apartment building . . . What did he know about you, Olivia? Why was he a threat? As I said to dear Gus, that very afternoon, mentioning his wife, trying to make him give something away – one person taking a swan dive within a twenty-yard radius could be seen as a coincidence, two is starting to look like more than carelessness.'

He looked up for a second then, as Poppet began a frantic flurry of yapping on the floor above and I heard Mr

Luigi shushing her before the upstairs window slammed down and I could think of yelling for help.

'Always thinking, aren't you, Olivia?' grinned Van Allen, giving me a little shake. 'Look at you right now. You're scared but not very. You're not crying or pleading and saying *this is all insane* – you're listening and thinking. Perhaps thinking, how much does he weigh? How far is it to the edge of that rail and can he pull me out? Can I pull this window shut on him first? Can I reach that broken jug on the floor behind me? No, don't try it,' gripping the back of my neck, clamping me in place as it struck me how, to any observer in the windows opposite, we might appear to be in a sudden embrace.

'Stop struggling now and listen to me,' ordered Van Allen. 'Listen to my truth. I think you found out Jenna was fucking your husband. I think that because the carpet in the photos the stalker sent to Jenna is the same as the Lowbeck carpet from Room 717 where those pervert videotapes were made. Unfortunately your husband is not on those videos and Jenna took the pictures away with her, so I have no proof.

'But there were other things, Olivia. Little things. You know, the sort of thing only a lover would know. Like, when Jenna came to see me at the precinct and I saw the book in her purse. Yeah, I snooped in her bag while she was in the bathroom, bad old me. But Jenna was never a reader. Never read anything longer than a magazine article about diet trends, and it was a poetry book. Like Jenna ever read Dylan Thomas in her life, the collected poems no less.

'And then she said the weirdest thing, when she explained she wanted me to find out who was sending her the porn.

She told me everything, and when she described what she remembered about the night at the Temple Hotel, with the spiked drink, she said, "Well I was mingling with the group, meeting and greeting and so forth . . ."'

He paused as if waiting for me to understand, 'And so forth,' he repeated. 'She actually used that phrase, a California girl, pure West Coast, and she says *and so forth*? And when she'd arrived at my desk she'd said it was because she wanted to talk to me about a terribly awkward matter. *Terribly awkward?* As if she'd swallowed a box set of *Downton Abbey* or something.

'Now, it makes sense, when you put it all together. People pick up on the speech patterns of the people they spend time with. Jenna always did. She once spent a whole summer saying *Ciao!*, referring to everything as *bella* because her college dormmate claimed her grandmother was some blueblood Florentine. So you see what I mean? *And so forth, terribly.* That's what you and your husband say, isn't it? It couldn't be more obvious what it all means.'

'Please let me go,' I yelled then, to make him stop, to make him shut up. 'Please, just come inside and talk. You've got this all wrong, Charles. But we can talk about it. I can see you're upset.'

'Upset? Is that what you call it? When it's the end of your world, the end of everything? You know how that feels, don't you? Come on now, Olivia, is there something you want to tell me? Say it, tell me the truth. So we can move inside. I mean, it's dangerous out here. Unsafe, someone should have a word with the borough safety department. I mean, someone could fall through this window so easily, slip over the rail, well, anything's possible . . .

'So say it, *I knew about the affair. I killed her.* Then I'll let you go. It was a moment of madness, wasn't it? Up there in the mountains, with no one watching? You weren't thinking rationally. Your heart was broken. You bumped into them. She was right there, rubbing your nose in it. Your husband was drinking with the Californians and it was all too much. You went to look for her, to challenge her, get things out in the open, then things got out of hand. She could be a handful. I know that.'

'No!' I couldn't bear to listen any more.

'Little wussy Gussy, though? That sorry excuse for a man with his lifelong victim complex? Always thinking people were out to get him because he was the wrong shade of self-obsessed instead of just a shiftless, useless dick. Was that really necessary? Surely someone as *persuasive* as you could have avoided that? It was easy enough for me to make him think that your husband might have hurt Jenna, that *you* might be in danger – I think he would've cracked and told me what he knew if I'd had one more day to work on him. But you saw to that, didn't you? That was an act of expediency. Cool and pre-meditated. Cleaning up and covering your tracks.'

'No!' I yelled again, thrashing in his grip. Laid out like that, Van Allen's story sounded insane even to me, the collected fantasies of an obsessive man, a list of coincidences and chance jumbled into something impossible and unlikely. No wonder Rawlins thought he'd fallen head-first off the sanity wagon. It seemed almost a coincidence that it happened to be almost true.

Perhaps he thought there'd be relief in hearing my confession, though hardly a confession worth anything,

286

not in court, not given the duress I was under, as he demanded, 'Say it, Olivia. Tell me I'm right. Own what you are! Say *I killed Jenna Parker. I killed Gustavo Rodriguez. I am a murderer.*'

But how could I say it, even to him, even to myself? Even though they were only words, slippery and deceitful, they couldn't show the whole story, explain what I'd been through over the months, the destruction of the quiet disaster that had unfolded within the four walls of our apartment, on those city streets, in my head, all because my husband had cheated on me.

Because it doesn't matter that it's a cliché, that it's commonplace, that it's glaringly mediocre. It still means the whole world and its end when it's happening to you. His truth was too simple a truth and saying it aloud would've split me right open. Luckily I didn't have to because at that moment there was a clatter of knocks at the apartment door and Mr Luigi was shouting, 'Mrs T, are you OK in there? Mrs T? Poppet was barking up a storm. I think there's someone on your fire escape. Close your windows, honey!'

'Franco! Call the police,' I managed to yell, finding my voice before Van Allen clapped his hand over my mouth and lifted me bodily through the wide window onto the flat grille of the fire escape. Losing my balance, my hands windmilled for something to hold on to, bloody fingers fixing on the rail before he pulled my wrist away and clasped me to him. Below, I could see the scurrying shoppers buzzing in and out of the boutiques and delis, oblivious to what was happening in the sky above them. It would be fitting, I thought, if this is how I end, hurtling after Gus in more ways than one.

But Van Allen wasn't done with me. He still needed to hear it. He needed to know the truth.

'Good neighbours, eh?' He smiled for a moment. 'But we have to finish our talk,' as the banging on the door stopped. 'Did she see you, Olivia, my Jenna? Did she look you in the eye at the last moment? Did you grant her any last words as I'm granting you yours? I know they won't believe anything I say, those dumb fucks I work with. I know how it all sounds, how they looked yesterday when they called me into the lieutenant's office, wouldn't even let me explain.

'They told me to take a break, suspended me right in front of Jenna's dad. This is the only justice I'll get but you have to say it. And you have to tell me who made you this way? Who hurt you?'

'Everyone,' I said, 'always,' suddenly wanting to cry.

'Yes. I understand that. I knew we were alike. You want to be free now though, don't you? To be safe? You'll thank me, I think.'

I wonder if he would have done it then, heaved me over the railing. I felt him brace his feet against the grille as the hammering started on the door again, except it wasn't Mr Luigi this time, it was Detective Rawlins, shouting, 'Open up, it's the police,' in his deep bass boom.

It must have been only a few seconds before the air split with the wail of splintering wood and the door burst open. I'm not sure who was more surprised, me, Van Allen or Rawlins as his eyes adjusted to the light and the scene at the window. As he demanded, 'Charles, son? What the holy fuck's going on?' all trace of the sad bear was gone, his eyes alert, 'Get in here right now and let the lady go before this gets out of hand.'

'Lady?' Van Allen sneered, twisting me around to face his boss. 'This is no lady, Lieutenant. What do you say, Olivia? Shall I tell him or will you?'

Seeing Van Allen's hand on my neck, the blood on the window frame and on my hand, Rawlins drew his gun, swift and smooth like water sliding up from his hip. It was the first gun I'd ever seen outside a pawnshop window and it didn't look real, even when it was pointed at my face. There's no way that will help me get out of this, I thought, despite the look of cool readiness on Rawlins's face. I have to save myself, even as the lieutenant demanded, 'She's bleeding, Charles. Let her go!'

So I answered Van Allen's question for him, turning my face to his ear, whispering gently, 'She was a whore, your Jenna. A dirty slut and she deserved to die. But she threw herself off that cliff because you didn't look after her. You didn't protect her and that's not my fault. It's yours.'

Van Allen gazed at me for a long second, primal fury dawning on his face, the 'truth' not what he wanted to hear after all. But if he'd wanted another answer, he should've asked another question. Either way, it was enough to give me the leverage I'd hoped for as he loosened his grip, shifting to look at Rawlins, yelling, 'It's not true. It's not true!' buying me enough time to push back against him with all my coiled force, making him stagger. Then I grabbed the wilted pot plant at my feet, the one I'd been watering off and on since we'd moved in, swung it up and smashed it into his face.

The blow wasn't as hard as I would've liked, being off balance, but it was enough, and he howled in anger at the sick cracking sound his nose made. As he shoved me aside, reaching for something in his belt that evidently wasn't there, I felt myself stumbling backwards, my foot losing contact with the iron edge of the step behind me, arms reeling, weight shifting.

At the same second that Van Allen brought up his empty hand in surprise, a shot rang out and the strip of apartment window glass above us exploded in a hundred shards of silver sunlight.

Then I was falling backwards.

Twenty-Seven

New York City

As I reeled away from Van Allen's shove, momentum carried me down the flight of steps behind me faster than I could have imagined. As I lost my footing, pin-wheeling backwards, there was just time to see Van Allen slump down against the railing above, a look of pained astonishment on his face. For a split second the sky above me was painfully blue, the breath I drew in cool and clean. I was fully expecting time to slow, for my life to flash a montage of images, all too brief, before my eyes, in the slow, drawn-out seconds before my weight carried backwards, and I tipped over the rail of the landing below to make contact with the sidewalk.

But somehow there wasn't time. Instead of falling further, momentum carrying me over the low rail and down into the alley, I was being grabbed from behind by two strong arms and rolled into a ball on the narrow landing. The breath thudded out of me, my left ankle cursing in pain, twisting under the muscular weight pinning me down.

My head turned awkwardly to the side, I could see Van
Allen, half on his feet above us, blood pouring from his
shoulder and his smashed face. For a second it looked as if
he was staggering, or maybe falling towards me, but then
Rawlins's arm came through the window, sliding through
the broken teeth of the shattered top pane to grab Van
Allen's shirt collar and yank it against the window.

I winced at the dull thump of his forehead hitting the
wood as Rawlins said, 'Give it up, kid!' sighing as his detective finally slumped on the grille, eyes unfocused. 'Talk to
me, Mrs Taylor, are you OK down there?' he called, head
bobbing out, no doubt thinking of the shitstorm that would
engulf him once everyone found the strength to move.
There was no brushing this one under the precinct rug, as,
from the street below, the hubbub started, upturned faces
already engaged in the drama the gunshot had kicked off
with such a flourish.

'I'm OK, I think,' I managed to wheeze, as the weight of
my rescuer finally rolled off me and the air returned to my
lungs.

'I never knew you writers led such exciting lives,' said
Pilar's boyfriend Beau, breathing hard, sitting up beside
me, white-faced. 'Guess I owed you one for keeping quiet
about my gardening hobby. Call it even?' his green eyes
twinkling. 'Good job I was in the building and saw that
prick on his way up here. Think you'll find a part for me in
the Great American Novel, then?'

'Least I can do,' I smiled back, letting him fold me in a
hug that smelled of herbal tea.

*

It was all very dramatic, the aftermath. I remember Beau helping me back up the fire escape on my bloated, already blackening ankle, stepping carefully over the litter of glass, and Van Allen's heavily breathing body. Climbing in through the shattered window, we made room for a lady paramedic to see to Van Allen before she, Rawlins and a colleague managed to hoist him back inside.

Barely protesting, slipping in and out of consciousness, Van Allen was laid on a stretcher and then cuffed to it, while I kept asking for someone to call Will and a flustered Mr Luigi poured me a brandy.

'I'm so sorry about this, ma'am,' sighed Rawlins, eventually returning from seeing Van Allen into an ambulance. 'I'm glad you're all right. What did he say to you out there? Van Allen? Did he tell you why he came here? What he wanted?'

'To be honest, I'm not really sure,' I offered, while a different paramedic swaddled my ankle, elevated on the sofa. 'He seemed unhinged, to be honest, confused, accused me of being involved in Jenna Parker's death. He said Gustavo Rodriguez had killed her and I was covering it up. It didn't make much sense. He kept saying, *tell the truth*. Is he . . . is he going to be OK? He seems . . . like a very troubled young man.'

'That's putting it mildly,' said Rawlins, the sad bear demeanour returning. 'This is strictly off the record but you deserve an explanation. He's made a lot of crazy accusations in the last twenty-four hours, Mrs Taylor. He's got an idea in his head about what happened up in Yosemite, about Mr Rodriguez hiding something and you and him "being in it together".

'He'd been speaking to the Parkers, filling their heads with plots and the idea that Mr Rodriguez was a violent, abusive man. It was incoherent, to be honest. Something about Jenna Parker being stalked and pornographic photographs – I think because, in relation to the other investigation, the voyeurism case, we discovered she'd been receiving some nasty texts. Most likely from the suspect we have in custody for making the tapes.

'He's conflated the two things, taken this all very badly, personally. Seeing conspiracies where there are none. It's not really the first time he's gone rogue. Just a few months ago he became overly involved with a girl who'd been assaulted by her father, made some threats against the man. He's been showing signs of stress for a while. That's why he was on station duty instead of being on the streets.

'I've had to explain all this to the Parkers and the Van Allens today. I've learned from his father he's been in counselling for years, since Jenna Parker left him. I suspect he only made it onto the force because his daddy greased the wheels. He'd never have passed the psych evaluation otherwise,' he grimaced, then looked flustered, having said too much. 'I mean, I shouldn't say that, of course. There's nothing wrong with going to therapy. He was a top-class cadet at the academy. Not everyone can take this lifestyle, the things you see. Goes to show you never know someone.

'Thank God we took his gun and badge away when we suspended him yesterday, or . . . well . . . I'm no psychiatrist, but this seems like a classic psychotic break – his father said something similar yesterday, though, like all fathers, he wants to protect his son, says this isn't his fault. Though whose fault it is then, is anyone's guess . . .'

It's mine, I should have said. And Will's. But I didn't. I said, 'I'm very glad you were here, Lieutenant, but how did you get here so quickly?'

'I was coming here anyway to tell you we've closed the voyeurism case. I can't really go into details for legal reasons, but I thought you'd want to know it's all cleared up, that the suspect will be charged.'

'Really, well, that's a bit of good news. So this man, I guess it's a man, had fixated on Jenna? Was harassing her with messages and so forth?'

'Well, we think so. He denies it. Says he didn't send her any texts or photos, but he would say that. Anyway, in the light of today I suppose that's the least of your concerns.'

Will burst into the room then, panicked and breathless, folding me into his arms and for the next few hours the rest of the world went away. As the apartment emptied of emergency strangers Rawlins promised to return when I was feeling better, to take my statement and 'consider options' regarding Van Allen. In light of what had happened there would have to be charges, he said, probably criminal, assault at the very least.

After Mr Luigi took his cue to go, sidling back upstairs, kissing my forehead on the way out, I let Will hold me and, for the next week, nurse me like the heroine he insisted I was. Even though all I'd done was be held hostage and given my captor a shove, that was enough for Will to want to look after me like Florence Nightingale, make sure I 'recovered from the shock' by feeding me endless Dominique Ansel cronuts and cinnamon buns alongside a stream of DVDs so I didn't have to hobble off the sofa.

'You were so brave,' he kept saying, 'my wife. No one gets the better of my wife.'

You did, I wanted to say, but it would have spoiled the mood.

And that was it, the end of the story, except for a few small matters that needed tying up.

The first was the disposal of Jenna's pendant, the one I had in my pocket the night I left the rooftop. I hadn't wanted to keep it on me so, when Mr Luigi offered me brandy and comfort in his apartment on the night that Gus died, I'd used his bathroom and hidden it behind the wall vent. Once I was sure the police weren't coming back to question me, or search my apartment, I popped in to see my good neighbour, thanked him for his timely actions with a bottle of Courvoisier, and retrieved it.

I knew I couldn't ever let Will see it. How would I have explained it away? And hiding it was too risky. So, on my way to the precinct to sign off my official statement, I dropped it into a storm drain, watched it swirl away into the sewers of the city.

The second thing I learned from Bonnie, when she popped around two days after my encounter with Van Allen, laden with flowers and barely contained excitement over my 'big police drama'. After I'd been through the scenario twice, in photographic detail, the conversation turned to the Lowbeck and how Bonnie had learned from an apologetic Sol that it was his nephew who'd turned out to be the mystery pervert voyeur.

He was one of the electricians who'd fitted the new suites and a bit of an IT amateur on the side. Sol, eager to help a relative, had got him the job, but he'd become suspicious about the number of times young Mack claimed he needed to carry out 'maintenance' in the new suites. When he checked, he found some non-regulation wiring, then little cameras in three of the rooms.

He'd confronted Mack at his apartment and forced him to reveal his little collection by promising to keep quiet about it, as long as he got rid of the recordings. But Sol's real loyalty was to his thirty-three-year employer. After he told Toby about Mack, Piper-Dewey, eager to protect the Lowbeck's reputation, had convinced the sixteen guests captured in 'compromising situations' not to seek publicity in exchange for a hefty private settlement. They were also reassured that the offender would quietly plead guilty to the less salacious charges of theft of company property, due to the IT equipment found hidden in his closet.

When I bumped into Sol, at the post fourth of July staff drinks reception two days later, I wasn't sure I should mention that Bonnie had shared his secret with me, but he looked like a man who needed someone to talk to.

'I'm sorry about . . . your nephew,' I said quietly, catching up with him in the bar. 'I'm probably not supposed to know but Bonnie mentioned it, discreetly of course. I think you did the right thing, for what it's worth.'

'Thank you, Mrs Taylor,' he said, grimacing as he knocked back what I suspected was the latest of several free whiskeys, adding, 'My brother's kid was always a no-good piece of crap, pardon my French, in trouble with the police since he was a teenager, and I need my job. I *like* my job. Besides, spying on people like that, recording their private moments, it just isn't right. That's not how it should be.'

I nodded, as he looked me up and down in my black silk dress and high heels (right ankle still in an inelegant support tube), and smiled. 'If you don't mind my saying so, you look very lovely tonight, Mrs Taylor, very classy. A real lady. But I'm real sorry about that crazy cop and all that stuff at your place. Bonnie said you were almost shot? Welcome to New York City, huh. Things can get crazy here so fast. People get crazy. Guess he picked on the wrong lady, though.'

He sighed then and, after a moment added, 'It was a nice memorial service and all, wasn't it?' speaking of the respectful gathering Piper-Dewey had held for Jenna in the lobby that afternoon, which Will and I had attended. 'She was just trouble, that girl, Ms Parker, I mean. I shouldn't say it, speak ill of the dead and all, but . . . married men. Other men. Oliver Sheldon and . . .' he stopped, blushing and, as his eyes flickered towards Will, across the room fetching us cocktails, I knew. I knew that he knew about Jenna and the affair. How could he not? The night manager and keeper of hotel secrets? He must have seen them, probably even leaving Room 717 that time, keeping check on what was occupied, officially or otherwise, like all good night managers would.

'It's OK, Sol,' I said, patting his arm. 'After Jenna died, Will told me about it . . . because of the investigation, you know, in case it came up in relation to it. In case . . . the tapes . . . in case they were part of that investigation.'

'I'm so sorry he did that,' said Sol, knocking back another slug of whiskey. 'He didn't need to. You've been so nice to me, Mrs Taylor, so friendly, and he was so nice too. I didn't want . . . that little tramp . . . When I went to

Mack's place and made him come clean I saw the CDs he was keeping, copying videos from the cameras before recording over them. I knew the date ... that one time, just one time when William and ... So I destroyed November ... no sense in ... I'd have got rid of Oliver's too, but that was still on the camera card, I didn't realise.

'I wanted to spare you, Mrs Taylor, and I know he's so sorry. William loves you so much. He talks about you all the time. Men are just stupid sometimes. It's a good job good women often forgive us.'

So Sol was the one who'd saved me, destroyed the video footage of Will and Jenna and with it any evidence of their affair and of my motive – all because of a kind word now and then, a jar of Marmite offered in exchange for a giant pretzel. As Will waved across the room, weaving towards us with glittering drinks, I threw my arms around Sol and hugged him.

No one believed Van Allen, of course, who kept up his stream of allegations from his hospital bed. He was diagnosed as having suffered a psychotic relapse, his ramblings dismissed as the delusions of a broken-hearted man. We didn't press charges. Van Allen wasn't in a fit mental state to answer them. He was removed from the NYPD and strings were pulled to let him return to his parents' house in Long Island, under the supervision of the family doctor. We learned this from Rawlins, who called round a few weeks later to formally ask if Will wanted his red anorak back, the one Jenna Parker must have picked up from the rec room the night she died – it had been professionally cleaned, he emphasised. But Will declined, asked Rawlins to dispose of it for him.

By the end of August we'd packed up our belongings from the apartment and Will had told Toby that, while he was very grateful for the offer of a renewed twelve-month contract, he simply couldn't stay in the city after what had happened to me; it was clearly time to pack up and move on, start another journey. So we left the gleaming spires and turrets of New York, reversed our steps past the Empire State and Chrysler buildings shrinking from view in the cab's rear-view mirror, flew homeward to Heathrow to be collected by Will's mum and dad and ferried to their house in Monmouth while we looked for a place to live.

Months later, we learned about the coroner's proceedings from Bonnie, still with Olly, via email. As Rawlins had indicated was likely, the coroner returned a verdict of accidental death in the case of Jenna Parker and suicide in the case of Gustavo Rodriguez.

Safely back in the reality of the United Kingdom, her words, sliding across the internet from so far away, already seemed unrelated to us, like snatches of dialogue from a film we'd once watched; a dark, macabre thing with unfamiliar actors we didn't recognise, about people making all kinds of bad choices and losing their minds in a foreign country.

One we were only too happy to forget.

Epilogue

So here we are, back in Wales, just about – straddling the border, braced against the Celtic west, facing England. It's been twelve months since we left New York. Six months of house hunting and job searching, then six more of setting up camp, building fences, circling the wagons, staying close to the fire.

It's true we are no longer pioneers in the way we once were, pinned again to this scrap of land tucked inside the leafy coat pocket of a former empire, but there is a sense of comfort where there are clear edges and boundaries and the possibilities are not endless. So I make the most of things, writing cheery features and articles promoting Welsh tourism from the desk in the spare bedroom, away from the hustle and bustle of city streets and cinematic skyscrapers, away from dreams and nightmares.

I work hardest on the travel package I'm developing for Piper-Dewey alongside their IT team, an app-based guide for Millennials who like a bit of adventure but think Airbnb is a terrifying prospect. I suspect they only offered me the commission because they feel bad about what happened in one of their official residences but they pay very well and I'm not complaining. They helped Will get his new job too, with the hotel development outside Chepstow. His commute takes just twenty minutes and his working day is nine to six, so the weeks are just busy enough and I take each day as it comes.

Except now and then at night, when the stillness is as complete as the darkness of the borderlands and the rolling hills sleep alongside the lazy River Wye, when I allow myself to think about what happened on the other side of the world, the other side of my life, to weigh it and balance it and see what I am left with. I think of it like that tally sheet I once wrote about Will, in the aftermath of his affair, always starting with the things I'd put in the tick column, of course, things such as:

1. Olivia is kind as often as she can be.
2. She looks after Will. She pays attention to the little things.
3. She supports him in his new job at the Castle Fields Country Spa and works with disadvantaged kids on weekends, kayaking and orienteering.
4. She looks after her mother and meets her for lunch every few weeks, like a good daughter, and they are becoming if not good, then better friends.
5. She does these things because they are the things people should do if they're really sorry. If they want to show it. If they are hopeful they can be forgiven.

That's usually as far as I get though, because how could such a list quantify what I am now? Do justice to the story I set out to tell? I suppose stories are like journeys in a way – they can lead you somewhere entirely different to where you thought you were heading.

And where is that? Where are we heading now? This smiling man and his wife, splashing on the River Wye together with a little gaggle of inner-city ducklings rowing in their wake at weekends; this pair of smart professionals living in a tiny cottage near Tintern Abbey, bought with his parents' generous down payment, with a view of soft green trees and the smell of running water.

As often as we can, Will and I have coffee or a glass of wine on the sun-kissed cobbles overlooking the riverbank, where wisteria grows and Welsh poppies cluster. In the early evening sunshine we tell each other about our days, discuss our next hike into the Brecon Beacons, think about our next holiday.

We are a great couple. We are happy, this ultimate selfie would say if someone were to capture the Instagram moment we lift our china cups to our lips, clink our wine glasses together before a cascade of purple blooms: *Married and loving it. Loving each other*, an advert for adventure and lasting partnership. *Here we are, laughing, smiling.*

Except . . .

Except civilisation is a fragile thing and you don't have to travel far to see it crumble, watch the old, dark shape of the beast emerge and bare its teeth. That's why I'm watchful now, on my guard. Every day when I look in the mirror, I look for signs. I check for changes – to see if I'm sprouting fangs, if a ridge of hair is prickling along my back, if my eyebrows are slowly uniting above my nose. I wait to see if, one day soon, I will wake in the night scratching at the bedroom door, slavering to be free, to run into the midnight forests and fields.

Because it was in me all along, I know that now, that thing with teeth and claws – something that showed itself to a teenage boy with a cruel smile, freed again by a broken marriage vow and a broken heart. So the last test for me, the test that never ends, is to make sure it never gets loose again.

Because I hear it at night sometimes, my dark, half-howling self, in my sleep, when I raise my face to the moon and bay silently at its bright, cold face.

I call to the wild and the wilderness answers.

Because that's where we are now, Will and I, on a journey into the unknown. There's no map for this uncharted path, no landmarks, no milestones. Nothing is sure underfoot, the destination uncertain. Because reality is not like fiction, no one gets to say when you've reached 'the end' – the end of the test, the end of the affair, the end of the world – because no one knows when that will be. Until that day comes all I can do is go up and go on, keep moving, keep watching and hope I never lose my way again, even though I might have to take some precautions along the way.

Because despite the promises Will has made me, despite the perfect house and circling the wagons again, it's not safe here either, it's never safe. I still need to protect what's mine from people who might try to steal it, from people like Laurie Harrison for instance, thirty-two-year-old development consultant; such a pretty smile, so *very* pleased to be working with someone like Will who truly appreciates the potential of ecotourism and sustainable development.

Something prickled on the back of my neck when Will introduced us at the hotel last week; something stirred in my gut when she showed me the designs for the eco spa she's developing. Something almost snarled when she placed her hand on Will's arm at the end of the meeting, when he smiled back.

I trust him, though. Of course I do. Only, her husband is not as good looking as Will. I took one peek at her Instagram and Facebook feeds to set my mind at rest, and they're not an obvious match; she's a sort of Hitchcock blonde with great legs and a tiny waist; he's an overweight bearded man who sells farming equipment. They seem happily married, but then doesn't everyone until they aren't?

That's why I'm not making any assumptions or taking any chances. That's why I've enabled the 'find my iPhone' app on Will's phone – on the off-chance I ever find myself wondering, in the dark of the night, if he's really where he says he is again. In case it ever pings his location near the sprawling barn conversion outside Chepstow where the Harrisons have installed solar panels on their roof and keep a state-of-the-art composter in their vegetable garden.

She was easy enough to follow in her bright green hybrid, though she drives like a short-sighted pensioner. I had to make just one quick visit to check out the lie of the land. So I know where to find her. Only if I need to, of course, only if it becomes necessary.

It's nothing as precise and picky as a plan, naturally, merely a matter of having contingencies at hand. Just in case Will ever needs to be shown that nowhere's safe.

That no one ever is.

Dream Holidays – Dark Visions:
How *Wilderness* Came to Life

As a child I loved concocting adventures, poring over books, fantasising about film locations, planning trips to far-flung places and inventing the stories I could find myself in when I arrived there. Yes, I was a kid with an active imagination – just as well since, growing up in post-industrial South Wales, I thought those journeys were dream trips I'd probably never make.

When I grew up and realised I could make them happen, it hit me that, even as adults, a holiday is more than just a break from routine. It still presents the possibility of a break from ourselves, a chance to be better, more interesting, more exciting than the nine-to five week allows our sensible selves to be.

Of course, writers are always looking for the dark currents beneath the tranquil aquamarine ocean or that picturesque holiday photo, and part of me was always wondering what might happen if a dream holiday turned sour. In that way the nubby little kernel of *Wilderness* lodged itself in my brain long before it had a title, an itinerary and a marriage in crisis at its heart. It was a feeling, an image of a character in their holiday best, lost and crying, that hung around the corners of my head for years, travelled with me in my suitcase.

I'd visited New York in my twenties, captivated by the cinematic landscape of steaming subways and gleaming skyline. It made perfect sense to make this the setting for the beginning and end of Olivia's journey where dreams and nightmares collide. But it was on a Californian road trip with my husband when my murderous story really began to take shape.

Travelling from San Francisco into the Sierras we experienced the scope of a country and its endless sky, so vast, that, like Olivia, I felt myself shrinking into insignificance before it. When we climbed the hairpin bends into Yosemite, the forests rising in ranks around us, it was like travelling into a wild, fairy-tale world, especially when jet lag makes everything weird, fuzzy, slightly off kilter.

This was before the interconnectivity of social media, of course, pretty much before smartphones too, and the sense of isolation was unnerving, even though, in reality, we were rarely more than half a mile from a ranger station or a sandwich stand. I remember that when we checked into our pioneer-style cabin, the huge map on the wall showed Yosemite Valley, or the bottom left-hand corner did – the rest was simply a rugged green expanse bearing the words 'Wilderness' – and suddenly a book title was born.

Over the next three days we gasped in wonder at waterfalls and granite cliffs, yet there was something alarming

under the skin of all that beauty – the idea that it might turn on you if you weren't looking, show you its teeth if you strayed from the path. There's a reason many fairy tales are set in dark, dark woods – believe me, real forests are scary, even on a sunny afternoon in good-quality hiking gear! So that was where I began forming a vision of a dreadful deed, done in a moment of madness, where no one was watching.

It took us four years to return to America, to explore the Grand Canyon, Monument Valley and the unrelenting desert. Arriving on the south rim late in the afternoon, we were astonished that we could walk right up to the edge, like grown-ups with the common sense to stay back from the dizzying drop. In a flash this became the ideal alternate reality situation for an accident or even a murder.

Unlike Olivia, when we hiked down to the Colorado River, I didn't fantasise about murdering my husband; I wouldn't have had the chance as, one minute we were alone, the next a young couple emerged from the rocks behind us. I've always been fascinated by the idea of chance meetings and mistaken identity, and, bumping into them in that seemingly lonely spot, two newlyweds, medical students due to start their residencies, made me wonder how we ever really know if people are who they say they are when we meet them. How did they know who we were? How did we know what the other might do if one of us had secrets? And then the plot took shape.

When I was reaching the end of my writing journey, try-ing to decide what to do with Olivia, I kept thinking of an exchange I'd once heard in an airport lounge, a little boy in tears because he didn't want to go back to England. 'Everyone has to go home eventually – holidays don't last for ever,' his grandmother counselled. Which was just as well in Olivia's case, as I tried to decide whether or not to send her home to Wales, carrying more than photos and cheap souvenirs, or let her loose in the wilderness she created for herself.

As for me, I've already planned my next holiday to America's Pacific Northwest – returning to the land of mountain peaks and dark woodlands. I'll be prepared though. I'll keep an ear to the ground because, whenever I'm somewhere new, there's always another story waiting to pounce.

Music to Murder Your Husband By – The *Wilderness* Road-trip Playlist

I've always liked to listen to music when I'm writing and certain songs are perfect for getting under a character's skin. Of course, I'm a sucker for a well-turned lyric but sometimes the subject of the song isn't as important as the mood it creates, something that resonates with the state of mind of a person in turmoil, considering questionable actions.

If you'd like a taste of Olivia's state of mind you could always listen to my ultimate road-trip playlist, songs to which I listened on the road and tracks to which I wrote Olivia's journey, emotional as well as physical. Be warned, it might not be an easy ride!

Monument Valley
　'Wake Up' – Arcade Fire
　'Time Go' – Caught a Ghost
　'Wide Open' – The Chemical Brothers featuring Beck
　'Looking Too Closely' – Fink
　'Monster' – Mumford and Sons

Grand Canyon
    'Heartbreak Warfare' – John Mayer
    'Indian Summer' – Stereophonics
    'Lights and Offerings' – Mirrors
    'Keep the Car Running' – Arcade Fire
    'About Today' – The National

Yosemite to Death Valley
    'Where the Streets Have No Name' – U2
    'I Still Haven't Found What I'm Looking For' – U2
    'For Reasons Unknown' – The Killers
    'God of Ocean Tides' – Counting Crows
    'Hurt' – Johnny Cash

On the New York Rooftop and the New York Streets
    'Mr Brightside' – The Killers
    'I'll Still Destroy You' – The National
    'Werewolf' – Magic Bronson
    'I Need My Girl' – The National
    'Hot Gates' – Mumford and Sons

Epilogue and Aftermath
    'Invisible Empire' – KT Tunstall
    'Right Where It Belongs' – Nine Inch Nails
    'Long Long Way' – Damien Rice
    'Hard to Find' – The National

TV journalist Melanie Black wakes up one morning next to a man she doesn't recognise. It's not the first time – but he ignores her even though she's in his bed. Yet when his wife walks in with a cup of tea he greets her with a smile and, to her horror, Melanie comes to realise that no one can see or her hear her – because she is dead.

But has she woken up next to her murderer? And where is her body? Why is she an invisible and uninvited guest in a house she can't leave; is she tied to this man for ever? Is Melanie being punished in some way, or being given a chance to make amends?

As she begins to piece together the last days of her life and circumstances leading up to her own death it becomes clear she has to make a choice: bring her killer to justice, or wreak her own punishment out to the man who murdered her.

Available now

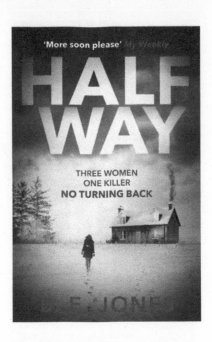

There's a killer behind and trouble ahead

The Halfway Inn is closed to customers, side-lined by a bypass and hidden in inhospitable countryside. One winter's night, deep in snow, two women end up knocking on the door, seeking refuge as the blizzard takes hold.

But why is the landlord less than pleased to see them? And what is his elderly father, upstairs in bed immobilised by a stroke, trying so hard to tell them?

At the local police station, PC Lissa Lloyd is holding the fort while the rest of her team share in the rare excitement of a brutal murder at an isolated farmhouse. A dangerous fugitive is on the run – but how can Lissa make a name for herself if she's stuck at her desk? When a call comes in saying the local district nurse is missing she jumps at the chance to escape the boredom and heads out into the snow.

The strangers at Halfway wait out the storm but soon realise they might have been safer on the road, especially when they find something disturbing in the cellar – which is nowhere near as disturbing as what's under the old man's bed . . .

Available now